A FINAL CROSSING:
MURDER
ON THE
S.S. BADGER

A Louis Searing and Margaret McMillan Mystery

By Richard L. Baldwin

© Buttonwood Press 2004

This novel is a product of the imagination of the author. The references to the S.S.
Badger are used with permission of the Lake Michigan Carferry, Inc. None of the
events described in this story occurred. Though settings, buildings, and businesses
exist, liberties may have been taken as to their actual location and description.
This story has no purpose other than to entertain the reader.

Badger cover photo was taken by Mr. Max Hanley and is
the property of Lake Michigan Carferry, Inc.

Published by Buttonwood Press
P.O. Box 716
Haslett, Michigan 48840
www.buttonwoodpress.com

Printed in the United States of America

OTHER BOOKS BY RICHARD L. BALDWIN

FICTION:

A Lesson Plan for Murder
ISBN: 0-9660685-0-5. (1998) Buttonwood Press

The Principal Cause of Death
ISBN: 0-9660685-2-1. (1999) Buttonwood Press

Administration Can Be Murder
ISBN: 0-9660685-4-8. (2000) Buttonwood Press

Buried Secrets of Bois Blanc: Murder in the Straits of Mackinac
ISBN: 0-9660685-5-6. (2001) Buttonwood Press

The Searing Mysteries: Three in One
ISBN: 0-9660685-6-4. (2001) Buttonwood Press

Ghostly Links
ISBN: 0-9660685-8-0. Buttonwood Press

The Moon Beach Mysteries
ISBN: 0-9660685-9-9. Buttonwood Press

The Detective Company (Written with Sandie Jones)
ISBN: 0-9742920-0-1. Buttonwood Press

Unity and the Children
ISBN: 0-9660685-3-X. (2000) Buttonwood Press

If A Child Picked A Flower Just For You
(2004) Buttonwood Press

NON-FICTION:

The Piano Recital
ISBN: 0-9660685-1-3. (1999) Buttonwood Press

A Story to Tell: Special Education in Michigan's Upper Peninsula 1902-1975
ISBN: 932212-77-8. (1994) Lake Superior Press

ABOUT THE BADGER

The S.S. Badger began service on March 21, 1953. It was built in Sturgeon Bay, Wisconsin. The ship is 410 feet 6 inches long, and is 59 feet and 6 inches wide. The cruising speed is 18 miles per hour with 50-60 officers and crew to manage a maximum of 620 passengers and 180 autos.

The Badger crosses Lake Michigan from mid-May to mid-October. It takes four hours to cross the lake. In the summer months the Badger makes two crossings a day with a 2:30 a.m. crossing from Manitowoc to Ludington.

Passengers can enjoy movies and television, food service, gift shopping in the Badger Boatique, learn history in the museum, or entertain children in a play area. Passengers who choose to stroll outside may do so or recline in chaise lounges. There is literally something for everyone.

For information about the Badger go to www.ssbadger.com or call 800-841-4243 for reservations and information.

A FINAL CROSSING:
MURDER
ON THE
S.S. BADGER

ACKNOWLEDGEMENTS

I want to thank the folks at the Lake Michigan Carferry Company, Inc. President Bob Manglitz allowed me to use the Badger as the setting for much action. Lynda Daugherty, Director of Media Relations was extremely helpful answering all of my questions promptly and thoroughly. Thanks too to Valerie Stapleton for her support of selling this book in the Badger Boatique.

I also wish to thank Eric Best, diving coach of MSU, for assistance in understanding the implications of jumping into turbulent water from great heights. Others who must be thanked are Patty Archambault who helped me understand captioning; Elaine Stanfield, psychologist, who advised me of the personalities of major characters; Dave Bachman, Police Chief for Manistee, Michigan, who once again provided enthusiasm and answers to questions about law enforcement activities.

The Buttonwood Press team must be thanked. The following worked in the best interests of the reader and the writer: Gail Garber, editor; writing consultants, Karen O'Connor, and Anne Ordiway; Joyce Wagner and Rudy, proofreaders; Sarah Thomas, cover designer and typesetter. Technical information was supplied by Sue at Sparrow Labs; Margie, Sparrow Hospital; Brian Bate, REI, Portland, Oregon; Eric Trap, Patrolman, Parker, Colorado Police Department. I wish to thank John Brown, Marge Fuller, Ben Hall, Scott Baldwin, Paul

Braun, and Don Flagg for technical assistance, as well as Ann Liming, and Maureen Wallace of the Division of the Deaf and Hard of Hearing within the Family Independence Agency, State of Michigan.

There were a number of law enforcement personnel who offered assistance in addition to Chief Backman. Thank you, Commander Smith of the Cleveland Coast Guard Investigations, and Lt. Carl Goeman, Michigan State Police, Traverse City.

Thank you to my good friend Hal Bate for the idea behind this novel. Thanks also to Bill and Joy Derengoski who provided information that added to the personality of this novel. Finally, I wish to thank my dear wife Patty for her belief in me, her love and support. I am so blessed to share life with the most beautiful human being on the face of the earth.

This book is dedicated to my beloved daughter Amanda Hoffmeister. Amanda is a creative woman, loving wife to Joe, and a marvelous mother to Hannah and Tom. My joy has been to watch her grow up, selflessly giving her energy and talents to helping others, and always being willing to listen to her dad tell his stories.

CHAPTER ONE

Wednesday, May 15, 2004

Lou Searing was watching television in his Grand Haven, Michigan, home. With the Detroit Tigers leading the Cleveland Indians 7-6 and the bases loaded, the game disappeared and the word BULLETIN filled the screen. Lou anticipated terrible news.

"We interrupt this program with a news bulletin. A house fire is raging out of control just north of Frankfort, Michigan. Unconfirmed reports indicate that the house fire is the work of eco-terrorists. Fire fighters and law enforcement personnel are on the scene. Apparently there were no witnesses. A crude sign in the driveway reads, 'You raped the land, you are the criminal, you pay the price.' This is one more in a long list of homes destroyed in environmentally sensitive areas, the fourth home destroyed by fire in the Great Lakes area within the past six months. All these homes were in the final stages of construction, and the loss is expected to be in the millions of dollars. We will have more news as it becomes available, but once again, authorities urge all home owners in pristine areas of the Great Lakes to take steps to protect their homes and neighborhoods. Authorities cannot predict where the terrorists might strike next. We now return you to your regularly scheduled broadcast."

The game reappeared and Lou noticed that the Tigers were now up 11-6. He'd have to catch the grand slam home run in the ESPN Baseball Tonight highlights.

Lou, retired from the State of Michigan's Department of Education, had found a double second career. He was a private investigator and also wrote novels under the pen name of Richard L. Baldwin. Lou was about six feet tall, had inherited male-patterned baldness, wore two hearing aids and a pair of bifocal specs. Since Lou hadn't been running regularly, his mid-section called for an occasional health lecture from his wife Carol. When Lou wasn't solving a murder or writing about a case, he could be found touring on his Harley.

Lou and Carol were living in the home of their dreams. The three-bedroom home with Lou's writing studio and Carol's quilting room on the second floor overlooking Lake Michigan was their gift to each other when they celebrated their retirements. "Ready to walk on the beach," shouted Carol Searing from the back porch.

Lou and Carol were best known to their neighbors as a lovely couple who walked along the shore with their golden retriever Samm. Samm eagerly fetched a piece of driftwood that Lou threw. Lou and Carol would walk hand in hand along the shore talking about grandchildren, plans for the next cruise, and any other topic that happened to be on their minds. On this particular evening, the conversation concerned a growth recently discovered on Lou's back. A biopsy would be conducted the next day and apprehension was high.

While Samm tried to play tag with a seagull, Lou asked Carol, "Did you have the TV on in your quilting room?"

"No, I was listening to a CD. Why?"

"There's a big fire north of Frankfort. Eco-terrorists again."

"That makes three homes hit in Michigan, right?" Carol asked.

"I think so," Lou replied. "It's so stupid. They make a statement, but nothing will change except insurance rates will go up and more trees will become homes."

"Will you get involved, Lou?" Carol asked apprehensively. Lou had been doing several investigations, but the lump on his back signaled possible ill health. Carol was hoping that he would finally settle down and act like a retired gentleman.

"I don't think so," Lou said. "Nobody has asked me to. Destruction of property is not my specialty. Now, if someone was murdered, I might get a call, but these people are bent on destroying property, not lives."

Lou's cell phone rang. "I forgot to leave this on the kitchen counter," Lou said, taking the phone from his hip.

"Let it ring. You can get the message later," Carol responded, concluding that the call and fire would be connected.

"Might be Scott or Amanda. I'll take it," Lou replied, referring to their son and daughter. "Hello."

"Lou? This is Mickey McFadden." Mickey was the Chief of Police in Manistee, Michigan, a beautiful city on the shore of Lake Michigan, about 20 miles north of Ludington. Chief McFadden was a 6-foot-2-inch good-looking gentleman in his late thirties. He had broad shoulders, was clean shaven, and commanded respect by the way he handled his responsibilities.

"Hi, Mickey. What's on your mind?" Lou asked.

"Are you on standby for some work?" Chief McFadden asked.

"Not really. What is this about? The fires?"

"Are you psychic or something?" Mickey said, with a chuckle.

"Carol and I are walking on the beach," Lou replied. "We were talking about the eco-terrorists and she was just asking me if I was going to get involved. I said, 'My guess is that my help won't be needed' and then my phone rang."

"Well, there are no reports of murders, but I want you ready to get in the game. I smell trouble up here. I'm calling to ask you to prioritize my request if and when I call."

"You make me sound like a donut shop – 'take a number, please,'" Lou said. Carol looked at him wondering what he could be referring to.

"You're a pretty popular guy, Lou, and I don't want to have to call and hear, 'Like to help you, Mickey, but I'm involved in another case.'"

"Hey, for you, Mickey McFadden, the world stops. You can count on my help whenever you need it."

"Thanks, Lou. Sorry to interrupt your walk. Tell Carol I said 'Hi', okay?"

"Will do." Lou returned his phone to its holster.

"For you the world stops?" Carol asked.

"Figure of speech. I was a little dramatic, but I like the man. I'd help him in a second."

"I take it you're off on another adventure?" Carol asked, not at all pleased with the possibility. "I really wish you would just write stories from your imagination. You don't need to get your material by actually solving the case. Why aren't you happy just to play cops and robbers in your mind?"

"I'm winding down. I can tell my second retirement is approaching. If Mickey needs me, I'll work one more case and then we'll let my imagination work full-time. I promise."

"Thank God you're finally coming to your senses. You're living much too close to danger for my comfort. Maggie's getting shot in the last case was my wake-up call, Lou. I'm putting my foot down. I tried to put my foot down when you wanted that Harley, but I wasn't strong enough. I'm strong enough now. That growth on your back and your chasing men with guns is scaring me, and you had better be a man of your word. This is it, Lou Searing. Solve this one quickly and grow old with me."

Lou knew that he had just gotten a talking to, but he knew it was from love. One more case and I'm calling it a career, he thought.

"So, does he want you up in Manistee?" Carol asked.

"Not yet. He's just putting me on alert that I may be needed. By the way, he said to say 'Hi' to you."

"He's a nice guy. I like Mickey," Carol said. "Taking you from me, that I don't like, though."

Lou took Carol's hand as they walked along with cool water splashing over their feet and ankles. Samm never seemed to grow tired of the run-and-fetch routine so common with his masters.

As the sun put on a color show in the western sky, Lou and Carol walked back to their home. Lou checked to make sure the Tigers won and they had. He retired to his studio to write another chapter in his latest book. Life was good. He and Carol were more in love than ever in their 30 years, children and grandchildren were doing okay, he was living in the home of his dreams, and he could write his stories in the most beautiful setting one could imagine. All was right with the world.

Actually, he thought, all was just too good for one man. For the first time, he hoped the phone wouldn't ring and call him to another case. Maybe he was stretching his luck. Maybe Carol was right, and he should forget the investigations and write his novels from his imagination.

While Lou was basically a positive thinker, he knew from his study of statistics for his doctorate work at Kansas University that things gravitate to the mean. His life had been skewed way out on the edge of the bell curve with health, income, family, and friends. It just made sense that, sooner or later, he'd be pulled back toward the center, into a life that was normal where things didn't always go as planned and every minute wasn't predictable. The growth on his back entered his consciousness and his heart quickened.

Lou didn't like what he was thinking. He ate some M&Ms and turned on the computer. One of the cats, Millie, rubbed his foot as he sat at the computer and composed his next chapter.

The next morning, Dr. Peg Lott greeted students on the first day of her class. She was tired and had a hard time staying on topic, for she hadn't gotten any sleep for 20 hours. Yesterday afternoon near Frankfort, Michigan, Peg had been quite sure that the house on top of the hill was free of people. Construction was nearly finished and the house appeared to be ready for furnishings. She walked a long and rugged path to the top of the dune rather than risk being seen on the winding road from the shore. The trail Peggy followed was one that had been used by hikers before the area was sold to a developer six years before. Much of the trail had filled in with thick branches and plant growth, but the path was still visible, and she could traverse it with little difficulty.

Taking it one step at a time, she finally arrived at the top. Peggy perspired heavily and her muscles were sore. Thankfully, the trip to the bottom would be quicker and much easier on her body. For one thing, she wouldn't be carrying a couple gallons of gasoline, which was a significant weight to take up a hillside.

Upon arriving, Peggy took a deep breath. Lake Michigan was stunningly beautiful on this spring afternoon. The land under her feet never should have been marred by the home owners who wanted this view to themselves, to say nothing of their destroying trees, uprooting the homes of wildlife, and taking over the natural beauty of the landscape. It was a crime and it would be met with another crime – arson.

As much as Peggy wanted to sit and watch the blue lake, whitecaps, and distant sailboats, she knew she had to act quickly. She took the containers of gasoline from her backpack and circled the nearly constructed home, leaving a trail of fuel under the log frame. Then she broke into the home by going through a window. Once inside she discretely put at least a pint of gasoline around the electrical box, hoping the arson investigators could be tricked into thinking the cause of the fire was electrical. She knew better, but that was what her Commander had instructed.

Peggy walked outside, lit a match, and set the gasoline on fire. She stood there for a few seconds admiring her work as the foundation began a slow burn that would eventually consume the home. The bright orange and yellow flames crept up the building toward the sky. Smoke began to billow upward. She admired the beauty of the fire. The sight was brilliant.

Peggy knew that the sun would set on a smoldering foundation; there was no way the fire department could put out the flames before the home was totally destroyed. If anything, the most that could be done was to contain the fire so the forestation would not be significantly harmed.

With one last look at the fire, Peggy picked up her backpack and headed down the trail. On her way to the bottom she could hear volunteer fire fighters' sirens piercing the air, and she caught a glimpse of their flashing red lights in the distance. She got into her car and began the five-hour drive home to East Lansing. Her fear was getting caught and all that would follow. She was slow to be convinced that this criminal behavior was the best way to cause change, but she agreed to be a part of the revenge.

Dr. Lott was a professor at Michigan State University. She was 37, single and, with an alley cat named Flame to keep her company, lived a rather lonely life. Peggy was not what most would call attractive, pretty, or even cute. She was thirty pounds overweight and her hair was stringy and usually pulled back in a ponytail or secured with a headband. She did not remove body hair – she saw no point in it. Her clothes were not in fashion; she didn't care what was stylish. Clothes were tools; they kept her warm and hid her body from judgmental eyes.

Peggy had lived outside the mainstream for a long time. Her parents were university professors at Dartmouth in the East. Peggy had rebelled as so many did in their youth, and her mother often told friends that she seemed to have changed overnight. One minute she was "normal," whatever that meant, and in the next she pulled into a cocoon and began a lifestyle foreign to her parents, friends, and most others her age. It wasn't drug use, her parents emphasized to friends who noticed the change, and they were right. The change in Peggy Lott came from the book A Timely Rebellion and its main character seemed to transfix Peggy; she needed to become the character and she did, overnight.

Peggy was brilliant, gifted actually, and in high school was quickly branded an intellectual, a label she was proud of. She wasn't like other girls with their petty concerns about their bodies, or boys, or whatever was the fad of the moment. Boys were repulsive and served no purpose on the face of the earth. The only boy she cared about was her brother, who was two years younger and deaf. She loved and was very protective of him. Her companions were books – lots of books. She was proud that she generally read a book a night before falling to sleep during the early hours of a new day.

Peggy completed high school in a year and a half. She was accepted and enrolled at the University of Michigan when she was fifteen; there she decided to major in biology, which she enjoyed in high school.

During a year at Harvard earning a master's degree in a specialized and individualized program of study, Peggy roomed with a young woman named Betty Taylor, whose love for cats was fanatical. The women were friends but had little time to develop a relationship because each was fully involved in her study. Betty was studying veterinary medicine.

Peggy returned to the University of Michigan to study with one of the world's greatest minds in ecology, Dr. Randolph Eberhard. She earned a Ph.D. in Environmental Ecology at the age of 22, one of the youngest students ever granted a doctorate at the U of M. She immediately went to work for Michigan State University teaching classes and supervising labs for students only a few years younger than she. Peggy was fascinated with research at Harvard and at the University of Michigan, so research opportunity was one of the factors that brought her to MSU where she could assist Professor Isaac Rosenberg. Drs. Lott and Rosenberg worked well together and within a few years became nationally known for their quality studies and published reports.

Dr. Lott's association with Dr. Rosenberg opened doors for her in a number of prestigious organizations. When not teaching, advising, or conducting research, Peggy Lott was flying to international and national conferences to give speeches or to soak up what peers had discovered through research that was impeccable in design.

Peggy never felt compelled to join Green Peace, the Sierra Club, or the action-oriented Earth Liberation Front, but she certainly shared a common spirit with them. As a student or a professor, Dr. Lott didn't join campus groups that were concerned with the environment. She wasn't a joiner who needed to be around people, could put up with immature comments and behaviors, and would listen to phony radicals not courageous enough to do something about a problem beyond bitching about it. She did participate with some students on occasion as they demonstrated for a cause, usually protesting the use of animals in research.

Ironically, for all her strong beliefs and all of the supporting behaviors, Peggy chose not to confront people and would not pass out handbills; nor did she write letters to legislators. She knew that carrying a placard or writing a letter would not change someone's ideas, but to take action and destroy the very structures that were defacing the land, that was advocacy, that was a contribution to the earth worthy of her talents and skill. She was private about her disdain for damaging the environment and expressed her advocacy in a very unorthodox way. Now she was an arsonist.

Peggy had been very careful to hide any indication that she could be capable of destructive behavior. Her colleagues at Michigan State knew of her advocacy on behalf of the earth. Peggy's students were divided in their feelings about her. Some saw her as a nut, but no one questioned her intelligence. In that respect, she was accepted. All of her students, even those who thought her off-center, hung on her every word, because she was a fascinating, walking encyclopedia on many subjects, not just biology and the eco-systems of the world.

Following her 10 A.M. class, Peggy found a television in the student center and watched intently to reports that the cause of the Frankfort fire was arson, and that a thorough investigation would be conducted. The home owners appeared devastated and were angry that their home was destroyed. If it were arson, they had no idea who was responsible, and they assured viewers that they would rebuild as soon as possible.

That evening, Peggy watched the Fox News, paying close attention to the captioning, and smiled when she read: "The stock market recovered today as the Dow jumped several points to close at a new high. The NASDAQ also was up. Good job and thanks. Our next story takes us to Miami, Florida where…"

Peggy knew that "Good job and thanks" was meant for her and was put into captions by her leader, the Commander of the eco-terrorist group of which she was a member, the Ring of Fire. Seeing the message meant that her work was perfect. There was nothing to tie her to the arson. The mission was accomplished. If investigators determined that arson was the cause of the fire, Dr. Peggy Lott would not be suspect. Once again, there was justice. People had been punished for raping the land.

CHAPTER TWO

Eight Weeks Later: July 14, 2004
Manitowoc, Wisconsin
2:30 A.M. CDT

As the S.S. Badger pulled away from the dock in Manitowoc, Wisconsin, a cold front was coming down from Canada. Storms would pierce the front and a rough crossing was expected.

Passengers were settling in for the four-hour crossing. Those who reserved staterooms were climbing into bunks hoping to sleep for the journey. Those without staterooms jockeyed for chair positions. Some sat in lounges in front of large-screen television sets. Those outside on the deck knew that the rain would soon chase them inside.

Two women on the Badger were targeted to die on this dark and wet night, but the two women didn't know each other. One was Professor Lott; the other was Stephanie Brooks, a high-ranking investigator with the FBI, coming to Michigan to conduct a multi-state drug raid.

At approximately 2:40 A.M. the two women conversed briefly in the lounge because Stephanie decided to ask Peggy a favor. Stephanie waited a few minutes till she could determine that Peggy had neither a travel companion nor was she traveling with children. Once she was fairly certain Peg was traveling alone, she approached.

"Excuse me. My name is Jane and I have a favor to ask. May I?" Stephanie never used her real name when talking to strangers.

"Sure."

"Do you have a stateroom for this crossing?"

"Yes," Peggy replied.

"I'm wondering if you would be willing to switch staterooms with me."

"Why?"

"Actually, I'm very superstitious. My stateroom is number 19, and I found out after coming on board that it is on the right side of the ship. I know it's silly, but that's the way I am. I can't stay in a room that is an odd number on the right side of the ship, or in a hotel or motel."

"My room is an even number on the left side," Peg said, doing some quick calculating of her room location. "Is this what you're looking for?"

"Yes. Would you mind switching staterooms with me?"

"Why don't you just go back to the cruise director and ask for another room?" Peg asked.

"If you agree to do this, I will inform the cruise director," Stephanie said, offering an alternative.

"No, I'd rather not switch," Peg said. "I'd like to help you, but I need that room."

"Need that room? They all look alike," Stephanie said, unable to understand why Peg would need the room.

"I'm set in there. It's the room assigned to me and I want to be there," Peg replied. "I'm sure you'll find someone else willing to switch with you."

"I can't even walk down the odd side of the ship, almost gives me an anxiety attack."

"I'm sorry," Peg replied. "Usually I'd be willing to help out, but this stateroom is where I want to be."

Peggy returned to her stateroom, settled in, and waited until it was time to begin her plan.

While Peggy and Stephanie were conversing, they were under the watchful eye of Todd Baxter who made it his job to know the whereabouts of Peggy Lott during every moment of the voyage. Another man had it as his mission to stalk Agent Brooks. He was as ordinary a passenger as one could imagine. He was very unassuming, quiet, and was as much a part of the surroundings as an empty chair on the deck of the Badger.

Stephanie was upset that the room switch had not worked out. It would have allowed her to successfully complete a double, and a double was important in her work. She had registered under an assumed name, and if someone sought her in Stateroom 19 she would not be there. The person looking for her would simply have the wrong room and be unclear where she was. Now, she'd have to find someone else to help her complete the double.

Stephanie remained among people in the lounge. Before the Badger left Manitowoc, the man stalking her had hung around the cruise director's office area which was always open. During a moment when the area was unoccupied, he glanced at the list upside down, but it was enough to get what he thought was the room number of Agent Brooks. The stalker wrote on a slip of paper, She is in 16.

At about 3:10 A.M., Peggy Lott was sitting in Stateroom 16, when she was startled to hear a rap on her door. She should have ignored it, but she was curious, and after a few seconds she opened the door. Nobody was there, but when she glanced to her left she saw, from behind, a large man, dressed in black leather.

Peg retreated to safety behind the locked stateroom door, her heart pounding. She knew she was targeted, and she was alone on the ship. She didn't recognize the man, but she felt that he was probably disguised. The thought that she was being toyed with caused an adrenaline rush, as if she had just seen a lion in front of her cave.

She heard a second knock, a sharp rap as if the person needed to talk to her, but she froze. Opening the door to this stranger was simply not safe. She made sure the door was locked and hoped he would go away. At approximately the same time, Stephanie Brooks walked down the aisle to the bathroom; she saw a large, bearded man in black leather, but she didn't think he was a threat to her.

Peggy was not alone in her eco-terrorist activities. There were two others plus the leader. Eve Summers was a member of the group. While at the University of Michigan, Eve was immediately drawn to Peggy because she saw in Peggy the free spirit that she wanted to be. However, she decided instead to always meet the expectations of others. College gave her the chance to be the woman that was always hidden in her soul.

Eve didn't exactly imitate Peggy; in fact, the two were still miles apart in so many ways. Eve was quite attractive and enjoyed the attention her figure and good looks brought from admiring males. After getting to know Peggy, she let go of makeup and dressed down considerably, but her bubbly personality and her beauty were unchanged.

What did change was Eve's attitude about who she was and what was important to her. What bonded Peg and Eve was the love of nature, an appreciation for the environment and a disdain for people who dug into Mother Earth to build mansions. The two women were repulsed that the wealthy would ruin the exquisite beauty of the wilderness to build homes on a mountain ledge high above a valley.

After graduating from the University of Michigan, Eve moved to Boulder, Colorado. She was not only passionate about the environment, but she was also an outdoor survivalist. She enrolled in an Outward Bound program and was one of their most honored graduates. In fact, she was asked by the leadership to join them in their highly regarded outdoor survival training program.

Eve's father, a successful businessman in a corrugated paper company, died of a heart attack, the direct result of working 20 hours a day and trying to make every decision for a huge corporation. Eve's mother, a well-known writer who sold her articles to travel magazines throughout the world, had died of breast cancer. While living, neither parent had had much time for Eve, so she sought attention in school by working on whatever it took to be accepted and popular. She did a good job because she was well-liked, talented, and athletic. With both parents buried, Eve found she had inherited a fortune that would support her lavish lifestyle.

The only male member of the Ring of Fire was Todd Baxter, the youngest of the four by at least a decade. Todd was shy and introverted. As starting tackle on the University of Pittsburgh football team, Todd was admired and feared by classmates and people who knew him. His strength and size coupled with his silent demeanor, caused people to keep him at a distance. While somewhat shy, he was quite comfortable on the Internet. He could "talk" to anyone via e-mail; he was a social butterfly on-line. Todd had many friends in chat rooms and among those who admired his football skill. But put him in front of a live human being, and he turned into a relatively quiet and introverted man. Todd's psychologist traced it all back to early childhood abuse.

Todd was ninety-five percent muscle and very strong. He didn't need to earn anyone's respect because his presence commanded respect.

Todd had long, dark brown hair. His neck was short and lined with muscle. There were tattoos on his biceps: one was of the Liberty Bell, because he was all-state football at Liberty Bell High School outside Philadelphia; and the second tattoo was "Norma," the name of the only girl he ever loved, who defined the word for him at an early age.

Todd saw those who damaged the environment in the same light as those who had abused him. There was no difference. Those who purchased plots of land, and then, for their selfish purposes, cut trees and built palaces, denying others the beauty of nature damaged the earth. He had no sympathy for these people, and burning their homes was his way of striking back.

The "Commander" of the Ring of Fire was Carrie Willoughby. Carrie lived in a suburb of Louisville, Kentucky, with her husband and two children, who were doing well in high school. She served as chairperson of the church circle, and she enjoyed her community quilting group.

At 36, Carrie was assertive, but not in an overbearing way. She simply had strong feelings about issues and voiced her opinions, an attribute that led many to suggest she run for the Louisville School Board. Carrie was attractive, slim, with long blonde hair that she usually wore pulled back and clasped at the nape of her neck.

Carrie worked for a Louisville company that provided captioning service to major networks. She picked up her skill by enrolling in a program at the local community college as a court reporter. There were additional opportunities in captioning and this work allowed her to work from her home.

Carrie had turned a small downstairs bedroom into an office. Her ergonomically correct office chair, a luxury she allowed herself since she spent so much time sitting, faced a collection of technology that was necessary for her job. A 17-inch RCA color television set was centered on a desk that was as deep as it was wide. A Dell computer sat to the left, and a steno machine rested on a small stand directly in front of her. She used a modem so that her captioned message could be sent directly to the studio.

Being asked to caption for the Fox Network was a compliment to Carrie because beginners with the company usually started by captioning Home Shopping or Headline News. Major networks of which Fox was a member and a handful of other shows were reserved for the more experienced captioners and Carrie was counted among the best the company had hired.

The steno machine that Carrie used had 22 keys that, when punched singly or in combination, allowed a typed message to scroll across the television screen with about a two second delay.

Every evening Carrie logged on to the show's web site about a half hour before the show so that she would know what would be presented. Twenty minutes before air time she would get a call from her employer to make sure she was preparing to caption and would in fact be able to do the show. Then, she would start the software for the program, make sure the settings were correct, and dial the modem which connected her to the studio.

Precisely at 5 P.M. she began captioning so that millions of people with impaired hearing would be able to understand the newscaster. But, Carrie knew that many normal hearing people who watched the show used the captions to clarify what was said. The service initially intended for deaf and hard of hearing people now actually served millions more than just those with impaired hearing.

At the end of the show, Carrie sent the file of her work to the Fox Network which kept archives of the captioning for approximately a month before destroying the file. Once the file was sent, Carrie would shut down her computer and modem, turn off the television monitor, and leave her office.

CHAPTER THREE

Twenty-One Months ago
Friday, October 4, 2002
Chicago, Illinois

The Ring of Fire got its start when Carrie, Peg, Eve, and Todd met at an environmental conference at the University of Chicago. The topic that caught their collective attention was titled, "Suburban Sprawl: A 9-11 of a Different Color." There were about twenty participants in the session. The speaker was a professor from the University of Oregon. During the question and answer portion of the program, Carrie looked throughout the group to see who in the audience was most passionate about the topic. It was obvious to her that Peggy and Eve were very interested. At the end of the session, as participants filed out of the room or approached the speaker to ask a follow-up question, Carrie walked up to Peggy and Eve.

"Makes you want to leave here and get to work, wouldn't you say?" Carrie said to the two women.

"Yes. I'm ready. We've done enough talking; it's time to put action behind our thoughts," Peggy said with conviction.

"My thoughts exactly," Carrie replied. "Dr. Lott, I'm Carrie Willoughby from Louisville, Kentucky. I am very familiar with your advocacy, research, and writings."

"Thank you. It's nice to meet you. This is Eve Summers, from Colorado. We were students together at the University of Michigan. Seems like awhile ago, right, Eve?"

"Hardly a few years ago, Peggy. I think it has been about fifteen now," Eve said, shaking her head. "Time sure flies."

"Nice to meet you, Eve," Carrie said with a smile. "I'd like to continue this conversation so that maybe we can put some energy into action. Will you join me?"

Both women nodded. As they were about to agree upon a time they heard from a hulking young man, "Would you mind if I joined you?" Todd stood looking at the floor, almost embarrassed to intrude.

Eve spoke up. "We're all in this bond of protecting the planet – of course you can join us." Eve felt a bit bold, given that she wasn't the one who had suggested a continued discussion. Peggy went along with Eve's suggestion, and Carrie seemed pleased with the expansion of the group.

Todd, sensitive to others, spoke up. "I don't mean to barge into your group. Really. Maybe you three want to be by yourselves."

"Not at all, please join us," Peg said. "We're only going to have a short discussion over some tea. Right, Carrie?"

"Yes. We'll just go to my room for some privacy. It'll only take a few moments," Carrie replied, knowing that in order for her plan to be successful she had to remain dominant and not have her ideas challenged.

Todd nodded positively. "Thanks. My name is Todd Baxter. I'm a student at the University of Pittsburgh." The three women introduced themselves and shook his hand.

"Let's all go to my room," Carrie said. "It is a suite that will allow us room to talk and be comfortable."

All four gathered up their materials and followed Carrie to the elevator. Once inside, she pushed the number 12. As the elevator rose, no one spoke a word.

In Room 1286, Carrie invited her guests to take a seat while she began to heat water in the coffee maker. She had an assortment of teas to offer her guests.

Peggy opened with, "That speaker was definitely motivational – one of the best I've heard."

"He said the same old thing in a new way," Eve replied. "He was preaching to the choir, but who else would you expect at a conference like this?"

"What did you think, Todd?" Peggy asked.

Todd nodded. "We don't need another pacifist, but he was okay, I guess."

"We don't need another pacifist?' By that you mean…" Eve asked.

"I'm ready for a war. We can meet and talk as we do every year. I've been coming here since I was in junior high and all this is, is a group of talkers – nice, well-meaning people, but they have no backbone, they take no action. I'm a football player. This is like a football game where we sit around like a bunch of cheerleaders, but no one is on the field taking it to the opponent, the enemy if you will."

"I agree, Todd," Carrie said. "I've reached a point where I'm about to give up. Talk, talk, talk. All the choir does is chat with each other. The choir needs to take over the church, if you know what I mean."

"I don't know what you mean," Peggy said.

"I mean take control!" Carrie bellowed like an old-time preacher. Todd smiled for the first time and nodded as he took a comb from his pocket and ran it through his long hair.

"Control?" Eve said. "What kind of control?"

"Action, retribution. Doing what makes people sit up and take notice."

"You sound a little harsh, Carrie," Peggy replied.

"No, what's harsh is developers buying the land. What's harsh is the wealthy raping the wilderness, killing animals, destroying the natural lay of the land, cutting down trees, robbing future generations of scenery. I've had it with talk, conferences, presentations, flyers, letters to congressmen. It's all a waste – a total waste, and year after year we gather to plan how to waste more time. It is time to act, not talk!" Carrie was passionate, and she began to connect with Peggy and Eve. Todd was already in her corner.

Carrie poured the hot water into mugs and gave her guests a choice of tea.

"What would you destroy, Carrie?" Eve asked.

"Homes. You need to hit the enemy where it hurts and since they covet money, taking from them what they covet hurts. If we hit enough of them, they'll begin to get the message." Carrie continued, "And to use Todd's analogy to football, what defense do they have, since we'd never be caught? We need to take the issue into our own hands to protect the land we love. Not only do we win, but nature wins, animals win, trees win. And, who loses? The wealthy, the developers, the construction companies, the loggers, that's who. We simply need to stop talking and go to war!"

Eve felt she had found the person who could take her frustration and unleash it in a way that would bring justice to a situation that was without justice.

"I'm not sure this is a wise course of action," Peggy said, thoughtfully. "Isn't there a better way?"

"Dr. Lott, you are the most respected advocate we have, and we love you for it. But do you see any chance for change? Do you see anything but the land being bought, surveyed, sold to developers, and then sold to the wealthy? Can you name any place in the country where those who love the land have been successful in keeping it from becoming just another neighborhood?"

"I guess I can't," Peg replied.

"My point exactly. How many years are we going to meet at these conferences to talk about it while nothing changes? The developers just see us as crazies getting in their way."

"I guess I agree that action is needed," Peggy said seriously. "But, if we get caught, we'll be jailed, and I'm not sure that I'm willing to risk that. You're sure this is the way to go?" Peg persisted. "This is criminal behavior, and if we're caught, we're in big trouble."

Todd replied, "We won't get caught."

"How can you be so sure?" Peg asked.

"Because of Carrie."

"Todd is right," Carrie added. "First, we won't be caught, and secondly, we are not the criminals; the criminals are the developers and the landowners and builders. They are the ones raping the land, not us."

Peggy persisted, "I appreciate your thought that we won't be caught, but we're amateurs, and all it takes is a slip."

"There will be no slip. Our bond will be so tight and our procedures so exact that no one will break the Ring of Fire!" Carrie replied with passion.

Group dynamics being what they were, the others convinced Peg that using arson as a means of destruction was justified and the only honorable way to fight the war against big government, big development companies, and people with big money.

Peggy was still concerned about getting caught. "I repeat: how can you be certain that we won't get caught?"

"Carrie," Todd said. "You weren't listening a moment ago. The woman is a genius, an absolute genius."

"How is that for a compliment, Carrie?" Eve said with a smile.

"Thank you, Todd," Carrie replied.

"Tell us how to proceed," Todd said.

"The new developments are listed on the Internet. All of the information we need sits right in our computers. We can even watch homes being built. I can scan those that will give us the best chance of wreaking havoc and striking at those who are killing our land. Peggy will be responsible for the Midwest, Todd for the East, and Eve for the

West. On a signal from me via captioning on TV, you three, acting from your regions, will go out and set fire to a designated house. You will burn the home, return to your place of residence and enjoy the media coverage while the authorities will have no clue – none whatsoever."

Todd then gave Carrie all the power she needed. "We simply take our directions from the Commander. She is responsible to stake out the homes, assure that the locations are remote, and give us directions. All we do is spread the flammable fluid and strike a match. Our offense is that simple. Nobody gets hurt, no fifteen yard penalties, just the joy of winning. Right, Commander? Just the joy of winning."

"Yes, finally some satisfaction," Carrie said, with a smile.

Todd continued, "The Commander has led another war that you probably don't know about. She led an effort to stop lumbering companies from cutting acres and acres of trees in Oregon. She organized, led, and directed the destruction of trucks, lumbering machinery, you name it and no one was caught. To this day, no further destruction of trees has taken place, and the authorities have no clue as to who set the fires."

"I am willing to go along with the plan, under one condition…" Peggy said.

"There are no conditions, Dr. Lott. You are a warrior or not – there is no middle ground."

"As long as you can assure that we will not be caught, I'll help. I'll burn for the sake of protecting the land," Peggy said. Eve was somewhat surprised at Peggy's agreement to go along with the plan, but, because of her respect for Dr. Lott, Eve agreed as well.

"Todd, I assume you are in?"

"Yes, Commander, I most certainly am."

"Thank you all," Carrie said. "We will act, and we will save the land. And in doing so, we will teach the wealthy that the land is not theirs to call their own, but the land belongs to the people."

"From this moment forth, we'll be known as the Ring of Fire. We must never use this phrase to another nor outside the private conversations of the four of us. From this moment forth, we shall never break the bond that we have established here. I'm sure you will understand that for this cause to be successful, we must bond forever. There is no backing out, there is no changing your mind, there is no thinking about it. You are soldiers for the earth in the Ring of Fire. If you understand and agree, nod and place your hands one upon another. By bonding together we will bring down the enemy."

The four nodded and piled hands one upon another and then hugged one another. Peggy was accepted in a new way; Todd could unleash his aggression; Eve would be doing something positive and exciting; and Carrie would be in control, total control. The four left the room planning a meeting for the next day, when they would discuss the details of how they would communicate.

Peggy was a bit surprised that she had agreed to this destructive plan, but she had been accepted into the group and it felt good, even though the group was intent on breaking the law. Now, at age 35, she was accepted by those who shared a common purpose. The fact that it was illegal was not inconsequential, but it seemed to be the answer to a problem that had concerned Peg for a long time.

Eve simply liked the excitement. It reminded her of her youth, of sneaking out of the house and riding with her boyfriend on his motorcycle, an activity that was absolutely forbidden by her parents. If they had ever found out, she would have been grounded for longer than she could imagine. It had been fun, exciting and dangerous, and now she would relive those feelings as a warrior in the Ring of Fire.

Todd was no stranger to Carrie. In fact, his approaching had been planned and orchestrated by Carrie. Todd was a good soldier in the war against timber foresters. He easily took orders from Carrie and had absolutely no guilt over crimes he had committed on behalf of the environment. He was ready to go and happy to have recruited two more people, which meant the number of homes that could be burned increased tremendously. This was exciting news to Todd.

The next morning Carrie approached Peggy and Eve as they were having breakfast in the hotel café. She handed Peggy a note. "We will meet in my room after the keynote address."

Later that morning the members of the Ring of Fire sat in Carrie's room taking copious notes about the communication plan. Carrie was teaching a code that would be communicated via captioning of the Fox News at 5 P.M. Each of the four members were taught the code and were instructed always to be in front of a television set with captioning during the half-hour news program. The coded message could come at any time during the half hour.

Todd, Peggy, and Eve would be sent notebooks containing specific instructions on how to burn the homes assigned to them. Also there would be procedures for responding to the police if they were ever caught.

Each was to carry out a burning following a coded message. Assignments would be given based on weather, completion schedule of the home, seclusion of the home, risk of forest fire, and distance from fire departments. Carrie would research all of this. The arsonist had to reach the assigned home, put flammable material in key places described in the notebook, strike the match, and get out of the area unnoticed.

The four once again committed to never break the bond and to carry out all of Carrie's instructions. There were a few questions and then the group disbanded. Over the next several weeks, the Ring of Fire polished its mode of operation. Carrie masterminded the selection of homes to be burned. She spent countless hours on the Internet locating housing developments in pristine areas of the country.

Peggy, Eve, and Todd practiced watching the 5 P.M. Fox Network News that Carrie captioned. They memorized the code and went over drills of how to decode and understand who was to burn, where, and when.

When Carrie was satisfied that the Ring of Fire was ready to begin the terrorism, she gave the signal for the first burning. The captioned message went to Peg. The home belonged to multi-millionaires in northern Wisconsin.

There was no pattern in Carrie's selections; the orders went out to the three warriors in random fashion. She knew that each assignment was a risk and that her warriors had other lives and spent much energy concealing their dark side. Carrie's assignments demanded action within 24 hours and, sometimes within 12 hours, of the signal to burn a home.

The thrill of Peg's success inspired Todd and Eve to do an equally good job when called upon. Carrie decided that Eve would be the second member of the Ring of Fire to taste the joy of a successful burning. Then Todd got his turn. After each burning, the Ring would talk via a conference telephone call to go over any glitches in the communication system and any suggestions for improvement based on their experience.

Between November 2002 and late May 2004, the group had successfully burned seventeen homes in the United States. Peggy had destroyed seven, Eve was responsible for six, and Todd had torched four.

The Ring of Fire was proud of its success. Especially satisfying was that no one suspected them. News reports indicated that the homes were definitely torched and an environmental terrorist group was suspect, but the authorities at the federal and state levels admitted they had no leads and no way of knowing who or what organization might be responsible for the destruction.

CHAPTER FOUR

June 27, 2004
Phoenix, Arizona and Gunnison, Colorado

In June 2004, Peggy applied to her department chair to attend a professional conference in Phoenix. The university, as well as her department, was supportive of Peg's attending national and international conferences because her presence was also that of Michigan State University. Her papers were often noted in distinguished proceedings.

In Phoenix, Peg would present a paper with Dr. Leonard Lowe of the University of Washington. Ironically, in this setting, Peggy was not as introverted as she was in her life outside these high profile meetings. She seemed to enjoy talking to other scholars and even attended an open house on occasion.

It was at the Phoenix conference on June 27 that Peggy Lott changed, almost as quickly as she had twenty odd years before as a teenager. Overnight she went from an introverted intellectual, without concern for appearance, to someone in love. The reason for this change was Len Miles. Leonard was wealthy, he loved the environment, he played in bridge tournaments, and he spent a lot of time at his mountain estate outside of Gunnison, Colorado.

Peggy and Leonard met at a conference session where the focus was on the compassionate use of land. The federal government had designated Phoenix as the southwestern site of a public hearing on the topic of land use. Peggy filled out a card to be a speaker. Because of her standing in the environmental community, she was chosen to testify.

The speaker following her was Len. He opened by saying, "Thank you for the opportunity to comment and especially to follow such an articulate and beautiful person as Peggy Lott. I have known Dr. Lott through her writings and lectures and admire her for much more than her beliefs."

To say that Peggy was floored would put it mildly. She had never heard anyone refer to her as a "beautiful person." Peggy listened carefully to Len's presentation and found his attitudes to be in sync with hers. She needed to meet this man, if only to thank him for his kind words.

Len was most willing to accept Peggy's appreciation. After they had talked for most of the afternoon, Len suggested they share an early evening meal. As they continued to get to know one another, they found they agreed on every major topic, from politics to religion, to abortion to peace in the Middle East.

Near the end of the meal Leonard said, "Would you consider going with me to Gunnison for a day or two? I'm leaving this evening around eight o'clock."

"I'd like to, Len, but I really must get back to MSU – I need to plan for the next term."

"No better place to do that than in the fresh mountain air of the Rockies," Len replied, looking deeply into Peg's eyes.

"I know. I'm tempted, but…"

"Then give in to the temptation, Peg," Len suggested. "It is a beautiful setting."

"I am sure it is, but I hardly know you. I really don't think it's appropriate to join a man at his mountain home for a couple of days, after knowing him for only half a day."

"I respect that, but you have nothing to be concerned about. You'll have your own room and my housekeeper lives there when I'm home. I also have a handyman who lives on the property as well, not in the house, but out back in a small cabin. We'll have plenty of company."

"Well, if that's the case, maybe it would work out." Peggy knew she had a couple of days before she had to be back to the university.

"You won't regret it, Peg. The setting is out of this world. We can take walks, see deer, gaze at stars you didn't know existed, and admire hummingbirds flitting here and there. Say no and you'll regret the decision for the rest of your life."

"Ok, sounds like fun," Peg said, a bit apprehensive.

"Great, we'll fly in my plane. I'll take you to the Denver airport the day after tomorrow so you can continue your trip back to Michigan."

"Your plane? Are you a pilot, or do you hire a pilot?"

"I'm a pilot. I simply couldn't handle waiting in airports and all the security. I got my own plane, took lessons, and got my license. That was about five years ago."

There was a moment of silence and then Peg said seriously, "Why, Len?"

"Why what?"

"Why this sudden interest in me? I must be the exact opposite of women you are usually attracted to."

"Opposites attract, I guess. No, seriously, I do know of your research on the environment. My sister is a professor in Oregon, and she holds you in high regard; whenever we get together, at some point in the conversation your name comes up and she talks eloquently about you and your work. She respects and admires you."

"Thank you. But, that's not enough of an explanation to know me for six hours and invite me to share a day or two at your home."

"I believe that the beauty in a person has little, if anything, to do with physical appearance, clothes, hairstyle. I know you are extremely bright and that is attractive to me. We think alike. We appreciate nature."

"I do enjoy being with you," Peg replied. "I've never known anyone like you. I've never dated, never been in love, never even gone out with a guy for coffee. I'm just kind of shocked that you would be so kind and want to be seen with me."

"Hey, I'm not proposing marriage," Len said with a smile. "I'm only suggesting we continue to learn about one another by escaping this smoggy city and retreating to a beautiful setting high in the mountains away from people. We both love the environment, so I'm suggesting we go to the environment and enjoy it."

"Okay, I guess so," Peggy said, acquiescing to Len's plan. "I've done what I came here to do, so I'll check out and meet you in the lobby shortly."

As the two walked from the elegant dining room, Peggy realized that she had missed the Fox News and the captioning which may have given her a command. She knew that Carrie gave orders in a rather routine fashion. Carrie knew that Peggy would be out of state, so it was safe to assume that if there was a message, it would have been for Eve or Todd. Later she found that she was right; the message was for Eve, and before dawn a multi-million dollar home nearing completion burned to the ground.

The Lear Jet set down on the Gunnison Airport runway about 8:30 P.M. Len took Peggy's luggage and led her to his Mercedes-Benz. The two drove through town and headed north on Route 168 for the twenty-five minute ride to one of the most beautiful estates in the mountains. On the way to the house, Len called his housekeeper Martha Hayden to let her know they were on their way. He asked her to have coffee, cookies, and some herb tea ready when they arrived.

As they went onto the property, Peggy could not believe the size of Len's mountain retreat. The home was huge and looked like a log cabin castle. The grounds were meticulously trimmed. Flowers of all colors were blooming everywhere. The road made its way between long rows of pines, then circled in front of the two-story house with its huge wooden doors and porch lights casting a warm and welcoming glow.

When Len opened the door for Peggy, she suddenly realized what Cinderella must have felt like getting out of her carriage. Walking in the front door, a smiling Martha greeted her as if the two had known each other for years. The handyman Phil Bryson stopped in, more out of curiosity than wondering if his services were needed. He, too, was kind and gracious in his greeting.

Martha showed Peggy to her room, and Phil carried her bag up the stairs. Peggy thanked both of them for their hospitality and then put on some comfortable clothes, washed her face, brushed her teeth, and combed her hair. When she came downstairs, Len and his German shepherd were sitting by the fire looking as comfortable and at peace as a man and his dog could look. He's handsome, Peg thought. As far as she was concerned, Len was her knight in shining armor.

After Len gave Peggy a tour of the house so she would feel comfortable, they went outside and walked on the veranda. It was dark and there wasn't much to see, so Len told her he would give her a full tour in the morning. The two returned to the den, sat in front of the fire and talked into the night.

When the conversation was about to end, Peggy realized that her secret bubble had to burst. She knew that sooner or later she would have to admit to her involvement in the Ring of Fire. Again comparing herself to Cinderella with the clock ticking toward midnight, she lived in the moment. She was convinced that Len would reject her as soon as he realized that she had burned seven homes. He had been kind, and Peggy should never have decided to come to this beautiful home in the mountains of Colorado. What a hypocrite I am, she thought, enjoying this home when in a matter of days I will deny others the beauty I now experience.

Len put his arm around Peggy. Everything in the last several hours was a first. No man had ever put his arm around her. She took a deep breath and savored the moment, allowing herself to enjoy being in Len's presence. She sipped the herb tea and enjoyed a cookie while the two talked not about intellectual topics but about the simple things in life: taking a walk in the forest, looking at a reflection in the pond, standing next to a tall pine and appreciating its survival in a world of storms, and man's encroachment onto the land and its resources.

Peggy didn't want to be pinched and awakened from the heaven she suddenly found herself in. But she felt a need to let someone know of her evil deeds, and Len was the first person in her life, outside of the Ring of Fire, in whom she felt she could confide.

Ironically, Peggy decided to talk about it in the glow of the fire. The two sat side by side, holding hands now, enjoying the dancing glow of the flames and the crackling of wood. Peggy took a deep breath, felt her heart pounding inside her chest and then began.

"Len, I want to tell you something. I hardly know you, and yet I feel I can trust you."

"You most certainly can, Peggy."

"This is hard for me because it involves a lot of risk, and I also realize that this magical time with you could burst like a soap bubble, but I want to tell you something."

"Go ahead. I'll put another piece of wood on the fire."

Peggy lowered her head praying for some wisdom to stop her or to allow her to proceed in trust. She looked up and said directly, "Len, I'm an arsonist. I burn homes, homes like yours."

Len tried not to allow any body language to express his shock. He stood by the fireplace. "That's quite a stretch from my image of you. I think you are testing me here, Peg. Is there a need to do that?"

"No, I'm not testing you or teasing you or playing games. I simply need to be honest with you. You have shown me more love in the last twelve hours than I've ever experienced in my adult life. I felt you had to know. I'm part of a small group of, some would say vigilantes, who have taken the law into their own hands, believing that people should be punished. I'm talking about people who are raping the land and building expansive homes where trees once grew, animals lived in natural habitats, pristine scenery stood for generations to enjoy."

"Tell me about your arson ring. I'm curious," Len said, as the fire snapped and glowed.

"We call ourselves the 'Ring of Fire.' We believe that the only way to combat the destruction of the land is to, as they say, 'Fight fire with fire.'"

"You never could see the uselessness of it all?" Len asked.

"Meaning?"

"Well, a key word is insurance," Len replied. "All these owners and building companies have insurance. All you are doing is delaying the inevitable, which is building a new home. In fact, one way to look at it is that you are destroying wood, and more trees, trees that you love, will replace those in the house you burned."

"I never thought of it that way, but you're right."

Len sat down next to Peggy, took her hand and with much compassion and with no condemnation said, "Peggy, for a woman of your intelligence, this makes no sense at all. I appreciate your desire to protect the environment, but what your Ring of Fire is doing is counterproductive to your goal. Not only that, but you put the environment at great risk by your action. Think of the pollution you cause, to say nothing of the possibility of forest fires or significant damage to adjoining land and wildlife."

"Len, you make good sense," Peggy said, now holding her head in her hands. "But, when we began, we were so angry with these people and what they were doing. We knew that responding politically got us nowhere. We couldn't counter with petitions. We had no power, and the only way anyone would listen was by seeing the destruction of what they valued."

"Pretty desperate, I'd say."

"Yes," Peg replied. "We're angry, and we want to do something to stop the violation. The only thing we could think of that seemed logical was to burn down homes."

Len listened thoughtfully. He could understand Peggy, but he simply couldn't believe that a woman of her intellect and stature in the professional community would be involved in a ring or a cult. And this one pursued a course of action that had no chance of changing behavior, public policy, or the future construction of homes on land being sold by developers.

"Do you see the error of your ways, Peg?" Len asked.

"I do now. I was hooked into the Ring of Fire from the moment the idea was proposed. I did question the violation of law but I guess I got caught up in the emotion of revenge. Now I realize how stupid I was and how my entire future is jeopardized because of my behavior. My biggest fear was getting caught, and it still is."

Len squeezed Peg's hand, and she looked into his eyes. "I hope you reconsider what you are doing, Peg. I love the environment as much as you do, but I work to set policy by playing within the system. I think it works. I really do, or I wouldn't spend as much time as I do advocating for it. I suppose we are two human beings compassionate about nature, but we differ on how best to preserve it. Even after hearing of your arson, my thoughts, respect, and admiration don't change one bit. I don't agree with your behavior, but you remain a beautiful, beautiful woman."

Peg started to cry. She was simply overwhelmed by his compassion. She had heard the phrase "unconditional love," but she had never understood it until now. She knew that her attitude had changed, not because a man accepted her, but because being a criminal was not in her nature, and what Len said made sense. All she was doing was causing more logs to be cut and more homes to be built, and that led her to realize how foolish she had been.

Peg and Len did not speak for several minutes as he held her. There were no words to express the emotions that consumed Peg as they sat in front of the glowing fire. She would put her head on her pillow that night as a new woman. A new life would begin, and somehow things would be okay.

Ten minutes later, Len stood up and taking Peggy's hand, said, "Come with me. I want to show you something you've probably never seen before."

He turned out the lights and the two stepped out onto the deck. There was only a sliver of a moon on the eastern horizon. The two stood in total darkness. All was quiet except for the brook that flowed in the valley below.

"Look up, Peg. Have you ever seen so many stars?"

Peggy looked into the heavens and couldn't believe it. The stars were brighter than she had ever recalled. They sparkled against an ebony canvas.

"I had no idea that the universe was so expansive," Peg said, amazed at the view. "The Milky Way's always just been faintly visible, but out here it's bright. This is awesome."

"I love to come out here on a clear night," Len replied. "I feel sorry for the millions of people who live in the cities and suburbs. They never get to see the heavens like this."

"It's spectacular, Len. You're right. I've never seen a sight like this. Thanks for inviting me here." She stood close to Len, reveling in his warmth. He put his arm around her. They stood like that for several minutes enjoying the cool, refreshing air.

The next morning, Peggy woke up before the others. Putting on her robe, she went out onto the deck to enjoy the quiet and watch the sun rise. She sat with her eyes closed for a few minutes. When she opened them, to her left a doe and two fawns moved cautiously across the lawn. The deer were skeptical of Peggy and kept her in their sight as they moved forward looking for berries. Within a few seconds, four more deer surrealistically appeared and quietly moved from Peggy's left to right. The view was filled with colorful aspens and bright Douglas firs, serving as a backdrop for the deer's morning walk.

Following breakfast, Len invited Peg to hold the hummingbird feeder.

"You mean hang it up on a hook?"

"No, I mean hold it so the hummingbirds can come up to you and drink."

"Really? They'll come that close?"

"Sure. You can hear the hum as they flit here and there. That, too, is quite an experience."

"How many come to feed, a couple?"

"Quite a few. Ten or fifteen, I'd say."

"I'll try it." She held the feeder and was amazed at the trust the magical birds had in her.

"You hold it up and I'll take a photo or two," Len said.

"I'd like that. Wait. Can Martha take a picture of the two of us? I simply can't leave here without a photo to remind me of Camelot."

"I'm sure she can," Len replied. Martha was happy to oblige.

They spent the rest of the morning hiking and fishing. Peg would have nothing to do with fishing, saying she was not capable of taking the life of such a beautiful creature. Len understood and accepted her feelings, but he had no problem reeling in a couple of beautiful trout. He would clean them and give them to Martha for a future meal.

In mid-afternoon, Len announced that he had invited some neighbors and friends over for cocktails and dinner. The friends were curious about his upcoming trip to China and wanted more information. Peg was apprehensive about being with so many strangers, but she knew this was important to Len. For the first time in years she wanted to look nice for the evening.

Martha agreed to drive Peg to town so she could get her hair done and buy an outfit for dinner. The two women went into Gunnison, where Martha was able to get Peggy an appointment with her hairdresser. The two women were like teenagers in the dress shop. Peg tried on various outfits and debated about her style and what colors looked best on her. Martha also helped her pick out some perfume.

With a new hair style, a new dress and shoes, Peg felt ready to go back to the estate and prepare for the evening. Through this experience, a bond had developed between Martha and Peggy. The two women were about the same age, but they couldn't have been more different in background and life experiences.

Once back in Camelot, Peggy walked into the guest bedroom to find on her nightstand a dozen red roses with a note from Len. "These roses are envious of your beauty. Love them, as they were grown solely to please you." She buried her face in the blossoms and inhaled deeply. The smell was intoxicating.

Peggy spent more time in the bathroom than a teenager preparing for the senior prom. When she finished and was about to make her grand entrance, she looked in the full-length mirror in her bedroom and almost didn't recognize the figure looking back at her.

The guests arrived around six, and Len proudly introduced Peggy to his friends. He was dressed in a silk shirt and linen slacks, looking casually elegant. He complimented Peg on her new look with her long, column dress and stylish new haircut.

Drinks were served, followed by dinner. Martha knew about Peggy's vegetarian preference, so she prepared a meal just for her. After-dinner drinks were served on the deck as guests watched deer below, white-water rapids off in the distance, and wildflowers in every direction. The birch and pine trees were stately right up to the tree line, and then the mountain peaks, white with snow, glistened against a dark blue sky, preparing for the evening show of color when the sun would set in the west signaling the end of another day.

As the temperature cooled, guests came inside for continued conversation around the fireplace. Peggy soon became the center of attention as she was asked about teaching at MSU and the research she was conducting. Peggy was not comfortable with small talk involving her profession, but she felt that she managed quite well.

When the last couple had left and the estate gate was closed and locked, Peggy and Len took off their shoes, took a deep breath, and gave each other a smile and hug signifying a successful party. "I am so proud of you, Peg. You looked marvelous in your dress and hair style. What a joy to introduce you to my friends and to have them so pleased to meet you and be with you."

"This has been the happiest I've ever been, Len. Thank you."

"I said you would enjoy the mountains."

"Enjoy doesn't begin to explain my feelings."

"I'm glad. They won't recognize you at the university tomorrow or whenever you are returning."

"Some people may wonder what happened, but I'll probably be the same old reclusive academician the staff and students have come to expect."

"Thanks for joining me here, Peg. You've made me very happy, very happy indeed."

"I guess the chariot awaits, or it will turn into a pumpkin," Peg said, squeezing Len's hand.

"I'll fly you to Denver and get you to your flight first thing in the morning. By the way, if you think some of the sights were out of this world from the deck, wait till you see the Rockies from the air. With the sun rising, the view is something to behold."

"Just being with you will make me happy, Len. Anything else is frosting on the cake."

"Speaking of which, let's have some coffee and a slice of Martha's wonderful cake before calling it a day."

The two talked into the early morning hours about the realities of their lives. Peggy learned that Len had been married, and had two grown sons who lived in California. His wife had died of cancer seven years before. He had made his millions in the business world and had found his passion for the environment as a student at the University of Idaho. At that time he had no problem organizing protests against lumber barons in the dark green forests of the Northwest. He was even arrested and jailed overnight for resisting arrest outside a lumber yard. Peggy told Len more about her past, about her family, and her deep roots in the world of academia.

The evening came to a close with a discussion of Peg's arson. There was no judgment, no advice, no condemnation, but Len did say once again that, as far as he was concerned, the avenue to changing attitudes was to work within the system. All arson did was to make people dig in deeper with their political connections and their deep pockets of money. They would also have the support of public opinion, because the truth was that the ordinary man on the street didn't agree with protestors, didn't value terrorists. And people's personal problems far outweighed their concern for a mountain view, or the home of a squirrel or a wetland habitat for a turtle or a bird.

Everything Len said made perfect sense. Peg would return to Michigan and withdraw from the group. If she was arrested for her crimes, she would pay whatever price society deemed appropriate for her acts. She could no longer participate in the Ring of Fire.

CHAPTER FIVE

Thursday, June 29, 2004
East Lansing, Michigan

Once back in Michigan, with more time to think about her change of attitude, Peggy decided the best way to end her involvement with the Ring of Fire was to talk to the members. It would be awkward and stressful, but she had always been one to talk to others about major decisions rather than talk behind their backs. She asked Carrie to set up a conference call.

"I don't think it's necessary," Carrie replied.

"How about a chat group on the computer?" Peg asked.

"That's worse than a phone call. You really feel you need to talk to everyone?" Carrie asked.

"Yes. I have some important information to share."

"You share it with me first. If I think it's important, I'll share it with the others."

"I'd really rather talk to everyone," Peg said, getting a bit perturbed with Carrie's attitude.

"Like I said, you tell me what's on your mind, and I'll decide if it needs to go to the group."

"I've given this a lot of thought and well, to put it bluntly, I'm out of the Ring, Carrie."

"Not possible. We agreed to this mission and that there would be no getting out. You swore to that at the ceremony, Peg. You are not getting out!"

"You're wrong, Carrie. I am getting out. I'm sorry not to meet my commitment, but things have changed. I've changed. I'm out."

"I hope you realize the consequences of this, Peg."

"What would that be?" Peg asked.

"This is a war we're fighting. We took up arms in the form of fire to fight and defeat those who rape the land. You are a traitor now. People shoot traitors, Peg."

"Shoot traitors? Oh, come on, get serious, Carrie!"

"I am serious."

"You're going to kill me?" Peg asked. "Being an arsonist is not enough? Now you want to tack on murder?"

"I don't want to tack on murder, but you have to realize that if you divulge any information to anyone that in any way jeopardizes what we do or in any way implicates Todd, Eve, or me, we really have no choice. I can't believe you are shocked."

"No, from you, this isn't a shock," Peg said. "I hope you realize that I can play the same card."

"Same card?"

"If any of you implicate me or give out any information that I have been a part of the Ring of Fire, I'll have no choice."

"That's fair, but picking a fight with three people is hardly something I think you should consider," Carrie said.

"I'm sorry this is ending this way," Peg said solemnly. "I expected you would be unhappy, but I didn't expect to be threatened. Even without your threat, I wouldn't call the police and report you."

"This is serious stuff, Peg. If the authorities get a hint that helps them track this perfect crime to us, our lives as we know them are over. We can't allow any leaks, any slips, or, in your case, any turncoats."

"I don't expect to talk to you again, Carrie," Peg said, upset that the conversation had not gone as she had hoped.

"I'm very angry with you," Carrie replied. "I counted on you to be in the Ring, to be a support for Eve and Todd. I never thought you would turn on us. I'm shocked and angry and there's nothing else I can say!"

"Goodbye, Carrie," Peg said, eager to end the conversation.

Peggy had communicated her wish to be out and now she was. Her only fears were that the authorities would crack this mess, and that Carrie and the others would think she had let the cat out of the bag.

Carrie, still furious with Peg, called Todd; he returned her call from a public phone in Pittsburgh.

"Peg is out of the Ring, Todd. I need your help."

"Sure. What do you need?"

"I don't trust Peg. She broke a solemn vow that the four of us made two years ago to start and finish this war. She broke that commitment, and I have every expectation that she will break another one."

"You mean by going to the cops?" Todd asked.

"Yes, I expect her to do or say something to implicate us."

"I agree."

"I want you to kill her." There were a few seconds of silence.

"When I got into this, I agreed to arson, but not to murder, Carrie," Todd responded. "That wasn't a vow I made."

"I realize that, but unfortunately Peg is now a part of the war."

"I'm not certain I can do this, Carrie," Todd admitted. "I can beat someone up, or smash a guy across the line in football, but murder? That's beyond what I want to do, or will do."

"Todd, listen to me. This is an order. You are to kill her," Carrie demanded.

"I don't think so, Carrie. I like Peg. I'm sorry she is leaving, and I hope we're not turned in, but I can't kill her."

"Todd Baxter, this is your Commander speaking to you!" shouted Carrie. "All our futures will be spent in prison if she slips. She has to pay a price. I'll handle all the details of how and when. You will do as I say!"

There was silence. Todd flashed back to his abuse. He felt he had no choice but to acquiesce to the person threatening him.

"I'll do what you ask, Carrie. Give me the directions and I'll kill her."

"That's better. I will give you directions at a later date."

"OK."

"We'll be in touch," Carrie concluded.

Todd could feel the adrenaline cursing through his veins. He was anxious, his heart quickened, and he had a funny feeling that could not be explained. He detested what he had just agreed to do.

Carrie called Peggy. As soon as Peggy answered she hung up. Peggy did not have caller ID so could not match a number with a name. At first, Peggy thought it was someone who had called a wrong number. But, every half hour the phone would ring and when she answered she could hear only breathing on the other end of the line. After four calls, she removed the plug and could only wonder what was happening.

That night she got a message on her computer. It didn't look like scam material, it looked personal. She opened it up and read, "You really blew it when you left the Ring of Fire. Life is precious; enjoy every minute." Peggy didn't recognize the sender's e-mail address. She deleted it and spent a few sleepless hours wondering if there was a connection between the phone calls and the e-mail message. Peggy's guess was that the actions were harassment strategies by Carrie, but without any evidence, she couldn't be certain.

The authorities had begun to see similarities between the fires that burned across the country. In each case they had no suspect, but like many crimes, a pattern was discernible. Each home was burned at about the same time in its development, and each fire was set by pouring gasoline around the foundation with extra fuel near a fuse box.

In a control and strategy room in the nation's capital, on a large United States map on a wall, pins showed locations. Looking at the pins, someone connected the dots. To everyone's amazement they formed concentric circles. One of the employees of the U.S. Department of Alcohol, Firearms and Tobacco said, "Looks like a ring of fire to me." The phrase stuck, and from that point on, any additional fire that fit the pattern was referred to as a burn in the Ring of Fire.

That night while Carrie was captioning the Fox News, she heard the following: "Now, a story about a series of burnings taking place around the country. We go to Houston and Tracy Sasso of WHOU."

"Thank you, Tom. I'm standing on the outskirts of Houston in an environmentally sensitive area where developers were recently allowed to purchase what had been pristine public land since the days of Sam Houston. As you can see behind me, many new and expensive homes are going up. At 3 A.M. this morning firefighters rushed to this scene, where, behind me and to my left, you can see the charred remains of a mansion.

"WHOU learned this afternoon that the federal government has now dubbed the terrorism as the Ring of Fire. When asked the meaning of that phrase, our informant, who refused to be identified, told us simply that the reference to 'Ring of Fire' is top secret.

"That's it from here, Tom. A lot of very nervous homeowners in the final stages of their dream homes now worry that in the pre-dawn hours their homes may become trophies of the Ring of Fire. Tracy Sasso, reporting from northwest Houston."

"Thank you, Tracy. The authorities ask that citizens contact their local police if they have any information about these home burnings. Now, a story from London, England…."

To say that Carrie was furious was to put it mildly. She could hardly finish captioning the newscast because she now knew that Peg had talked, had violated the bond, and she would have to pay the price. For as intelligent as Peg Lott is, you'd think she could keep her mouth shut in order to live, Carrie thought.

As soon as Carrie finished captioning the news, she reached Todd on the phone.

"She's done it, Todd. It was on the news. She told the authorities about the Ring."

"That can't be, she's smarter than that," Todd replied, surprised at what he had heard.

"I captioned it myself," Carrie said.

"You mean we're being called the Ring of Fire?" Todd asked.

"Yes, and it's because Peg told them about us."

"We're in trouble now. Big trouble."

"I'll continue planning the murder," Carrie said.

"Okay, but I'd give anything not to have to do this," Todd replied.

"Well, if you don't, you'll be playing football for some prison team till you're an old man. It's just a matter of time till the cops knock on our doors."

"Let me get this straight. You know for sure that she told the cops our names?"

"No, but she told them about the Ring of Fire because it was on TV. I'm only using common sense in believing that she told them about us."

"I'll wait for your directions."

Peggy felt it right that she contact Eve and tell her she was out of the Ring of Fire, for Eve had only agreed to join the group because of Peggy's influence. Peggy called Eve late that evening.

"Hi, Eve. This is Peggy. I'm calling because I wanted to tell you that I…"

"Left the Ring. I know. Carrie told me."

"Are you curious about why I made that decision?" Peg asked.

"Well, yeah, you were our model, so to speak," Eve replied.

"I decided I was going down a road that was heading only to terrifying consequences."

"I agree, but only if we get caught, and Carrie assured us that that would not happen," Eve said.

"Theoretically, that's correct. But, we're dealing with a world of very sophisticated technology. The chances of keeping this operation a secret are really next to nil. The more time that passes, the greater the risk of discovery."

"I'm staying in," Eve replied. "I believe in what we're doing."

"I respect your feelings, Eve, but even though I've committed the same criminal acts, I can't respect your actions."

"I know. Peggy, I'm concerned for your safety," Eve admitted.

"My safety?" Peg asked.

"Yes, Carrie is convinced that you talked to the authorities and will implicate the three of us in a plea bargain, if you haven't already."

"That will not happen, Eve."

"I told her that, but she has it in her head that you ratted on us. And Peg, Carrie would kill me if she ever found out that I told you this, but you could soon be killed."

"Well, that's not going to happen either," Peg said. "I know Carrie is angry and sends a strong message, but I doubt she would act. Even if she did, it would only be if I talked, and I'm not going to go there, so I've nothing to fear."

"You are not hearing me, Peg. She heard on TV that the cops call us the Ring of Fire, and she's convinced that you went and told them about us."

"That's not true. I don't know where they got that phrase, but it wasn't from me!"

"I don't know who to believe, Peg. I ask that you be very careful."

"Please believe me, Eve."

"OK. But, take care of yourself."

"I will. Before we hang up, please tell me how I'm to be killed."

"Well, it won't be by me, and you know that the Commander won't dirty her hands."

"Todd?" Peg asked.

"He's the only one left."

"Eve, I am going to begin a new life, and when that happens, no one will be able to contact me. I'll miss you."

"Wherever you go, please stay in touch," Eve asked. "It's important to me."

"I can't promise you that. Perhaps some day we'll reconnect."

"Please don't disappear."

"I may have to, Eve. Thanks for the warning. I've got to go."

Eve called Carrie and reported that she had heard from Peggy. Peg was her friend, but the bond of the Ring of Fire was stronger. Open communication had been burned into their minds, and any information concerning one was of concern to all.

At seven in the evening, Peggy was startled out of her deep thoughts by a sharp meow from Flame. Someone was at the door. This was odd because practically nobody knew where she lived and solicitors never bothered her.

Peggy went to the door and cautiously asked who was there.

"Flowers, ma'am."

She opened the door to a delivery man who held a dozen red roses in a tall vase. "Dr. Lott?"

"Yes."

"These are for you."

"Thank you."

Peggy was surprised at this. Her mind quickly went to a mental calendar. This wasn't her birthday or any significant day. There could be a mistake.

While Peggy carried the roses to her kitchen table, she noticed an envelope with her name on it. She removed the card; on the front was a newborn baby wrapped in a pink blanket. The card read, "As you begin a brand new life, know that I love you." It was signed, "Len."

Peggy looked at the card again, looked at the bright red flowers so full of beauty and life, and then broke down and had a good cry. No one had ever sent her flowers. Peggy literally reached to pinch her forearm. She needed to feel a twinge of pain to be assured that she was not dreaming this.

Once Peggy recovered, she called Len.

"The flowers are beautiful, Len. Thank you so much. Your note was so sweet."

"I just wanted you to know I was thinking of you, Peg."

"You will never know what this means to me. I broke down with tears of joy."

"That's wonderful. I'm happy you're happy."

"I'm very happy, Len. Thank you so very much."

"You're welcome, Peg. I'll be in touch."

"Goodbye. Oh, Len. I love you." What did I say, Peg thought. I just told Len I loved him. I said it and it sounded wonderful!

The next day brought a frightening experience. When the phone rang late in the morning, Peggy answered it and heard "Just wondering if you're still alive," and then the phone went dead.

That evening, when Peggy returned home from a graduate seminar, she called Len. She told him about the threat on her life. For over an hour the two talked about how best to respond. There was talk of aggression and of escape. What grew out of the long conversation was a plan to think about, to sleep on, to consider the pros and cons of, and to discuss the next evening.

Len favored using some of his resources simply to have Peg relocate, change her name, and live quietly in a small community in Idaho or rural Oregon. As tempting as that was, Peg thought it to be a cop out, and an escape that didn't bring any justice to those who had taken the law into their own hands. Now they planned to go further by destroying a life, hers.

Peggy concocted a plan that initially sounded ridiculous: she would jump into Lake Michigan in the middle of the night from a car ferry, the S.S. Badger. She then would be picked up by someone hired to do so. But first, she would lure her killer onto the Badger and set a trap. It was sure to break up the Ring of Fire and bring justice where there had been none.

The complication was the timing. Peggy wanted to carry out her plan during the early morning hours of July 14. Len had a commitment at that time in China. Besides not wanting Peggy to risk her life by jumping off a ship into Lake Michigan, he also didn't like not being there to help her. She finally convinced him that the plan would go without a hitch, and she'd be waiting for him in Colorado when he returned.

The next day Len set about making sure that this plan would succeed. He needed a charter boat captain he could trust to snatch Peggy from Lake Michigan, take her to the airport in Green Bay, and keep his mouth shut. With Len's contacts, influence, and money, he accomplished these goals in a matter of hours.

Central to this plan was Dick Warren, the captain of a charter fishing service in Manitowoc, Wisconsin. Once Len was assured that Dick was reliable and able to work effectively with them, he called Captain Warren to discuss the details of the proposed rescue. Len would pay him ten thousand dollars to do the job and to keep his mouth shut.

"Dick, what we want you to do is to pick up a woman from Lake Michigan in the early hours of the morning of July 14, after she jumps from the stern of the Badger."

"Jumps from the Badger? Are you serious?" Dick asked, surprised to hear such a thing.

"She knows what to do," Len said.

"She'll kill herself. She could be pulled into the propellers."

"We understand the possibilities," Len replied.

"She'll be hitting turbulent water at quite a fast clip. Not an activity for an amateur."

"She plans to get some instruction from a professional diving coach."

"Does he know this woman's going to jump from the Badger?"

"No, she told him she was going to go to a resort in Mexico where people can jump into water from great heights."

"Well, going into a tropical pond is quite different from going into Lake Michigan. The waters are cold and choppy at best, without adding turbulence from powerful propellers."

Len responded, "We appreciate your concern, but we think this is not going to be a problem. We wouldn't risk her life. We'll take precautions. She'll wear a wet suit and carry a flotation device when she jumps, and she'll have a strobe light with which to signal you."

"I was wondering how I would know when she is in the water," Dick said. "You see, I can't be close to the Badger. They'll just get on the radio and tell me to clear the area, and if I don't, they'll send the Coast Guard out."

"How far do you need to be away from the Badger?" Len asked.

"About a mile, and that's when I'm going in the same direction. If I head toward her, I'd better be a few miles away. The Badger pilot house has a radar screen that can pick me up. He'll wonder what I'm doing at 3 o'clock in the morning, following or going parallel to him."

"He doesn't own the lake, does he?" Len asked sarcastically.

"No, but after 9-11, he keeps a good eye on what is going on around him. I'd be wondering what a fishing boat was doing out there at that hour. He's got just as powerful a pair of binoculars as I have."

"Can you see a light signal from the Badger at a mile?" Len asked.

"Not a problem. I'd see a light flashing, but I obviously wouldn't see a person."

"Ok. Here's the plan," Len said. "When Peg is sure no one is around or in any position to see her jump, she'll signal with three flashes of light. We are planning the jump for 3:30 A.M. central daylight time. She will activate her flotation device and once she's in the water, she'll signal you with a strobe light."

"I guess it could work, but I'm not real sure," Dick responded.

"Peg will call you the evening of the 13th to make sure everything is okay at your end," Len said. "I assume there are some conditions that would prohibit you from going out in the lake."

"A bad storm would be about it. My boat can handle pretty rough water."

"I want to make this perfectly clear," Len said, his voice serious. "Not one word can be said about this to anyone."

"That won't be a problem," Dick replied. "You have my word on it."

"Are we set then?" Len asked.

"I have a few questions, please," Dick said.

"Go ahead," Len replied.

"Where do I take Peg when we get back to Manitowoc?"

"You'll drive her to the airport in Green Bay. She will be on her own then. You do not need to stay with her."

"Are you my contact during all of this?" Dick asked Len.

"No. I will be in Beijing when all of this happens. I fully trust it will go perfectly and I can honor my long standing commitment to an important environmental meeting with the Asian leaders."

"I see."

"When do you expect to arrive at the airport?" Len asked.

"If Peg jumps at three-thirty, I should have her to the airport in Green Bay around seven-thirty at the latest."

"OK."

"Next question. What if the Coast Guard stops us, or we're met by the police in Manitowoc?" Dick asked.

"If that happens, we don't expect you to go to any heroic lengths to hide Peg or to lie. If that happens, we've failed, not you. Just go ahead and cooperate with them."

"OK. Can Peg call me, say, about fifteen minutes before the jump, so I can be assured all is on schedule?"

"Yes, she'll do that," Len said. "Once Peg jumps, she'll have no means of contacting you other than the strobe light."

"I understand. If the jump is cancelled, I can still call her to confirm. Correct?"

"That's right.

"Okay, I think I'm all set."

"Thank you, Captain," Len said. "Your compensation will be adequate, I presume."

"Yes, much more than necessary, but I will assure you a successful pickup and silence which is what you are paying me for."

"Good."

That evening Len and Peggy talked again. Len repeated that it would be easier and safer to just disappear and he would pay for her relocation. He also said once again that he favored changing the date so he could be there.

Peggy appreciated his concerns on both matters but held firm. She knew what she wanted to do, and as long as she could be pulled from Lake Michigan and taken to Green Bay, she was certain that the plan would be successful.

CHAPTER SIX

Saturday, July 1, 2004
Pittsburgh, Pennsylvania

The first part of the plan to implicate the Ring of Fire involved Todd Baxter. Peggy contacted Todd and arranged to meet him at a restaurant in the Pittsburgh airport. Peg knew that a setting in a public place with security around would be a safe place to meet. If Todd was planning to kill her, he would not do it in an airport. Peggy arranged her flights so that she had an hour and a half in the airport, plenty of time to say what she needed to say.

The two met at a restaurant, The Fish Ladder. Peggy was fairly certain that Todd would record the meeting, and she didn't like knowing that Carrie would hear every word.

Peggy's plane landed on time, so she walked to the restaurant and was seated at a table when Todd arrived. He greeted Peggy coldly, as if it was an imposition for him to meet her.

"Thanks for meeting with me," Peggy said sincerely.

"What's to talk about?" Todd asked.

"As you no doubt know, I told Carrie that I'm out of the group."

"Yeah, not a good idea, but I know about that."

"Well, we all change, Todd."

"We don't all change when it comes to commitments."

The waitress interrupted to see if the couple wanted anything to drink or eat.

"I'd like some tea, decaf, maybe some lemon Constant Comment – do you have that?" Peg asked.

"Yes," the waitress replied. "And you, sir?"

Todd didn't respond to the waitress, only shook his head negatively. The waitress left to get Peg's tea.

"Nothing?" Peg asked. "Todd Baxter in a meeting without coffee? That's unheard of," Peggy said.

"Not in the mood," Todd replied. "Tell me what you came here to say and then I'll be on my way."

"I'm sorry to rob you of your valuable time, Todd. I thought we were friends."

"Not any more. Once you decided to break the bond, you became a stranger. This must be pretty important to you, since you were willing to come all the way from Michigan."

"Yes, talking to you is important to me. First, I'd like to show you this magazine." Peggy handed Todd a perfect copy of the most recent Environmental Speeches magazine. Todd took it and began to flip through the pages. "I brought it to show you the article by William Nichols. You know he's at MIT, and he presents some interesting theories. When I read it, I thought of you and wanted to tell you about it."

"You are giving this to me?" Todd asked.

"No, only bringing it to your attention. You can note the volume number if you like. I want to take it with me."

Todd closed the magazine and handed it back to Peggy. "Thanks."

Peggy put the magazine in a freezer bag and shut it with the plastic zipper.

"You've gone to quite a bit of trouble to protect that magazine," Todd said.

"I treat magazines as friends, and, with the rain expected, I don't want it damaged."

"You were always strange, Peggy," Todd said, shaking his head at her behavior. "I guess your quitting the Ring of Fire shouldn't have shocked us. I suppose it is the real you." Peggy nodded.

The waitress brought the tea to the table. "Sure I can't get you something, sir?"

Once again Todd shook his head. In doing so, his hair fell slightly out of place, so Todd took out his comb and smoothed his long hair. Peg often wondered why he didn't look like other athletes of today with shaved heads. He seemed to fixate on combing his hair.

The waitress turned and walked away as Todd said, "Tell me what you want to say. I've got things to do."

"Sure. What I wanted to say, Todd, is that while I admire our cause, I think we're making bad decisions in the long run."

"Bad decisions?"

"Not many crimes can be repeated often before the criminals get caught. There's too much technology out there these days. It's simply a matter of time before someone makes a mistake or says something to the wrong person. I don't want to spend the rest of my life in some women's penitentiary. I wanted to meet with you to try to get you and the others to see the danger in what you are doing, and to join me in stopping all of this burning before we're discovered."

"You think we'll get caught?" Todd asked, astounded at Peggy's thought.

"I'm certain of it, and if you knew about the cutting-edge technology and surveillance surrounding arson, you'd reach the same conclusion. Maybe before September 11 chances were good of not getting caught. These days, a criminal might get away with several fires, but to do this in a systematic fashion makes us putty in their hands, and they're waiting for someone to slip."

"The only slip that will kill us, Peggy, is you. You are the only one who might cause the 'slip,' as you call it. You are the one to fear."

"You fear me?" Peggy asked, chuckling. "Todd, be serious."

"I am serious. You are our only fear. Quite frankly, the three of us believe you have already talked to the cops."

"What do you plan to do about it?"

Todd looked down at the table for a moment, then said, "The success of our work demands perfect allegiance to each other. Once that bond is broken, you slip up, say something to someone, or do something to arouse curiosity, the cause for justice is over."

"I didn't realize I had so much power, Todd."

"Well, you do. As long as you keep quiet and reveal nothing, everything is fine."

"And if I do reveal something?"

"That would be too bad. Listen, Peg, you hold a lot of power, and at the same time you hold in your hands your ability to live. If you give up your power and become an informant, or say something that leads the authorities to one of us, you're dead. I can't make it any simpler than that. Like I said, we're still pretty certain that you've already gone to the cops."

"Then why would I come all the way to Pittsburgh to try and get you to come to your senses?" Peg asked. "If you were right, I would have told the police I would be meeting with you, and you'd be off to jail before I could get to my gate. Wake up, Todd! You're a bright guy. I've not talked to anyone about the Ring of Fire. I'll not talk to anyone. How stupid do you think I am?"

"The TV report talked about the Ring of Fire."

"Oh, somebody hears three words and you jump on the idea I'm an informant."

"It's not a common phrase," Todd replied. "It's our bond."

"Well, you can listen to Carrie, or you can listen to me. I can't form your opinion; only you can do that."

"Carrie is in the bond, and you've left us. I believe Carrie."

Peggy shook her head in anger, took her scarf from her head and revealed hair that looked like it had not been combed recently. "Well, you've made it clear that if I want to live, I need to develop complete and immediate amnesia about everything the four of us ever said or did."

"It may be too late, but if you haven't gone to the cops, then, yes."

"In that case, here's my notebook. It contains all of the information I collected for potential burnings. I'm giving you everything I have related to our efforts to destroy what belonged to those who destroyed the land that we love. You, Eve, and Carrie can be assured that I have nothing related to the work we did. I have totally cleaned my laptop and my at-home computer, and I've destroyed anything in writing. It is all in this notebook."

Todd accepted the material and put it into his large black case. "You're sure this is everything?"

"Yes, I'm absolutely certain. My hands are clean of it all."

"OK. I'll be on my way then."

"Todd, one more favor, if you will. May I borrow your comb?"

"My comb?" Todd asked.

"I've misplaced mine and my hair is a mess. Do you mind?"

Todd reached into his breast coat pocket for his long brown comb and handed it to Peg. She tapped the comb on the table allowing a couple of strands of hair to fall.

"I didn't give you a drumstick, Peg. Comb your hair and give it back. I'm on my way."

Peggy drew the comb, smelling of hair spray, through her medium-length brown hair. After swiping it through her hair a few times, she handed the comb back to Todd.

"Thanks. It was nice to know you, Todd. Sorry we're leaving this way. You're a man who fights for his beliefs and I admire that about you."

"I admire commitment, Peg. I wish you wouldn't leave us. We'll meet again – I can assure you of that."

"Would you kill me, Todd?" Peg asked, looking him in the eye.

There was a pause before Todd said, "Our cause is greater than life."

"You'd create the perfect murder to match the perfect arson, is that it? That would take some planning, Todd. It could be that murder would be your downfall – ever think of that? You know, murder is a lot different than arson. Investigating murder involves different technology, more tactics, and to be honest, it's much easier to slip up in a murder than it is in arson. Then I won't be the 'slip,' will I, Todd?"

Todd couldn't bring himself to look Peg in the eye. He merely looked down at the table.

"Todd, I am going to Wisconsin in a couple of weeks on the car ferry out of Ludington to begin a new life. Nobody in the Ring of Fire will ever hear from me again."

"I guess I should thank you for coming here, but I'm so angry with you that I can't even bring myself to do that," Todd said. He stood up, put his comb in his pocket, and walked away.

As she watched Todd leave, Peg opened a plastic bag and brushed the hairs into the bag, and sealed it; then she finished her tea and walked from the restaurant. Her life had been threatened, and from this moment on, the challenge would be to survive.

As Todd drove away he couldn't help thinking of what Peg had said and that it made a lot of sense. If she had talked to the cops, he would have been arrested by now. He thought she had met him just to place all of the incriminating evidence into his hands. It allowed the police the opportunity to catch him. For all he knew, they could be following him right now, ready to pounce at any moment. Peg was the enemy, she did rat, and he would kill her. One life was not as valuable as the passion for bringing justice on behalf of nature.

Once home, Todd called Carrie and told her about the meeting he'd just had with Peg and of her plans to cross Lake Michigan on a car ferry.

Peg flew back to Lansing, drove home, and called Eve because she forgot to tell her about Len when they talked recently. She knew Eve would be happy for her.

"I have good news to share, Eve."

"What's that?"

"I've met a wonderful man. His name is Len Miles. He lives in Colorado, in a beautiful home in the mountains."

"Well, that's a change for you, isn't it?" Eve said, referring to Peg's arson of similar homes as they were being built.

"Yes, it is, but Len has literally changed my life. I love him and want to be with him."

"That's wonderful, Peggy. I'm very happy for you. I never thought I'd hear you say that you loved a man."

"I know, but life deals you cards and you play them," Peg said.

"I wish you both much happiness."

"Thanks."

"Can I have his name again, and an address?" Eve asked. "I'd like to send him a note telling him how happy I am for you both."

"Sure. His name is Len Miles, and he lives northwest of Gunnison. I don't have his address. You can get that easily, I'm sure."

"I can. You'll be hearing from me."

"That's nice, Eve. Thanks."

CHAPTER SEVEN

July 9, 2004
Green Bay, Wisconsin

Before Peg began a new life, she needed to arrange care for her cat Flame. After weighing a number of options, she recalled that her Harvard roommate Betty Taylor was a cat lover – fanatic would be a better descriptor. They had remained in touch over several years via annual Christmas cards. Peg knew that Betty was a recognized veterinarian in Green Bay. Flame's care and happiness were uppermost in Peg's mind; she would do anything to be assured of Flame's comfort. She convinced herself that the only place for Flame would be in Betty's care. Peg called, and Betty was happy to take Flame. She told Betty that she would call back to let her know the details of her arrival.

Once that decision was made and arrangements complete, Peg looked up the S.S. Badger on the Internet to check the crossing times. She made a reservation for the 7:30 A.M. crossing to Manitowoc on July 13th. At the same time, she inquired about their pet policy. She would stay overnight on the Badger, at what the company called the Badger Boatel. For a reasonable fee, she could stay in a stateroom, have a continental breakfast, and be ready to go in the morning. It was either that or stay in a Ludington motel, and the Boatel seemed original and convenient.

On July 11th, Carrie called the Badger Reservations Office and told the clerk that she was organizing a surprise for a friend's birthday. "May I please have the date and times of Peg Lott's departure and return?" Carrie asked. "And, if Peg requested a stateroom, may I please have the number so that I can have some flowers delivered?"

"It's our policy not to give out that information," the clerk said.

"I can appreciate your concerns but we work with Peg, and we'd like her to have a nice surprise. We can ask her for her room number, but we'd like to surprise her. So, is there any way you can please bend your policy a little?"

"I'll need to get an okay from my supervisor. Do you want to wait?"

"Yes, but please tell your supervisor that it's very important to us to honor our friend."

"Okay, one moment please."

The inquiry took longer than Carrie expected, but since she had called on an eight hundred number, it wasn't costing a dime. Soon she heard the phone being picked up.

"Ma'am?"

"Yes."

"My supervisor said under no conditions will we give out the number of our passenger's stateroom."

"That's ridiculous!" Carrie shot back. "We just want to make our friend happy. You really mean you can't help me?"

"That's right. I'm sorry, but it is our policy."

"Can you tell me if she has a stateroom? I think she told us at the staff meeting that that was her plan."

"One minute."

"She is crossing to Manitowoc on July 13th at 7:30 A.M. without a stateroom. She returns on the 2:30 A.M. July 14th crossing from Manitowoc to Ludington, and she has booked a stateroom for that crossing."

"Thank you so very much. We're working hard to make it a memorable trip for her."

Carrie then called Todd and gave him his orders. "Peggy will be in a stateroom during the crossing from Manitowoc to Ludington, July 14, 2:30 A.M. central daylight time departure. Find a way to get into her cabin, put a pillow over her head, and suffocate her. Report to me as soon as you arrive in Ludington. For her, it will be a final crossing."

Todd drove to Ludington on Wednesday July 12th to make the round trip on the Badger from Ludington. He took his car so he could spend time in the Manitowoc area waiting for the return trip July 14. He requested a stateroom and was assigned to 25. He needed to see the layout of the typical stateroom so he could plan exactly how he would surprise his victim and carry out the murder.

Peg and Flame took the Badger to Manitowoc, drove to Green Bay and arrived at the Taylor Veterinary Clinic about one o'clock on the afternoon of July 13. Peg told the receptionist that she was there to see Dr. Taylor and took a seat. Flame complained in a pet carrier at her feet. A couple of dogs in the waiting room gave Flame a reason to voice her displeasure.

"Dr. Lott, please come with me."

Peggy carried Flame into an examination room, put the carrier up on the table, and opened the cage door. Flame could tell by the smells that this was not a place she wanted to be. She fought getting out of the carrier, but eventually she acquiesced to her master's coaxing.

Betty Taylor entered and warmly greeted Peg. "Well, I never thought I'd see my old roommate here in Green Bay. How are you? My goodness, you haven't changed a bit."

"Oh, come on, Betty. You're kind, but the years have done a number on this body," Peg replied. "You, though, really haven't changed. You look great, and obviously you followed your dreams of being a veterinarian."

"Yes, I think I'm the only female Harvard post-grad who became a veterinarian. How's that for a note of distinction?"

"We all need our claim to fame. I'm proud of you. With your fascination with cats back in Massachusetts, I knew that you would do something in the world of animals. Becoming a vet is a wonderful expression of your compassion, your intelligence, and your skills."

"Let's not get too carried away, Peg, but thanks. When you called you asked me to care for Flame. How long will this be?"

"I need to ask you to do me a huge favor."

"I'll help if I can."

"I'm in a position where I can no longer care for Flame. I can't satisfy your curiosity about why, but please understand that circumstances are such that I can't. I tried to think of someone who might be willing to help me out and you came to mind."

"Do you want me to care for Flame temporarily? Is that it?" Betty asked.

"No, I'd like you to find a permanent home for her, or maybe to even adopt her yourself. I'm quite certain that I won't be coming back for her."

Flame meowed and rubbed her nose against Peg's hand, almost as if she understood what had been said. Peg fought back a tear as she petted Flame, realizing that very shortly she would be without her companion of many years.

"I can keep her here; often a client will be looking for a nice cat to adopt," Betty said. "I don't think I'll have any trouble finding her a home, Peg."

"Good. She's a good cat, a good companion. I'll miss her terribly."

"Do you want me to let you know where Flame goes, once I find a family or someone to care for her?"

"Normally I would, but I really don't expect to be able to receive that message."

"Peg, listen, I can keep a secret, and I'm not asking you to tell me what you want to keep to yourself, but you sound like someone about to commit suicide."

"Betty, I'd like to be able to share my plans with you, but I can't. You may see my name in the paper, but only if my plan fails."

"I see. No more questions. I'll take care of Flame."

"Thanks, Betty. Do I owe you anything for doing this?" Peg asked.

"Don't be ridiculous. I'm happy to help an old roommate."

"I appreciate your kindness. Oh, one more thing: this will only add to the curiosity, but if anyone calls or comes here wanting to know if I was here, or if you saw me, I would appreciate it if you would not tell anyone you've seen me."

"You were never here, Peg," Betty said, reaching out to touch her shoulder. "You can leave knowing that Flame will be well-cared for and that nothing will be said about you and Flame being in Green Bay today or any day."

"Thanks." Peg picked up Flame, gave her a hug, and stroked her several times as tears rolled down her cheeks. "Thank you, dear Flame, thank you for listening, for being my companion, for all the smiles you gave me, and for all the snuggles. I'll miss you very much." Peg set Flame on the table, smiled to Betty, who gave her a hug, and walked out to her car. Peg knew the separation would be trying, and the tug on her heartstrings was strong. As she drove, Peg continued to sob and wipe tears from her eyes.

Peg's next destination was a restaurant in Green Bay. It didn't matter where she stopped. She wanted some coffee and a piece of pie and a chance to think about something other than losing Flame.

Walking into Bill's Diner, Peg was greeted by one of the waitresses.

"Just one? Smoking?"

"Just one and no smoking, please," Peg replied.

"Follow me." The waitress led Peg to a table near the salad bar but as far away from the smoking section as she could be.

A waitress approached and placed a glass of water and a menu in front of Peg. "My name's Sue. I'll take care of you. Need a minute, honey?"

"No, I'll have coffee and a slice of apple pie."

"With ice cream and warmed up?" Sue asked.

"Sure. That's all."

"Coming up. You haven't been in here before. You live in Green Bay?" Sue asked.

"No. I live in Michigan. I'm here visiting a friend."

"We're glad you're here. Coffee and pie coming up."

When Sue returned with the hot coffee and melting ice cream on a huge slice of apple pie, she said, "You must be a Lions fan. We sure rang your bell this year."

"A Lions fan? Rang our bell?" Peg asked, confused.

"Yeah, Detroit Lions – pro football. Thanksgiving Day game and all of that. You with me, honey?" Sue asked, surprised that Peg didn't know about the Detroit Lions.

"Not exactly. I'm not a sports fan at all. I'm incensed by all the attention, money, and glamour that surround men playing games. Terrible misdirected energy."

"Well, welcome to cheesehead country," Sue said with a grin.

"Cheesehead? Oh, I get it, Wisconsin is known for its dairy products."

"Not exactly, hon," Sue replied. "I'm referring to the Packers, the greatest football team in the land and owned by the people of Green Bay, I might add."

"Packers? I don't get it," Peg replied, feeling uncomfortable with the conversation and wanting to enjoy her coffee and pie.

"The team is named after meat packers."

"They named a football team after slaughterhouse people?" Peg asked, shivering with the thought of the violence against animals.

"I guess you could say that," Sue said, laughing. "Makes good sense to me, after all, they play with a pigskin filled with air. You mean you haven't heard of our Green Bay Packers?"

"No, I haven't," Peg said, hoping Sue would leave and attend to other diners. "Their colors must be green and gold, right? That's all I see around town."

"Now you're getting in the spirit. By the time you leave here we'll have you knowing about Lambeau Field, Brett Favre, Paul Hornung, Bart Starr, Vince Lombardi, and since you are from Michigan, I'll toss in Ron Kramer."

"I think I'll just enjoy my coffee," Peg said, wishing Sue would leave her alone.

"And who knows, our Packers might chop up your Lions in a Super Bowl some day," Sue said enjoying the banter.

"The what bowl?" Peg asked.

"Oh, I give up," Sue said, shaking her head. "You enjoy the pie and I'll leave you alone. I talk about the Packers to most everyone who comes in here, but I'm knocking on the wrong door – not your cup of tea, honey." Sue left to wait on other customers while Peg enjoyed the delicious pie and hot coffee.

A few minutes later, Sue came up to her. "How we doing here? Need a warm up, another slice for the road?"

"Nothing more thanks. Just my bill."

"I'll give you ten percent off if you promise to be a cheesehead," Sue said with a chuckle. She knew she was getting under Peg's skin and the banter was fun.

"What do I need to do to be a cheesehead?" Peg asked.

"Just cheer for our guys to go all the way to the Super Bowl," Sue replied with a smile.

"For a discount, sure, I'll cheer for your Packers," Peg replied, anxious to once again be rid of the waitress who was unlike any waitress she had ever known.

"Safe trip home now, you hear, honey."

Peg smiled, and shaking her head, walked from the non-smoking section of Bill's Diner. What a character, Peg thought while walking to her car, ready to drive to Manitowoc and what would hopefully be the start of a new life.

Four motorcyclists were meeting a drug runner south of Green Bay in a county rest area that was rarely used by travelers. One of the riders, Randy, was an undercover agent working for the Manistee Police and Chief Mickey McFadden. The other three were mean-looking, tough, and effective at what they did. It was their job to load contraband into their saddlebags, ride from rural Manistee up and across the Mackinac Bridge to northern Wisconsin, drop off their supplies near Green Bay, and then ride to Manitowoc, where they would catch the red-eye car ferry back to Ludington.

It would be easier to take the drugs across to Wisconsin on the Badger, but security was tight, and sniffing dogs would surely send the runners to the slammer. Coming back to Michigan was a piece of cake, a nice diversion from riding in a saddle for several hours.

One of the riders was Gary "Moe" Green, big, obnoxious, and paranoid. Because of his allergies to feathers, mold, and many seasonal allergens, he practically lived with a soiled handkerchief at his nose. Another rider was Jeff, the leader of the tribe, so to speak. Equally tough-looking and -acting, he was really a pussy cat. The third rider was Lucky, the quiet one. His appearance wasn't threatening or unkempt. In fact, Lucky looked like a successful businessman turned motorcycle fanatic. Randy, the undercover officer, didn't look anything like the police officer he was. It was imperative that the other three never suspect his real purpose for being among the group. Thanks to Randy, the information needed for a multi-state drug bust was secure and reliable. The riders were paid handsomely for their work and also given drugs as a perk for their job.

As serious as the four were about moving drugs, they were absolutely passionate about poker. On some ferry crossings, nobody left the table in the lounge during the entire trip. Toothpicks represented kilos of cocaine or hundreds of dollars in their poker games, and only the four knew the symbolism of the fragments of wood.

CHAPTER EIGHT

Thursday, July 13, 2004
Manitowoc, Wisconsin

Peg drove to Manitowoc for her return trip on the Badger. She stopped at an art supply store on the outskirts of town. She went in, made a purchase, and headed for her motel. If all went well, she'd be baptized into rebirth about 3:30 A.M. CDT. Peg rented a room at the Comfort Inn in Manitowoc, using her mother's maiden name. After registering, Peg knew she had a good four hours until she needed to get to the Badger so she ordered a pay-per-view movie. She needed a distraction from the imminent drama.

The movie ended at nearly 11 P.M. Peggy took her cell phone from the top of the dresser, turned the volume down on the TV, dialed a number, and waited for an answer.

"Hello," Captain Warren said.

"Dick?"

"Yeah."

"This is Peg Lott."

"Yes, Peg."

"Just checking in. I want to go over the plans one more time."

"Can't rehearse it enough, Peg."

"I will call you fifteen minutes before the jump. That should be around three-fifteen. I will flash a light from the stern of the ship toward the north three times, meaning I'm planning to jump at three-thirty. If you see five flashes, the jump is cancelled for whatever reason. If I don't jump, I'll call you on my cell phone and explain that the mission is called off."

"OK. That's the plan I have."

"Good. Once I'm in the water and the Badger has moved a bit east, I'll activate a strobe light. Assuming all goes as planned, you will follow parallel to the Badger and turn south to get me when you see the strobe light. Do we agree on this?"

"Yes."

"What do you know about the lake's condition?" Peg asked.

"It won't be smooth as glass. I expect three-foot waves. We've got a cold front coming through. You might be doing some bobbing, but I'll see the strobe and will come right to you."

"Good."

"Don't be concerned if it takes several minutes," Dick said. "I'll be a mile or two north and can't be there instantly."

"OK. The next you will hear from me is around three-fifteen when I give you my indication that all is going well or that there are some problems," Peg said. She took a deep breath, realizing that the plan was in the final stages.

"That's right."

"See you in the boat. And, I assure you, you'll be a welcome sight."

"I'll have towels, blankets, and some dry clothes."

"Thanks. You have my cell phone number if you need to call. I'll leave the motel close to one o'clock," Peg said.

"Good luck to you."

"Thanks."

While Peggy and Captain Warren were talking, Todd Baxter was confirming his plans with Carrie.

"Just checking in from Manitowoc. I bought my ticket about 8 o'clock. The dock area was pretty quiet. There's activity from about eleven on, and I don't want to be anywhere around the place until I board in disguise."

"Sounds like all is set," Carrie said. "You are registering with a phony name?"

"Yeah, that's right."

"You'll be in a stateroom?" Carrie asked.

"Yeah."

"Good. Things are going as planned then."

"You'll undoubtedly hear of my success on the news. I'll be in touch in the morning," Todd said.

"You're driving right on to Pittsburgh?" Carrie asked.

"Yeah, but I'll probably hang around a few blocks from the Badger to watch all the action."

"Action?"

"Well, yeah, police, ambulance, the whole works. I'll have an opportunity to admire my ability to cause a lot of commotion."

"Don't get yourself identified," Carrie warned. "It's important to be isolated. You know that, Todd."

"Not a problem. My black leather outfit and disguise plus the phony name I used when I bought my ticket, will give me all the privacy I need."

It was 12:10 A.M. CDT when Peg called Len, who was at lunch in Beijing with the President of China and a large delegation of Chinese and American government representatives. He was sensitive to the drama that was about to unfold in Wisconsin and wanted to take the call. He excused himself and went out into the hall.

"Len, I'm sorry to bother you, but I'm about to head to the Badger."

"Are you feeling okay, Peg?"

"I'm a little nervous because I have no experience jumping off car ferries into Lake Michigan in the dark with two-foot waves while knowing that a future NFL lineman who wants to kill me is on the ship, but I'm confident that all will go well."

"That's a lot to carry, Peg. Are you sure you're up to this?" Len asked.

"Yes. I'm just hoping that no one is at the stern of the ship at three-thirty. It's possible that someone could see me."

"Definitely. And, it is critical that you not be seen. I can't emphasize this enough," Len said seriously. "If anyone sees you go over, the whole thing is botched. The ship has detailed procedures, and they are sure to rescue you, so the jig will definitely be up. So, take whatever precautions you need to take, delay the jump if you need to. Once you decide to jump, you've got to go – you can't hesitate. Once the way is clear and you've decided to go over, do it swiftly, and don't make a sound on the way down."

"The Badger shouldn't be concerned about Dick's boat to the north, right?" Peg asked.

"I don't think the Badger captain will see him. I've researched that. The size of Dick's boat will not register on the radar screen. It's too small."

"Won't the captain of the Badger see the lights on Dick's boat?" Peg wondered.

"He's not going to have any lights."

"Will he be safe?"

"Not a problem. He knows the freighter routes. Besides, he has his own radar, and he'll be able to spot anything in his area. And, the possibility that anyone will be out that far in Lake Michigan at three in the morning is remote at best."

"Okay, I think we're all set."

"Yes. You've gone over the jump in your mind many times, I'm sure," Len said.

"I've gone off the high dive at the university countless times. They can't replicate the choppy conditions, but I shouldn't have any trouble."

"Got the wet suit, inflatable life preserver and strobe light?" Len asked.

"It's right here," Peggy replied.

"The magazine, hair, and note?"

"Right here in my bag."

"Good."

"We've been over it so many times, it all should be automatic."

"It'll go without a hitch," Len said, offering assurance.

"You're certain that Todd won't kill me on the Badger?"

"Very certain, Peg. He would be crazy to do it on that ship."

"I guess I don't follow," Peg said, needing Len's explanation.

"First, the ship has a record of everyone on board, so if you were killed, the police have a closed number of suspects. Second, there is a risk of noise and commotion, and a killer won't want that. So, no, he won't attempt to kill you on the Badger. Now, once you're off, that's when I would expect him to try it, but, of course, you will not be on the ship when it docks in Ludington."

"Why is he on board then? Why won't he just be in Ludington when I arrive?"

"Good point. I can't answer that, but I do know that no killer in his right mind would act on a ship where every passenger's name and address is recorded."

"I'm not having second thoughts, Len. I just want it over. It's the waiting that's nerve-wracking."

"Try to relax. Everything will be fine," Len said, trying to be reassuring. There was a pause while Peg collected her thoughts.

"Len, if something happens, thank you for everything. Since the moment we met, I've been the happiest woman on earth."

"Peg, you're sounding like you are on your last legs. Our life together is just beginning. In several hours you'll be in Colorado waiting for me to return from Beijing and we'll be in each other's arms."

"I hope you're right."

"Trust me. I am."

"But if something happens, I want you to know that you made me happy and I also want you to know that I love you very much."

"I love you too, Peg. Tonight, tomorrow, and for all eternity."

"Thank you."

"I'll talk to you when you're in Colorado," Len said. "I want very much to hear your voice, the voice of a new woman, starting a new life, with a new opportunity to live life to the fullest."

"I love you, Len. Goodbye."

"I love you, too."

CHAPTER NINE

Friday, July 14, 2004
On the S.S. Badger

Peggy pulled up to the ferry dock at 1:15 A.M. Travelers were requested to arrive one hour before departure. She noticed that the cars were being checked by a leashed German shepherd guided by a woman with a security badge on her blue shirt. It was the same procedure used in Ludington prior to her trip to Green Bay, so she wasn't surprised.

The dog circled her car and moved on. She gave her name to the worker who greeted her with a smile. Peg was told to pull up behind a white Toyota. She did so, left the key in the ignition, and took belongings from the back seat. With purse in one hand and a small tote bag in the other, she walked to the ticket office, checked in, and was told she could board. Peggy joined a short line and eventually came up to another worker who took her ticket and checked her name off.

"Excuse me, could I ask if Todd Baxter has checked in yet?"

"Name again?"

"Todd Baxter. We're friends and we're going to meet on board."

"Let me see," she replied as she looked at her alphabetical list of passengers. "We don't show a Todd Baxter as a passenger. He could be checking in late. No one by that name has boarded."

"Thanks," Peggy said. She walked up the steps knowing that she would not see Todd on the way to her stateroom.

Todd was away from the ship, watching the passengers arrive. He saw Peggy's car and watched her every step, from check-in to boarding. He waited about fifteen minutes and then approached the line, gave the worker his ticket, and boarded the ship. Disguised in black leather, beard, and Harley skull cap, he felt comfortable walking freely around the ship, certain that Peggy would not recognize him.

Peggy went to her stateroom and once again went over the plan. Then she left for the lounge area thinking she would be safer being with people, lessening the probability that Todd would threaten her. Peg walked around the Badger, always staying close to people. She saw some passengers leaning on the rail, looking at the lights of Manitowoc.

"First time crossing on the Badger?" asked a short, stocky, older man with a neatly trimmed goatee.

"I came over this morning. Or, I guess that would be yesterday morning. But, yes, this is my first time over and back," Peg replied.

"My name is Bill Yancy and this is my wife Joy. We're heading home – been up in Ellison Bay."

"Hi, I'm Peg Lott."

"Pleased to meet you. You must live in Michigan then?" Bill asked.

"I teach at Michigan State."

"Oh, my goodness. We live in Williamston. What do you teach?"

"Ecology."

"I see. Looks like a storm will be traveling across with us," Bill said, watching some lightning approaching the shore of Lake Michigan.

"Yes, it does."

"I used to work on a car ferry when I was eighteen years old," Bill reminisced. "I worked on the Midland. In fact, I saw this ship, the Badger, being built in Sturgeon Bay, Wisconsin. My grandfather was the president of the Manitowoc Ship Building Company, which built the Midland. That's how I got the job. It helped having a relative in high places."

Peg nodded and listened politely. "Yeah, a lot of memories on the Midland," Bill continued. "I got my first kiss on that ship."

"Excuse me," Joy said. "I've heard this story so many times that I can't bear to listen to it again. I'm going for a walk." She leaned over and whispered in Peg's ear, "Listen, dear, any time you've had enough, just excuse yourself and get on with your life. Bill will talk to anyone who will listen, and he hardly ever comes up for air."

"Thanks for the warning, but I enjoy good stories," Peg replied. Then turning to Bill she said, "Now tell me about this kiss."

"I stole my first kiss on the Midland when I was eighteen. I was with this pretty girl up on the top deck by the big smokestack. I put my arms around her and was right in the middle of this romantic moment when the ship's fog horn went off. I mean, that baby is designed to be heard twenty miles away."

"That probably interrupted things a bit," Peggy said with a chuckle.

"It sure did. We were not only stunned but practically deaf for a few moments."

"They say everyone remembers the first kiss," Peg said. "I remember mine and it was just a few weeks ago, believe it or not. Mine was memorable, but not like yours."

"Oh, I remember it all right, happened about fifty years ago, and I can still hear it if I listen," Bill said with a chuckle.

"You said you used to work on one of these car ferries?" Peg asked.

"Yeah, lived and worked on the ship for twenty days straight, and then we were off eight days. In those days you could drink alcohol in Wisconsin at age eighteen, and in Michigan the age was twenty-one, so I recall a lot of stories from the crew after visiting the bars in Manitowoc. I'll spare you those stories."

"Thanks, I think," Peg said with a smile.

"In those days we slept in tight quarters under the part of the car ferry where the trains were housed. These ferries took train cars across

Lake Michigan. The original meaning of car ferry referred to railroad cars, not passenger cars like today."

"I see. I read the historical marker on the Michigan side. When I got on in Ludington, I looked down and saw several railroad tracks coming into the ship and thought that had been the case."

"Yeah, this used to be a shortcut for the railroads, and now it is a shortcut for people in cars. Same purpose, just diversified a bit as the years went by."

"Looks like we might get some rain," Peggy said looking up.

"Yeah, seeing this storm coming in reminds me of the time I got terribly seasick. Oh, was that a miserable experience. They say that people who never get sick on the ocean can get sick on a Great Lake. I think it's because the ship doesn't have stabilizers like the cruise ships have. The ship sort of roll like a figure-eight, if you know what I mean," Bill said, using his hand to simulate the ship fighting through waves and rocking to and fro.

"I didn't need that reminder," Peg replied. "Do you think we'll be tossed around tonight?"

"We'll be fine. There's a storm brewing, but it shouldn't be too rough," Bill replied.

"Good."

"Yeah, lots of memories of Manitowoc. Many years ago the tower of Lincoln High School was the last thing to disappear from sight and the first thing that you saw coming to Manitowoc. It used to be lit up. My mother graduated from there. My dad played for Notre Dame and my mom went to Northwestern in Chicago. They met at Notre Dame. Yeah, once I get in this area all the memories come back. Hope I'm not boring you."

"No, I enjoy listening to people's stories." Peg knew she was being less than honest, as she didn't generally like listening to people, but he was company, and she needed to be around people, so this was working out just fine.

"Yeah, I look at that town, and I think of the Yindras Bakery where I used to get a kolache."

"A what?"

"A kolache. It's a hollowed out hunk of bread dough with some type of fruit filling; prune was the most popular back then, but they also had apricot. And then there is Lates Restaurant, it's still there today, but I remember back in my youth getting a charcoal-grilled bratwurst on a cut-open hard roll with butter and ketchup. Man, I thought I'd died and gone to heaven."

"Now you're making me hungry," Peg said. "We've gone from kissing, to seasick, to a delicious brat!"

"Well, I cover the waterfront with stories, pun intended," Bill said with a laugh.

"You sure do."

"Is this man still telling his stories?" Joy asked, walking toward the two.

"Oh, yes," Peg replied. "He's full of fond memories."

"Well, don't get him going about Door County, or you'll be standing out here half way to Michigan," Joy said. "He'll be telling you stories of Johnson's Swedish Restaurant in Sister Bay where they serve the best pancakes in the world. Actually, they are the best, I can't disagree there. People come from hundreds of miles just to get those pancakes."

"Yeah, and the story is that the building was put together in Sweden and then taken apart, crated, brought over here, and reassembled," Bill added. "The place has a grass roof, and goats feed up there in the summer."

"Really? You eat pancakes inside while goats graze on the roof?" Peg asked.

"Yup, it's quite a place. Joy's right, I've never tasted pancakes so good in my life, and I've lived a lot of years."

As Peg's conversation with Bill and Joy continued, the Lake Michigan Carferry workers were following routine jobs. Standing at the rail and looking down at the cars and the motorcycles disappearing into the belly of the ship was Stephanie Brooks, an FBI agent in charge of a soon-to-be conducted multi-state drug bust. She recognized the four bikers and expected them to be on board, since her informants had tracked their every move for the past several weeks. Stephanie, 38, traveled alone, used disguises, carried little luggage, and would often take multiple steps to confuse anyone who might be following her.

Stephanie had been driven to the Lake Michigan Carferry dock by undercover drug agents from Sheboygan. In Michigan, she would contact Manistee Chief of Police Mickey McFadden.

The passenger list was checked to make sure everyone was on board. The captain, first mate, and the wheelsman were going through pre-sailing procedures. The sailing went like clockwork every night, and tonight would be no exception.

As a horn blew signaling departure, a crack of thunder was heard by those still awake. It seemed like a signal to begin the drama, like the firing of the gun by a track official. Slowly the Badger pulled away from the dock with powerful engines churning allowing the wheelsman to guide the ship from its moorings into Manitowoc Harbor and then out into Lake Michigan. Rain fell as the Badger moved with the storm into the lake.

Dick Warren sat in his charter fishing boat and waited before leaving about ten minutes after the Badger headed for Michigan. While the Badger could only move at 18 miles per hour, he could move much faster, so he waited a bit before heading into the lake. Despite the thunder and lightning and rain, the lake was not terribly rough.

There was little activity for the first 30 minutes of the journey. Shortly after the ship left the harbor, Peggy returned to her stateroom.

But, after a half hour, she began to get cabin fever. She felt safe going out into the lounge area, and she was curious how many people were up and around. She hoped nobody would be outside in the stern of the ship. Even if Todd saw her, it wouldn't matter, as he no doubt knew she was on the ship. Being out in a lounge would be safer than confined to a small room.

At 3:15 A.M. Peg used her cell phone to call Captain Warren. "This is Peg Lott calling. Are you ready?"

"Yeah, I'll be watching for the light flashes."

"Good, see you soon."

About five minutes before Peggy was to leave her stateroom, she took a sharp knife from her purse. She sterilized the blade with a lighter. She then carefully slit her middle finger on her left hand. As hoped, a steady flow of blood oozed from the wound. Peg began to smear her blood on the door, on the mirror, and on one wall of the stateroom. When she finished it looked like quite a disturbance had occurred in the room. She carefully wrapped the finger, applied some antiseptic and then put a tight bandage over the wound.

Having created a bloody scene, she took the magazine she had Todd look at in the Pittsburgh airport out of the plastic bag and set it on the floor. She placed the hair from Todd's comb on top of the magazine on a light portion of the cover photo, thinking any detective would see it without much trouble. She threw some things about so it looked as if something violent had occurred in the cabin. The DNA from the hair and the fingerprints on the magazine would match Todd's. His presence on the ship would be documented and in a nutshell, he would be suspected of her murder.

It was time to get to her location and flash the light three times, meaning she was about to jump. Peg put on her wet suit, nylon jogging outfit, and running shoes. Peg fastened the strobe light to her waist. Underneath her nylon top was an inflatable vest to keep her afloat.

Peggy opened the door to check that no one was in the corridor. She closed the door behind her, but it didn't close completely. In fact, with the ship rocking, it opened and closed like a loose screen door in the summer.

As Peggy walked past the lounge area, she saw the couple she had talked to earlier. They were awake, but they didn't seem to notice her. She stepped outside onto the deck and walked to the spot in the stern where she was to jump. She looked up and saw no one by the rail above her. A man was smoking a cigarette, but he turned, put it out in an ashtray, and walked into the lounge area. She pointed her flashlight to the north and flashed it three times. It was 3:18 A.M. Captain Warren saw the three flashes and knew that the plan was a go.

Dick had cut his engine and bobbed in a sea of darkness. There were no boats or freighters in the area. Other than some rain and two-foot waves, the setting was near perfect.

Peg stayed in the general area of where she planned to jump, constantly surveying the area above and behind her. Frequently she walked around the stern of the ship, watching for anything to disrupt her plan.

Peggy was so intent on thinking about the jump, she didn't notice that an electrical short was causing the light near the lounge door to go on for a few seconds and then off for a few seconds. The bulb could simply have been loose, or an occasional jolt may have caused the light to go on and off.

Dick Warren spent most of the time between three-eighteen and three-thirty watching the Badger from a distance. When Dick saw the irregular flashing light, he believed that it was a signal from Peg that the jump was called off. He had seen at least five flashes of light; there could have been more, but not less, and he couldn't be sure when the five flashes started. He realized that the light was not the same as he had seen at 3:15, but then again, he wasn't told a flashlight would be used, only that five flashes of light would cancel the jump.

At the very moment that Peg decided to pull herself up onto the railing to jump, Bill Yancy appeared and surprised her when he said, "Good to see you. Got time to listen to one more story?"

Peggy was upset with this unexpected presence. "I don't mean to be offensive, but I really don't want to hear a story. I just want to be alone. Do you mind?"

Bill was a bit stunned by Peggy's disinterest in him and his story, so he turned and left. Peggy glanced at her watch and saw that it was 3:40.

Alone now and a bit past the scheduled jump time, she had to drop into the lake believing that once Captain Warren saw the strobe light, he would easily head south and pick her up. She visualized the jump one more time. She was no longer under the watchful eye of the Michigan State University diving coach. There would be no help should she black out or injure herself as she entered the water.

Before her jump, she threw her belongings, including phone and flashlight, into the water. She looked around one last time, saw no one. She stepped up, took a deep breath and jumped. Looking straight ahead as the cool air and rain seemed to wrap around her and chill her, she let go of the railing and went into a free fall for thirty or forty feet. The jump had been rehearsed many times from the high platform at the MSU outdoor pool facility. However, that was quiet and the water was warm.

When Peg hit the water, the turbulence from the boat caused much more of an impact than she had anticipated. Swirling water from the back of the Badger held her under water longer than expected; the jump was nothing like what she had experienced in training. She tried to calm herself and managed to activate her inflatable life vest. She surfaced, coughing violently, but was able to get air into her lungs. When she realized she would live, she reached for the strobe light attached to her belt and was horrified to realize that it must have been ripped off on impact.

Peg Lott was alone in Lake Michigan, lucky to be alive, but wet, scared, and in almost total darkness. She couldn't see anything because her head was at the water level and Captain Warren's boat would show no lights.

At three-thirty, and for the next fifteen minutes, Captain Warren looked for the strobe light, but there was none. Putting two and two together, he believed that the jump had been cancelled. He would later recall that he saw what appeared to be a light going on and off, but in his mind he had seen the five flashes and decided he no longer needed to pay close attention. When he did notice the flashes he had no idea if he was seeing the first, the second or the third.

As far as Captain Warren was concerned, Peggy was still on the Badger. Though he saw no strobe light, he knew it was possible that Peggy had jumped because he had not received a phone call nor seen a flashlight signal from the Badger. He began to move the boat south where he would eventually intersect the path of the Badger, and if Peggy had jumped, he would no doubt find her. He continued to try to reach her by phone, but there was no response.

At this point, Captain Warren turned on his lights. His only goal was to get to the spot where Peggy was supposed to have jumped.

Peggy was safely buoyant, but cold. The choppy water began to subside as the Badger continued east. At least being in Lake Michigan meant she didn't have to fear sharks.

Captain Dick Warren proceeded to where he thought Peggy should be if she had jumped. He cut the engine, but heard nothing. He stayed in the general area where she should have been at three-thirty for at least a half hour, circling the area and then decided to return to Manitowoc. The fact that Peggy was in Lake Michigan in danger of losing her life did not occur to Captain Warren. If she had jumped, he would have seen the strobe light and picked her up.

At approximately, 4 P.M. Stephanie was very tired and unable to stay awake. She walked down the left aisle, and, noticing the door ajar to Room 16, she looked in, ready to profusely apologize if she startled someone. Seeing nobody, she decided to lie on the bunk, thinking the room had not been assigned to anyone.

Around a table on the upper deck sat four poker players. Moe Green reached into his coat pocket and took out the slip of paper that read, She's in 16. He announced he was going for another beer and left the group. Randy noticed he was gone about 10 minutes, longer than it would take to get a beer. When he returned he didn't have a beer in hand, and he was blowing his nose and snorting as if he had a bad cold.

Todd Baxter decided that the time was right to honor his promise to kill Peg. He had put it off long enough. Early in the crossing he had lost track of her, but he knew that she was in Stateroom 16. He'd seen her go into the room and even tried some tactics to scare her a bit. At ten minutes after four he opened the door and quietly walked in.

CHAPTER TEN

Friday, July 14, 2004
Ludington, Michigan

At 5:30 A.M. the employees of the Lake Michigan Carferry service in Ludington, Michigan, began driving cars off the S.S. Badger. Passengers who had eagerly disembarked watched for their vehicles to arrive from the hold of the huge ship, so that they could pile in and be on their way.

The morning was crisp and cool with a slight breeze. The sun was up and a rather warm day was on tap for the tourists eager to enjoy a summer day in Ludington. Pulling away from the Badger dock, with the sun in their eyes, most drivers were glad they had been spared that long drive around the Upper Peninsula of Michigan, or heaven forbid, a drive through Chicago and around the southern part of Lake Michigan, a nightmare trip if ever there was one.

Todd Baxter disembarked along with the rest of the passengers. He carried a gym bag with a University of Pittsburgh logo on the side, and he wore his black motorcycle jacket. Todd walked down the long flight of stairs, and once his car appeared on the dock, he drove into the downtown area.

Todd picked up his cell phone and called Carrie.

"This is Todd. I'm in Ludington."

"Mission accomplished?" Carrie asked, anxious to hear that Peg Lott was dead and no longer a threat.

"The Ring of Fire is once again anonymous."

Before Carrie could say anything, Todd disconnected. It was a long drive to Pittsburgh, and he wasted no time getting out of town.

One car sat on the dock of the Lake Michigan Carferry Company after all passengers had left the area. The authorities were not immediately concerned for two reasons. The first was that some folks take their time. Many have families and it takes a while to round up children. Some don't like standing in line to make the slow exit from the boat. The second reason is that the ship sails from Manitowoc at 2:30 A.M. and sails when people are used to being sound asleep. Some deep sleepers just don't hear the announcements, the ship's horn, or the bustle of folks around them.

It's not uncommon for a car or two to sit in the parking area waiting for owners. However, thirty minutes after most passengers had left, a stranded car was rare. Bob Carter, one of three principal owners of Lake Michigan Carferry, Inc., was briefed by radio. "Mr. C, we've got a red late model Chevrolet, license MI 448-SKI, still awaiting its driver," Pat, the cruise director, said matter-of-factly.

"This is the third cruise in a row," Bob said, shaking his head. "There's truth to things happening in threes. Pull up the record on the vehicle."

"Will do." About three minutes later Pat reported to Bob, "Stranded vehicle belongs to Peg Lott of East Lansing, Michigan. She was traveling alone, assigned Stateroom 16."

"Send someone to check on the room and if it's empty, I want the ship checked from stem to stern. Understand?"

"Yes, sir. I'm sure this passenger is sleeping like all the others. She'll be embarrassed when we wake her up, as they all are," Pat replied. She had six years of experience as a cruise director and was a proponent of the "Do it yourself if you want it done right and on time" school of thinking. She decided to handle this one herself.

"Let me know when she's found and the car leaves the area," Bob directed.

"Yes, sir."

Pat put her radio in its belt holder, grabbed the master key, and headed for Stateroom 16. When she arrived, she knocked on the stateroom door, but there was no answer. She knocked again, then louder. Still nothing. Pat used the master key to open the door. Realizing she was about to violate someone's privacy, she knocked on the door, now ajar, said in a raised voice, "Peg Lott?" and then slowly opened the door the rest of the way.

A body was on the bed, face up.

Pat knew the body was lifeless as soon as she saw it. The face, pale with eyes open and staring at nothing, had death written all over it. To be absolutely certain, Pat checked the woman's wrist for a pulse. Nothing. "I hate these things!" she said to no one. The blood in the stateroom hinted at foul play. Not only had there probably been a murder, but the paperwork would be tremendous, not to mention the commotion of the paramedics, and contacting the funeral home people and next of kin. A dead woman on the Badger was simply a huge inconvenience, to say nothing of the media attention.

Pat prepared to send the message she had sent only once before when an elderly man had died of a heart attack during a crossing a few years ago. At that time, the dead man's family had been on board, so things went smoothly. All passengers had left, as was the case this morning, so there was no one to gawk and get upset with all the emergency vehicles and all the rumors of what had happened.

"Got the reason for that stranded vehicle, Mr. C.," Pat reported. "Passenger is asleep all right, but for eternity. We've got a dead body in 16. Room looks like it was a murder. Please put procedures in place. I'll stay here and keep maintenance out."

"Murder?" Bob asked, not wanting to believe what he had heard.

"That'd be my guess. She's lying in bed. Looks kind of peaceful, actually."

"Ok. Thanks, Pat. So much for a routine docking."

Within seconds, the wailing of sirens could be heard in Ludington. The police, ambulance, and fire trucks were making their way down South Rath Street toward the dock. People at the Water Plaza Condos expected the vehicles to enter their complex, believing a resident had a medical problem, but the vehicles passed, heading toward the Badger.

Ludington Chief of Police Harry Grether, in the lead vehicle, was met by Mr. Carter. "Good morning, Chief."

"Hi, Bob. Got some business for us?"

"Yeah, could be a murder. Body is in 16. Name is Peg Lott. That car is hers," Bob said, pointing to the red Chevrolet.

"I assume we've got permission to go aboard," Harry said, knowing the age old practice of asking permission from the captain to board his vessel.

"Most definitely. Do what you need to do."

"Thanks, Bob. The Coast Guard has jurisdiction if this is anything but natural causes. I called the commander and he asked me to take the lead. They're over their heads with national security issues. Unless it's a senator who's dead on board, he'd just as soon have us work this one."

Chief Grether turned to the paramedic who had emerged from the ambulance, "Body is in 16. Word is that she's dead, possibly murdered. I want her left where she is, understand?"

"Yes, Chief."

While waiting for the police and paramedics, Pat looked around the stateroom. A feather pillow and a magazine lay on the floor, and a small carry-on bag was also on the floor at the foot of the bed. She did not want to be accused of tampering with evidence or anything that might be associated with alleged criminal activity, so she left everything as it was. But, on this quiet summer morning if ever there was a classic case of murder, this seemed to be it.

Pat didn't need to worry about a crowd with the arrival of the authorities because no one was on board except the maintenance crew. When the paramedics and Chief Grether arrived at Stateroom 16, they nodded to Pat, who pointed to the body and said, "She's in here. Nothing has been disturbed."

The paramedics nodded and immediately went to work to verify that the woman in the bed was dead. There was no pulse or respiration, the body was cold and pale.

As instructed by Chief Grether, the body was left as it was found. He called the medical examiner and then directed his officers to begin their investigation. While photos were being taken, the room was dusted for prints and evidence was bagged. The magazine was carefully lifted from the floor, and the hairs resting on the magazine were carefully picked up with a tweezers-like instrument and put in an evidence bag. Blood samples from the floor and the sink were also carefully lifted for analysis.

Harry tried to verify the identity of the victim. It was helpful that the car ferry company had listed the passenger as Peg Lott, but he needed something more than the ship's registration. A purse with no identification inside was found at the base of the cot. Wearing latex gloves, Chief Grether went through the carry-on bag. He found some toiletries and a change of clothes but nothing to identify the victim. This is strange, he thought. Things are not adding up.

Shortly after the police and paramedics arrived, news media pulled up to the Lake Michigan Carferry dock. The Ludington Daily News sent head reporter Rick Danville to the scene. Dana Worthy, who covered Ludington news for the Grand Rapids Press arrived next. A film crew and reporter from Channel 7/12 out of Cadillac arrived. The media were not permitted on board the Badger while emergency personnel were investigating.

Lynda Shaffer, the Director of Media Relations, was doing what she could to answer questions, but she didn't have a clue about what had happened, other than that a woman's body was in Stateroom 16. Lynda was the youngest member of the administrative team, having earned her position by serving as a cruise director for several years as well as a stint as a reservations clerk. She had long, shiny blond hair, and was smartly and professionally dressed in a white blouse, slacks, and company blazer.

Lynda gathered the news people in a meeting room in the LMC, Inc. offices. "We'll prepare a press release as soon as we have information for you," Lynda announced. "Most likely we'll have something within the next half hour. There will be a press conference once the body has been identified and taken from the ship. Police Chief Grether and our company president Bob Carter will make statements and answer your questions. Between now and then, I'll be your source for information, but if your questions now are about the death of the woman, you know what I know."

"Is this the first death on the Badger?" Dana Worthy asked.

"No, there was an accident several years ago and then a couple of years ago a man died of a heart attack during a crossing."

"What was the accident?" Dana inquired.

"I believe someone dropped a glass that shattered and severed a blood vessel in his foot. The passenger was a hemophiliac and bled to death before medical personnel could respond," Lynda replied.

"Anyone ever murdered on the Badger?" Rick Danville shouted from the back of the expanding crowd.

"No, a murder has never occurred on our ship, and, as of now, I have not been told that this is a murder," Lynda answered. "We have a body in one of our staterooms. I don't know the cause of death nor do I believe the police know at this point. But, that's conjecture on my part."

"What was the name of the passenger, Lynda?" Dana asked.

"She has not been positively identified at this point. Obviously we know who was assigned to that stateroom but we'll not release the name until the victim's identity is confirmed."

"Was she shot?" Rick asked.

"I said I only know that the woman is dead. I don't know how she died. We did not receive any report of commotion, noise, or anything that would indicate that there was a confrontation."

"When did the death occur?" Tom Evans, a reporter for the Traverse City paper, asked.

"Tom, when are you going to believe me?" Lynda asked, a bit perturbed with the incessant questioning, when she had made it clear that she had shared sufficient information. "I don't know when she died. You'll have to wait till the press conference, or, if I find that out, I'll put it in the press release."

After the medical examiner certified death, the Ludington police completed their investigation while the body was taken to the hospital for autopsy and identification. Bob Carter and his staff completed all the necessary paperwork.

Fortunately, the body had been removed without a lot of fanfare. Hundreds of people had reservations for the Saturday morning crossing. If the Badger could not sail that morning, it would have meant a huge financial loss for the Lake Michigan Carferry Company, to say nothing of dealing with a lot of angry and upset passengers who still expected to be in Wisconsin by early afternoon.

Lynda drafted a press release for Mr. Carter to review. The press release read:

> The owners and management of the Lake Michigan Carferry Company, Inc. are saddened and deeply concerned about the mysterious death of a passenger on board the S.S. Badger during her voyage from Manitowoc to Ludington in the early morning hours of July 14, 2004. The Company will cooperate fully with the investigation. We wish to assure our customers that travel on the Badger is safe, and all steps are being taken to assure that security is in place. The Badger is expected to continue her scheduled departure as soon as officials have concluded their work and are certain that the ship poses no potential threat to passengers.
>
> In the unlikely event that the S.S. Badger is not able to sail as scheduled, full refunds will be provided to ticketed passengers, or credit for a future crossing can be arranged. We regret any inconvenience this may have caused our customers. We will resume safe and secure passage as soon as possible. Updates will be posted on our web site www.acrossthelakequickly.com or persons are encouraged to call 1-800-555-6666. Signed: Bob Carter, President and CEO of Lake Michigan Carferry, Inc.

Once the press release was approved, Lynda Shaffer immediately made sure that it was provided to her long list of media people and put on the Associated Press wire as well. Next on the agenda was the press conference with Chief Grether.

CHAPTER ELEVEN

July 14, 2004

Manistee, Grand Haven, Ludington, and Manitowoc

At 8 A.M. on July 14, Manistee Chief of Police Mickey McFadden was in his office waiting for a phone call. Mickey was a tall, muscular, dominating figure with a pleasant personality. He was the epitome of a small-town police chief that children and the towns folk admired, and one who held both citizens and tourists accountable to the law.

Mickey was expecting to hear from Stephanie Brooks who was coming to Ludington from Wisconsin. Her job of late was to visit the members of the team supporting the Great Lakes network. She was supposed to have taken the car ferry after meeting with the police in Sheboygan, Wisconsin.

One of the major figures in the drug operation, Laurence "Big Guy" Renaldo, spent summers in the Manistee area. Acting on information from Stephanie, Mickey and his men had been tracking Renaldo and reporting his movements to people in the FBI, as well as state and local law enforcement agencies.

All of the drug-related problems in Manistee and in the surrounding areas could be traced back to the work of Renaldo and his pushers. Mickey was looking forward to the sweep because he knew that many problems would be history with the Renaldo folks out of town and behind bars. The investigation was full of double agents and at any given time, one couldn't be one hundred percent certain who was the bad guy and who was the good guy.

Chief McFadden's phone still hadn't rung more than an hour beyond the expected time. He realized that in undercover drug work, you always expect the unexpected, but he was getting uneasy. After two hours, he dialed the chief of police in Sheboygan, Wisconsin, because Mickey knew Stephanie had planned to be with the Sheboygan chief before the crossing.

"Chief Eckhart, please?" Mickey asked.

"One moment."

"This is Chief Eckhart. How can I help you?"

"Mickey McFadden across the pond in Manistee."

"Mickey. Good to hear from you. What's on your mind?"

"I was expecting a phone call from Stephanie this morning, but so far nothing."

"Hmmm, she left here on time. One of my officers took her to Manitowoc and stayed till the ship left for Ludington. I know she was on the Badger and was looking forward to seeing you."

"I called the car ferry company and know that the ship arrived on time. She was to give me a call when the ship docked."

"That's strange. Can't help you. If she calls me, I'll give you a call and tell her you're not too happy about being stood up."

"I'm sure there's a reasonable explanation, but I'm a bit uneasy. From what I know of her, it's not like her to be late or not to call."

"You're right. She sees the guy in your backyard, Renaldo, as the key to starting this line of dominoes falling from the streets to prison cells."

"That's my impression as well. OK, thanks. I'll keep you posted."

Carol Searing was sleeping in. Last night a Maeve Binchy novel had kept her in its grasp. She didn't turn off the light on her nightstand till almost 2 A.M. As is often the case when one doesn't want to be disturbed, the phone pierced the quiet. Carol awoke and glanced at the clock to see 8:52. In a groggy voice, she answered.

"Sorry to wake you, Carol."

"Oh, that's okay, I needed to get up," she replied, lying, but trying to put the caller at ease. "Who am I talking to?"

"This is Mickey McFadden in Manistee."

"Oh, hi, Mickey. You need Lou, right?" Carol asked.

"Yeah, I'd like to talk with him if I could."

"He's in the hospital, Mickey."

"Hospital?"

"Yes. The doctor found a malignant tumor in his back. He's due to come home today."

"Oh, I didn't know. I'm sorry."

"They got it early. Lou's itching to get out. He needs something to get his mind off of this thing. He took it pretty hard. Guess that's normal."

"Sure he would. We all would."

"I suppose you've got a job for him?" Carol asked.

"Yeah, but not now. He needs to be quiet and rest."

"He told me to take the cover off his Harley so I don't think he will be resting long."

"Do you think he'll want to investigate if I need him?" Mickey asked.

"My guess is, if you need him, he's yours."

"That's great, but is it too soon after surgery?"

"I dread the thought of his doing anything dangerous, but I can't live his life for him. He's got his cell phone in the hospital. You should give him a call. Do you have his number?"

"Yeah, I do, but I'll wait till he gets home."

"You can call him at the hospital, Mickey. He's ready to do something besides give the nurses headaches."

"If you think it's okay to call, I will."

"Has there been a murder, Mickey?" Carol asked.

"I'm not sure, but I'm putting two and two together and coming up with four. If I'm right, and I usually am when it comes to discerning crime, I'm going to need Lou and Maggie."

"Looks like you'll be seeing more of him than I will in the next few weeks. He's yours, Mickey. Just send him back healthier than when you get him, okay?"

"I'll do my best, Carol."

Lou had just finished talking to the oncologist. He had been released to go home and was getting into his trousers when his phone rang.

"Lou Searing."

"Hi, Lou. This is Mickey."

"Hey, thanks for the call. I didn't get any flowers from you, Mickey," Lou said with a chuckle.

"Flowers are not in my budget," Mickey said, trying to make light of a serious matter.

"I get out of here as soon as Carol can come and get me," Lou said, sounding upbeat. "I talked to Carol. She told me what you've been through. Sorry to hear it, Lou."

"Yeah, not fun, and worry is worse than the stitches."

"I guess you're right."

"Why are you calling?"

"Might need you, Lou. I can't locate an FBI investigator who was due to arrive on the Badger this morning."

"Could she be the person who died, Mickey?"

"Died? Somebody died?"

"Yeah, I got a call from a Ludington Daily News reporter, guy by the name of Rick Danville, telling me about a death on the Badger."

"This morning?"

"Yeah, the reporter called about two hours ago. He was wondering if I was going to be involved if there was a murder. I told him, contrary to what some might think, I don't investigate every murder in the state of Michigan."

"You seem to get the high profile cases, Lou. Did this reporter tell you the name of the person who died?"

"Yeah, Peg Lott. They don't have much information. No ID found, but she was assigned the stateroom where the body was found, and her car was left unclaimed on the Badger dock."

"You said it was a murder?" Mickey asked.

"I didn't say she was murdered, but that's what the police think happened. The body was found when the cruise director went looking for the owner of an unclaimed car."

"Hmmm, Peg Lott is not the person I'm looking for," Chief McFadden replied.

"Could it be an alias?" Lou asked.

"No, I don't think so. And, besides, she doesn't have a vehicle, so we're mixing apples and oranges."

"At any rate, you need some help finding this person, right?" Lou asked.

"I'm not asking you to get involved at this point, but if my colleague is found murdered, I'll sure want you working on the case."

"I'll do whatever I can, Mickey. Your dad and my brother go way back, and you led the investigation into the Marina Murders. You know I'll be there for you."

"Thanks. I'll monitor the situation up here, and if there was a murder, I'll let you know. I'm going to call the Ludington Police Chief and see what he knows."

"OK. In the meantime, I'm going home to Carol, take a walk on the beach, eat a normal breakfast and take the Harley out for a ride."

"Doesn't sound like any kind of prescribed post-op procedure to me."

"Doc wouldn't approve, but it's not his place to tell me how to live my life."

"Take care of yourself, Lou. I've got the feeling I'm going to need you."

Mickey McFadden called the Ludington Police Chief.

"Harry, Mickey McFadden here. I hear you've got a suspicious death on the Badger."

"I'm not sure if it's suspicious. She appears to have died of natural causes. We can't seem to find any information about her. We found some blood in the stateroom. It's being analyzed now but the early indication is that the body has no stab wounds."

"Peg Lott?"

"Yeah, that's what the stateroom registration form says, and I have no reason to doubt that's who she is. We traced the car registration and know that she lives in East Lansing. I've got a call into the East Lansing Police to check on the residence. We don't even know a next of kin to inform of the death or to identify the body for us. Technically she's Jane Doe right now."

"I see."

"And, I'm not releasing anything to the media until I get confirmation that the dead woman is Peg Lott and can inform a relative."

"I understand. Can I view the body?" Mickey asked.

"Why?" Chief Grether asked.

"I was expecting a visitor this morning and I haven't heard from her. Strange of her not to call or make some contact. I'm wondering if the woman you have there may be my visitor and not Peg Lott."

"Would you recognize your visitor?"

"No, I haven't met her, but I can get a description. I'll call the chief of police in Sheboygan, Wisconsin, and see if I can get that information."

"Okay, when you're ready, come down here and I'll clear it with the folks conducting the autopsy."

"Thanks. I'll be there soon. Do I come to your office or to a hospital?"

"Go to the hospital and have me paged. You shouldn't take more than forty minutes, right?"

"Right. Thanks, Harry."

Harry had just hung up when he received a call from the Chief of Police in East Lansing.

"We found the residence of Peg Lott and have information about her."

"Good. What have you got?"

"She is a highly regarded MSU professor who lives alone in an apartment. She keeps to herself, and has few, if any, friends. She is a staunch environmentalist. She has no record – no traffic tickets, no arrests. Model citizen, I'd say."

"Hmmm, can anyone in the area identify the body?"

"I suggest you ask the head of her department at MSU, Dr. Lorraine Hutchinson at 517-555-6677. I alerted her to the possibility of your call. I also asked her to keep this quiet for the time being since relatives have not been notified, nor has the body been positively identified."

"Good. Did her records at the university list an emergency contact?"

"The form has a blank space by that question. Dr. Hutchinson said Dr. Lott had mentioned parents in the past, but Dr. Hutchinson has no idea where they live."

"OK. I'll ask Dr. Hutchinson to come up and identify the body."

"As I said, she's expecting your call."

"Thanks for the information."

Peg had been in Lake Michigan for almost eight hours, and the thought of death had been constantly on her mind. She probably would have given in to that fate, except for her love of Len Miles, the person who seemed to truly love and care about her. Not only did she want to be with him forever, but she also felt a need to bring some justice to the Ring of Fire without getting herself killed.

In early afternoon, Peggy saw a huge, white yacht coming in her direction. It was the closest yacht she had seen, and the possibility of being spotted was better than before. She knew she couldn't be heard if she shouted, but if she splashed to the extent that her energy allowed, if someone were looking in that direction, perhaps they would know that a fish wouldn't make such a disturbance in the water.

Peggy flailed her arms, splashing as much as she could. She thought she saw the huge boat slow and turn, but maybe it was an illusion, and for all she knew, she was seeing a mirage. Maybe there was no yacht, and it was just wishful thinking.

When she looked again, the boat was still there but had not turned. Apparently no one had seen her. Peggy stopped flailing. She shut her eyes and, although not a religious woman, asked God to allow her to live.

A group of seagulls drew the attention of the yacht's captain, LeRoy Billups. What could be of interest to that many seagulls so far out in Lake Michigan, so far from a source of food? LeRoy thought. His experience with seagulls was that they were all about food. Something had to interest them, since they were not following his yacht.

LeRoy Billups was the owner of a toy company in Los Angeles, a millionaire several times over. He was sailing with his wife Mary and son Brad on a tour of the Great Lakes. LeRoy had been around the world many times, but the Great Lakes still fascinated him. This was the first time he had ever sailed the five largest freshwater lakes in the country. Brad, a geology major at the University of Southern California, was making this trip with his parents so that he could write a paper on the historical development of the Great Lakes.

The family sailed in the daytime, and in the evening they would stop at a popular marina. LeRoy and his wife Mary would dine at the most fashionable restaurant they could find while Brad stayed on the yacht and read, wrote and studied volumes on the development of the Great Lakes. On occasion, Brad would take his Honda Spree off the yacht and drive around the port city looking for excitement. Each day the Billups would move to another spot for more research.

"I'm circling around," LeRoy said to Mary.

"Why?"

"Those seagulls over there. Something must be in the water and I can't imagine what. Also, they don't go down to the water, they stay up in the air circling. If something were dead and a source of food, they would go down to it. Since they are hovering, something has their attention, and I'm curious."

"Brad hopes to get to Door County by dark, LeRoy. Won't this delay us?" Mary asked, clad in a bright yellow bikini.

"Hardly. I can catch up by pushing the speed up a bit – the lake is calm."

Peggy had become exhausted trying to get the attention of someone on the yacht. She was beginning to lose consciousness, but her head stayed above water because of her flotation device. In prayer, she accepted that death was no doubt her fate, and she prepared to give up.

LeRoy guided his yacht toward the seagulls, asking Brad to use powerful binoculars to see whatever might be of interest to the seagulls.

"Something's there, Dad," Brad called out.

"What is it?"

"Can't tell yet – there's no movement. Something's floating is all I can tell right now."

The yacht continued toward the object that Brad had spotted and the seagulls were getting closer and closer.

"It's a person, Dad. I can't tell if he is dead or alive – there is no movement."

LeRoy tooted his horn. The only response was that the seagulls seemed momentarily frightened. The yacht continued to move closer to Peg.

"I think it's a woman!" Brad said, just before he jumped in the water and swam over to Peg. LeRoy cut the engines so he and Mary could assist Brad. They were able to pull her up onto the ledge at the back of the yacht. From there they brought her on board. Brad had had some first aid training at USC and immediately tried to find a pulse.

"She's got a pulse, but it's weak," Brad said.

They wrapped blankets around Peg while Mary began to prepare some soup. When Peg came to, she didn't know where she was or what was going on around her. She didn't say anything, just reveled in the warmth of the blankets.

LeRoy thought it best to contact the Coast Guard, so this woman could be airlifted to a hospital in Wisconsin. She was alive but clearly in need of medical attention. He had moved toward his radio when Peg muttered something. He couldn't make it out, so he stopped and went to Peg's side.

"You okay, lady? Can you tell us who you are?"

"Where am I?" Peg asked weakly.

"You're on my yacht out in Lake Michigan. Did your boat sink or something?" LeRoy asked.

"Who are you?" Peg asked.

"We are the Billups. We found you floating out here. You've got the seagulls to thank for our seeing you."

"Thanks," Peg murmured as she began to realize that she was now safe.

"We're getting some soup for you. We've got to get you warm and then get some help from the Coast Guard."

"No, please, no. I'll be killed."

"Killed?" LeRoy was surprised at what he heard. "Are you wanted for something?"

"No, no, nothing like that. But, if certain people find out that I am alive, they'll find me and kill me. Please don't call. Please. If you can get me to shore, I'll be okay."

"I won't call the Coast Guard if that's what you want, but you've got to have some medical attention. You almost died out there in that water, lady."

Around noon, Dr. Hutchinson was pulling into the hospital parking lot in Ludington. Chief Grether met her and introduced her to Mickey McFadden, with whom he had been talking prior to seeing the body. He asked Dr. Hutchinson if she had any experience viewing a dead body.

"Yes, I've studied lots of cadavers over the years," she replied.

"Just asking. Some folks are not used to this, and it can be a bit troublesome, especially when they are looking at a relative or a good friend."

"I understand."

"Let's take a look and see if we have Peg Lott here," Chief Grether said, as the three walked up to the cold metal table in the autopsy room of the hospital. The white sheet was pulled back and the face of the victim exposed.

"That's not Peg Lott," Dr. Hutchinson said, firmly shaking her head from side to side.

"It isn't?" Chief Grether asked, surprised to hear that this was not the owner of the vehicle left stranded at the Badger dock.

"No. I brought a photo of her from the university in case you might need it to help in identifying the body."

"You're right. This woman has a different hair color, and appears to be smaller than Peg Lott."

"I appreciate your making the trip up here," Chief Grether replied. "Guess you don't have a vacancy in your department, Doctor."

"No, but I'm concerned. Peg said she would call me this morning on her way home from Ludington."

Mickey McFadden had talked to the police chief in Sheboygan who described the FBI agent Stephanie Brooks. As soon as Chief McFadden saw the corpse, he knew it was Stephanie. Mickey said to Harry, "We'll need to verify the identity of the woman, but I'm almost one hundred percent certain that the dead woman is Stephanie Brooks, a high-ranking FBI Supervisor."

"That's reassuring," Chief Grether replied. "At least I have another name to put on this corpse."

"Yeah, but why was this woman in Peg Lott's stateroom? And, where is Peg Lott? And, why didn't she pick up her car?" Harry asked.

"She would be my first suspect in this murder," Mickey offered. "After all, the stateroom was assigned to her, right?"

"Right," Harry agreed. "Maybe Peg got off the Badger and got out of town as fast as possible, thinking that standing around waiting for her car would allow the body to be discovered, and it sure wouldn't look good for her."

"But why leave your car?" Mickey asked. "Isn't it sort of putting your calling card on the murder scene?"

"Good point."

"If you want the best detective working on this, I suggest Lou Searing. I'm going to call Lou to ask his help in figuring out why Agent Brooks is dead," Mickey said with conviction. "My guess is that the missing Peg Lott is a part of this story."

"I've got a good detective," Harry replied. "I'm going to stick with my team but I'll cooperate with Lou if he's helping you, Mickey."

"Thanks. This is your jurisdiction, but I'll tell you this, Agent Brooks being murdered means that some heavy hitters in the drug scene smelled that their jig was up. I'm going to expect the Feds to get involved in this, Harry."

"Not a problem. I've got a murder to solve. I think I can do it with my team, but if you, Lou Searing and the Feds beat me to the solution, not a problem – as long as the crime gets solved. You can count on me for full support. Is that understood?"

"Thanks, Harry. I appreciate it."

Mickey informed Lou that he needed him as soon as possible. Lou packed an overnight bag, strapped it onto his Harley-Davidson, kissed Carol, patted Samm on the head, and left Grand Haven. While Lou wasn't in a hurry to begin another murder investigation, he knew he would love the fast and exciting ride on his Harley. Lou always anticipated solving the crime, but this time he had the feeling that something wouldn't work out well. He felt an intuitive urge to leave this investigation to the police and stay home. But he kept on going. He got out to U.S. 31 North and, pushing 75 mph, headed toward Ludington, where, by mid-afternoon, he'd be well into his sixth murder investigation. He hoped his gut feeling was wrong, but most of the time it was right.

While Mickey was talking to Lou, Harry talked to the FBI who would send someone up to positively identify the suspected victim, Stephanie Brooks. The FBI would also assign someone, probably Joan Nelson, to investigate the agent's murder.

Lou was without his partner, Maggie McMillan, who had worked with him in solving the previous five murders that he had investigated. This would test Lou's investigative skills, as it was usually Maggie who discovered the pattern of evidence and then guided the investigation to a successful conclusion.

Maggie, 46, was attractive and had a pleasant personality. She became a wheelchair user after a knife attack by a man suspected of insurance fraud had left her paralyzed. Lou considered Maggie the brains of the duo, but this case looked like it would be his to solve as Maggie was caring for an aunt in Denver. Lou would no doubt call Maggie for advice, but for the most part, this case would be his and Mickey's.

Lou met Mickey at The House of Flavors Restaurant in Manistee, a favorite ice cream parlor of area residents as well as travelers along U.S. 31. They greeted one another, exchanged small talk about their families, and then Mickey briefed Lou on the case.

"Let's start with the car," Lou said, anxious to get into the investigation. "Have you inspected it?"

"No. I have no jurisdiction in the case," Mickey answered.

"In the event there is a connection between Peg Lott and Stephanie Brooks' death, I'd like to know as much about this Peg Lott as I can," Lou replied.

"Harry has pledged his full cooperation, and I expect the Feds will be involved at some point."

"Good, let's look at that car."

The two men finished their coffee, paid, and headed for the Ludington Police Department where Harry had impounded the late-model Chevrolet.

Mickey introduced Lou to Harry. Chief McFadden then asked for permission to inspect the Lott vehicle. Harry said that the Ludington police had thoroughly gone over the vehicle, but he gave them directions to the impound lot anyway.

After examining the car for several minutes, Lou said, "There's a lot of information in this car, Mickey."

"Yeah, I agree. If she's not a career criminal and I doubt an MSU professor is, she'll leave her information about herself all over this car."

"Precisely, and we'll start with some affiliations."

"You mean like the sticker from Harvard?"

"Right. We need to find out if Peg is the original owner of this car. If not, a lot of these connections could lead us on a wild goose chase."

"Here's an oil change sticker," Mickey said, looking toward the upper left corner of the windshield. "Looks like Valvoline in Okemos, Michigan; they could have some information."

"Here's a map of Colorado and a map of Wisconsin in the door storage area. And, bingo! Here's a trip-tic from AAA from East Lansing to Green Bay. If she made that trip, there is undoubtedly some connection to that part of the country."

"This is strange," Mickey said, looking in the trunk. "Here's a set of old TV Guides. She must have been a Fox Network groupie. All of these newscasts are highlighted."

"Probably likes the announcer," Lou surmised. "Some folks just can't believe the news unless Rather, or Brokaw or Jennings is talking. They look at these guys as trusted friends and unless they hear the news from them, it's not true."

"I guess so," Mickey replied, although not paying attention to what Lou was saying.

"Ok, now I need to get on the Badger," Lou said, ready for the next step in the investigation.

Mickey's cell phone rang.

"Yeah, McFadden here."

"This is Harry. The autopsy report has been faxed. The cause of Stephanie Brooks' death is suffocation."

"Hmmm. Murder."

"Yup. Someone got in that stateroom and covered her face with something, probably a pillow."

"Could have been Peg Lott."

"Suspect number one, Mickey," Harry replied.

"While you're on the line, Lou will want to look around on the Badger when it gets in this evening."

"Not a problem. Call President Bob Carter and alert him. He is cooperating fully."

"Thanks, Harry. We'll be in touch."

Mickey called Mr. Carter. "Hello. This is Bob Carter."

"Mr. Carter, this is Mickey McFadden, Police Chief of Manistee. I have permission from Chief Grether to inquire about a missing person who was to meet me after crossing on the Badger."

"You need to come on the Badger? Is that it?" Bob asked matter of factly.

"I'd like permission, sir. Yes."

"Not a problem. The ship is in Wisconsin right now, but it is due this evening around six. Come to my office around six-thirty. The ship should be vacated by then. Do you have any information about the lady who supposedly was killed?" Bob asked.

"You should probably call Chief Grether for an update on the cause of death," Mickey said, thinking it was not his place to release that information.

"It had better be natural causes, whatever it is – I don't need a murder on my ship."

"Chief Grether should be the one to inform you, sir. Give him a call."

"I will. See you about six-thirty this evening."

"Thanks. And, by the way, I'll be bringing Lou Searing with me."

"I know him. Searing is working on this, is he?"

"Yes, he is."

"Fine man. Excellent investigator. If there has been some foul play in this mess, Lou'll get to the bottom of it," Bob said confidently.

"I agree. See you later."

CHAPTER TWELVE

July 14, 2004
Manistee, Michigan

Larry Renaldo was responsible for drug distribution in the northern part of Michigan's Lower Peninsula. The visit by Agent Stephanie Brooks was to set a trap to finally catch the "Big Guy" in the act. The FBI, Manistee County Sheriff, and the Manistee Police were ready for the stakeout and the arrests which would surely follow.

Renaldo had fallen into a pattern. He would begin his distribution of drugs on Monday mornings. A shipment would come into Michigan from Canada via Port Huron. Truck drivers were unsuspecting carriers of the contraband; smugglers would attach a device that would track the truck as it headed into Michigan. When the truck driver pulled into a rest area and was in the bathroom or had gone into the truck's cab for a nap, a member of the ring would remove the magnetized container from underneath the trailer bed and be gone.

There were three drug runners working out of Port Huron. Each vehicle had magnetic door signs which read, "Medical Supply Carrier." One runner was responsible for trucks going west on I-69, another for trucks heading north and south from Port Huron.

Once the runner had a supply of drugs, he took them to Lansing, where additional runners picked up the expensive cargo for distribution. One runner handled the southwest part of the state from an operation based in a little town called Paw Paw, known for its vineyards and delicious wine. The southeast operation was based in Milan. Mid-Michigan distribution was based in Leslie, and drugs were supplied to the northern part of the Lower Peninsula based in Grayling. In each case, Renaldo based the regional operation in a small town so as to limit speculation regarding their whereabouts. Most people would expect the supplier to be in a large metropolitan area.

Mickey was responsible for monitoring the work of Larry Renaldo in Manistee. Mickey's staff had infiltrated the operation and was able to identify Renaldo's network and the major players in the drug operation.

Agent Brooks was coming to Manistee to put the final pieces of the dragnet together. The trap needed to be sprung simultaneously all across the region in order to shut this operation down. It was important for Stephanie to meet with Mickey to set up the last part of the operation, and once that was in place, federal and state authorities in the Great Lakes States were ready to make arrests in concert and expose the operation.

With Stephanie missing, the plans to make mass arrests in Operation Waterfall, or 'OW' for short, were on hold. And, the speculation of those high in the federal and state operation was that Stephanie was killed by one of the motorcyclist runners coming into Michigan from Manitowoc.

Mickey met with Randy, his officer who had infiltrated the operation, in the afternoon of July 14th. The two met in The House of Flavors Restaurant in Manistee. Both had a cup of coffee in front of them. Only a few customers were in the restaurant, so the two men could talk quietly without fear that their conversation would be overheard.

"You've heard that our principal agent was killed last night on the Badger, right?" Mickey asked.

"No, I didn't know that."

"Yeah, she was suffocated in a stateroom assigned to an MSU professor, who's also missing."

"Probably was Moe," Randy said matter of factly.

"Moe?" Mickey asked.

"Yeah, in hindsight, I suppose it was just a matter of time. He's the paranoid one. With every person who passed us on deck, Moe would say something like, 'That's an agent on our case,' or 'He's onto us, man. We're dead ducks.'

"He didn't realize that people stared at him. There he was all decked out in black leather and looking like the meanest guy on the ship. I tried to convince him that if he'd look in a mirror, he'd know why people were staring at him. I kept telling him we were clean. Nobody was suspecting anything, other than that we were a tough group of riders."

"Were you able to keep track of the other three at all times?" Mickey asked.

"No. That trip last night was like all the other trips – drive the bike on, cross the lake, drive the bike off, and get out of the area. On board, the four of us played cards, took naps, walked around a bit. We don't keep tabs on one another."

"Moe could have done this, huh?" Mickey asked.

"Sure. Probably did do it. He's mean and he's got no morals. I mean he'd kill you as soon as loan you a cigarette. Just depends on his mood."

"He got a record?"

"Does Baskin-Robbins have ice cream? Call the chief of police in Mount Pleasant, mention Moe's name, and you won't have enough time to listen to everything in his folder. Moe can't get a job because of his record and reputation, let alone how he looks. So, he runs drugs for money. He also sells a lot of it and takes in at least double your salary, Mickey. I know that for a fact."

"I need you to find out if this Moe killed Agent Brooks."

"Yes, sir."

"I need more than just Moe's involvement. Find out if anyone in Renaldo's operation knows about her being murdered."

"Yes, sir. Got a timetable?"

"I want it yesterday!"

"I'll get on it, Chief. Talk with you as soon as I know something."

Other than Dr. Hutchinson, no one at MSU would miss Peggy Lott. A few students had appointments with her on Monday, but Peg was a professor who didn't keep her office hours, and those students with appointments would check back in a day or two.

Dr. Hutchinson was concerned. She knew the dead body was not Peg Lott, but she kept tossing around the fact that Peg had never claimed her car.

Dr. Hutchinson tried to reach Lou Searing. Not only did she enjoy his novels, but she was familiar with his investigations because she was a Friend of the East Lansing Library to whose members Lou would speak. His personality was such that she felt she could call him and explain her concern. She called Lou's home in Grand Haven, talked to Carol for a few minutes, only to find he was not home. Carol gave her Lou's cell phone number, which she dialed.

"Lou Searing."

"Mr. Searing, this is Dr. Hutchinson, Chair of the Ecology Department at MSU. I've heard you speak at our Friends of the Library meeting."

"I always enjoy that group," Lou replied.

"Yes, we're a good group, if I might say so myself. Thank you. Anyway, I'm calling you because I have a staff member who is missing and I'm concerned."

"What's this person's name?" Lou asked.

"Dr. Peggy Lott. She was thought to have died in Ludington after coming over on the Badger. They asked me to identify her. When I saw the body, I told the police chief that it was not Dr. Lott."

"I see."

"I call her apartment every couple of hours or so but all I get is her answering machine."

"I happen to be involved with that case and I'm in the Ludington area now," Lou explained. "Actually, I'm working on trying to figure out who may have killed the woman in Dr. Lott's stateroom."

"Killed? They think it was murder?"

"Yes, so the autopsy report indicates."

"Oh, my. Peg Lott didn't do this, Mr. Searing. She wouldn't swat a fly. Granted, she's different, but she is not one to harm another."

"We have no indication that she did or would. We're trying to locate her as well. Do you know anyone who knows where she is?"

"I really don't. She is a loner here. She has no friends, at least none that I know about. She has mentioned parents, but I don't know where they live. If it weren't for her cat, I would doubt there is anyone around her that she communicates with outside of her teaching and research responsibilities. Usually a professor will have a good friend on staff, but in Peg's case, she doesn't talk to anyone, hates to serve on committees, and seems to be most content when she's alone."

"Let me ask a few questions," Lou asked. "Why was she gone from MSU?"

"I approved her to go to a conference in Minneapolis."

"She drove?"

"Well, we'll reimburse up to a certain amount, and whether the professor drives, flies, or walks, is up to them. She drove, because her car was left on the Badger dock in Ludington."

"Do you know if she knew anyone at the conference?" Lou asked.

"No."

"Did she present a paper with a colleague?"

"That I don't know. She filled out a form to request reimbursement for the trip. Let me pull that up and see."

A minute later, Dr. Hutchinson came back on the line. "Yes. She was presenting with a professor from the University of Washington, a Dr. Willard Lowe."

"Do you have a contact for him?"

"No."

"Do you have a contact for this conference in Minneapolis?"

"Yes." She gave Lou the number for information.

"Thanks. I'll be in touch, and you call me if you have any information and especially if she shows up. OK?"

"Certainly, Mr. Searing. Thank you."

"Have a good day."

CHAPTER THIRTEEN

July 14, 2004
Late Sunday Afternoon

Following up on his assignment from Chief McFadden, Randy rode his motorcycle out of Manistee to a bar named Chaser, the meeting place for the four drug runners. Randy knew the guys were there, because he recognized the bikes as he drove up to the bar. The guys were seated in the back of the smoke-filled room.

Randy got right to the point. "Some lady was killed on the Badger."

"Yeah, little action. Gives the cops something to do besides wonder how they can trip us up," Moe replied.

"You do it, Moe?" Randy asked bluntly.

Moe laughed out loud and drank half a mug of beer. "Are you joking, or are you serious?"

"I'm serious," Randy replied. "You're always so paranoid, thinking everybody who looks at you is doing you in. I figured this woman must have pissed you off, and you took care of business."

Jeff laughed. "He looks mean and ugly and if I didn't know he was a pussy cat, I'd think he killed her." Jeff could talk this way because he was the only one Moe feared. Jeff was strong and intelligent.

"What if I did?" Moe fired back. "I can smell a Fed a mile away. I watched her go into her stateroom and figured I'd pay her a visit, you know, just to make sure we weren't bothered."

"You're playing with us, Moe," Lucky said, laughing. "You didn't kill that woman."

"Okay, I didn't kill her. I'm foolin' with you. But, she was a Fed and if I was going to get hit up by the cops as we drove off that ship, I wanted to be in control. You guys understand control, right? Why you want to know anyway?" Moe asked Randy.

"Just asking," Randy said.

"That little stateroom was the perfect place for murder," Moe continued. "You greet the lady, tell her she dies if she makes a sound, throw her on the bed, and put the pillow over her face. Quick and quiet. She's history, and we don't have to worry about her."

"Who was she?" Jeff asked.

"I told ya, she was a Fed," Moe said.

"I'm talking to Randy," Jeff fired back. "Was she a Fed? Do you know for sure?"

"I don't know. How should I know?" Randy asked, careful not to blow his cover.

"We need more beer, and I want to play pool," said Lucky, the fourth member of the drug runners.

"I'll get a pitcher," Randy said, heading for the bar. "Lucky, you get the pool cues and get those kids out of our way. I'll beat your butt when I get back."

Randy walked to the bar while Lucky picked up two cues and told the kids to beat it. When Lucky played pool, each game, win or lose, was $100, and debts were paid and paid on time. The rule was, if you're dumb enough to gamble, you're smart enough to pay, because not paying a debt to a brother was worth getting your brains kicked in.

Randy still wasn't sure whether Moe was pulling his leg. He wouldn't have put it past him, killing the agent on the Badger. After he shot some pool and played some cards, Randy told the guys he needed to get home. It was his daughter's birthday, and he had promised her he would be at her party.

Once he was well away from the Chaser, Randy called Mickey on his private phone line.

"I talked to the guys and asked Moe right to his face if he killed the woman on the Badger. First he said he did, but then he told the guys he was foolin' with them. I hear this kind of talk all the time from Moe. He talks tough when he really is as far from the truth as we are from the moon."

"Do we have any evidence that he did it?" Chief McFadden asked.

"I wouldn't know. I was with him during the crossing, but wasn't with him every minute of the trip. On the witness stand, or even in interrogation by the prosecutor, I couldn't give any information that would lead to Moe as the killer. Once when he left the group and said he was going for a beer, he didn't come back with a beer. But, he can stand at the bar and down a beer in seconds."

"He said he did it, right?" Mickey asked, wanting to believe he had a suspect.

"Yeah, but then he recanted. His reputation is lousy for telling the truth. In fact, ninety percent of the time I listen to him, I know the opposite of what he says is true."

"Anything he said lead you to believe he could be the murderer?" Mickey asked.

"He said she was killed in a stateroom, but I didn't say that. I just said she was killed on the Badger. I don't know how he knew she was killed in a stateroom."

"Interesting. Okay, thanks for your work. Keep your eyes and ears open for anything else that could tie any of these guys to the murder," Mickey said.

Joan Nelson, an FBI Supervisor from D.C., was on her way to Ludington to identify and claim the body of Agent Stephanie Brooks. She would also interview members of the Great Lakes team, who had provided much information for the investigation of drug trafficking in the upper Midwest.

Joan was in her early 40s and was strikingly beautiful. While she kept the information to herself, those close to her knew that she had been Miss Virginia twenty years ago. As a college student, Joan was fascinated by forensic science. She earned a degree in criminal justice with a major in forensic science. She was hired by the FBI, and after a couple of successful investigations, she was promoted to headquarters in D.C. where she discovered a talent for administration.

Joan was met at the Ludington airport by a couple of agents assigned to Grand Rapids. She would handle all the paperwork related to the death of Agent Brooks and then assume the role of leader of the drug take-down in a matter of days. Her key contact would be Chief McFadden in Manistee. She had placed a call to Mickey and would see him soon.

Lou, Mickey, and Joan joined Bob Carter on the Badger after it arrived from Manitowoc at 6:30 P.M.. They only had a short time. In Stateroom 16, Lou and Joan took turns looking around the room. They found nothing out of the ordinary, nothing to help them with their investigation. As they were about to leave, Joan said to Mickey, "I want every piece of dust on this floor."

"I thought you would say that. I'll arrange for it." Lou, in an effort to be helpful, put on his latex gloves, and using forensic materials, retrieved dust, hair, and whatever hadn't been picked up by maintenance in their routine cleaning of the tile floor.

Bob was a bit anxious for his guests to leave. They were about to board passengers for the evening trip back to Manitowoc, and he didn't want them seeing a police uniform along with several other people. Rumors start over the slightest thing, and already many passengers had heard through various media that a murder had occurred on the Badger.

Lou had a couple more things to do. He wanted to know if the walls were thin enough so that people could hear any confrontation from an adjoining stateroom, so he asked Mickey to go next door, and bang around and shout. Bob allowed Mickey into Stateroom 18, and Lou, realizing that his hearing loss would not provide a true assessment of the soundproof status of the staterooms, asked Joan to listen. She could hear some sounds, and she believed that someone in an adjoining room with normal hearing could hear a verbal confrontation or banging on the walls.

The second thing Lou wanted to do was walk from the stateroom to the deck looking carefully for any clues. When he got to the stern, he looked over toward Ludington. Down below he could see cars lining up and people standing around waiting for the signal to board. They would immediately stake claims to tables, pull chairs to favorite viewing spots, and line up at the concession stands. Some had made the crossing many times and had established their routines. Others were making the crossing for the first time and had no idea what awaited them.

Lou took out his pen to note an observation when the pen slipped out of his hand, hit the rail and fell on the deck. He almost lost it in the harbor which would have been most unfortunate because the pen was a treasured gift from Carol. Lou bent down to get the pen and, in doing so, noticed a dark stain. Chances are it was simply some spilled soft drink that had dried. While he was looking at the spot, Mickey appeared. "We've got to go. Bob wants to get these anxious people on board and thinks we've had enough time to get what we need."

"Yeah, I know. Look at this, Mickey. Is this blood?" Lou asked.

"Could be."

As Mickey had gotten every piece of foreign matter from the floor of 16, he also managed to scrape up the possible blood from the deck.

"Okay, I've got what I need. Let's go."

Lou and Mickey joined Joan and Bob and left the ship as people began to board, anxious to get across the lake to spend the night in motels in and around Manitowoc.

W hile Lou, Joan, and Mickey walked to Mickey's police cruiser, Lou's cell phone rang. "Hello."

"Lou, this is Maggie."

"Well, hello. You're missed here in Ludington. Are you still in Denver? How is your aunt?" Lou inquired.

"Thanks for asking, Lou. She's not doing well. Hospice folks have been coming in. I'm not much help, but I'm glad I'm here. I've been thinking about you working on the Badger case. Have you got any good clues?" Maggie asked.

"We've got a body, but that's about it. An FBI agent was suffocated according to the pathologist. We also have a missing woman, Dr. Peg Lott, an MSU professor, and we haven't a clue where she is. She may be dead too, but nothing indicates that."

Lou and Maggie did nothing more than chit chat. Maggie, lonely for the excitement of working on a case, had called Lou to see how he was doing and hopefully to hear that she was missed.

As the three pulled away from the downtown Ludington area, Lou asked, "When the crew went through the ship looking for Peggy Lott, was the door to her stateroom open or locked?"

"Not sure," Joan replied. "I didn't see that information in Grether's report."

"What are you thinking, Lou?" Mickey asked.

"Well, it would be logical for the door to be open," Lou responded. "I'd be surprised if it was locked. I can't imagine him or her taking the time to lock the door after killing Stephanie. Nor can I imagine the murderer returning to the scene of the crime to lock the door."

"Why not, Lou? That makes sense to me," Chief McFadden responded. "The murderer wouldn't want someone coming into the room out on the lake because that would cause problems. The last thing he or she would want is for everyone on board to be confined to the ship in Ludington. It makes sense to lock the door."

"I guess you're right," Lou said, giving it more thought.

"Why can't you imagine the murderer returning?" Mickey asked Lou.

"I was thinking that once away from the stateroom, the killer wouldn't return because of the risk of being seen by someone. If I were the killer, I'd get out of the area, consider myself extremely lucky not to be seen, and I wouldn't take the risk of being seen again by returning to the stateroom. A cat has nine lives, but a murderer rarely gets two lucky breaks."

"That's a good point, Lou."

"If the stateroom were locked, that would mean that the passenger key to that stateroom is somewhere," Lou reasoned.

"I agree, and that place, no doubt, is on the bottom of Lake Michigan," Joan said.

"Yup, if there is a key, it's on the bottom of the pond," Mickey replied.

"However, there is the possibility that it's in the bottom of the killer's pants pocket," Lou said.

"I doubt it," Mickey replied. "But yes, it's possible."

As the three neared Manistee, they decided their next steps. The three agreed that Lou would do some legwork on the case. Jurisdiction was really with Chief Grether and not with Chief McFadden. Joan had decided to leave the murder investigation to Michigan law enforcement agencies. She would be traveling around the Great Lakes by plane, with bodyguards with her at all times. She could pick up where Stephanie left off and prepare for a successful multi-state drug bust.

Lou learned from the LMC the name and number of the person who had Stateroom 18. He then called a Mrs. Hogan of Elyria, Ohio, to find out what, if anything, she had heard. "Hello."

"Mrs. Hogan?"

"Yes."

"This is Lou Searing calling from Michigan. I'm a private investigator looking into a missing person case on the Badger. I'm sure you're aware that a woman was found dead in the stateroom next to yours after you crossed last Friday morning."

"I heard that on the news, but I didn't know the body was in the stateroom next to mine."

"Yes. The body was found in 16."

"Oh, my. I've never been so close to a dead body in my life."

"I'm calling to ask a few questions. Can you talk for a moment or two?" Lou asked.

"Yes, but I didn't do anything. You're not suggesting that I had anything to do with it, are you?"

"No. We're trying to get some information."

"Okay, what do you want to know?" Mrs. Hogan asked, sounding reticent about getting involved.

"How many people were crossing with you?" Lou asked. "Or were you alone?"

"My granddaughter was with me."

"Were you in the stateroom for most of the voyage?"

"Yes, most of it."

"Did you go out to look around or get a bite to eat?" Lou asked.

"This was the middle of the night, and my granddaughter wasn't feeling very well. We got on the ship, found our stateroom, settled in for the trip, and stayed in the room except for going out a couple of times to get some pop."

"Were you up all night?" Lou asked.

"I did get some sleep; around five o'clock, I'd say."

"Did you hear any commotion in the stateroom next to yours?"

"Oh, yes. It sounded like a bad argument," Mrs. Hogan replied.

"How long did this noise last?"

"It was only a few seconds."

"Did you hear voices?"

"A scream actually."

"A scream?"

"Well, not a loud scream. There was some sort of back and forth talking, then a muffled scream, and then nothing."

"Did you contact the cruise director?" Lou inquired.

"Oh no, I wasn't going to get involved. It quieted down, and I figured they were done, but it disturbed me. I don't like to hear stuff like that."

"About what time did you hear this scream?" Lou asked.

"I'd say it was around 4 o'clock; between four and four-thirty for sure."

"Did you ever see the person or people in 16?"

"No, I didn't. Well, I did see this big guy, looked like a motorcycle guy."

"Dressed in black leather?"

"Yes, chains, leather cap, the works. A mean-looking man."

"You saw him go into 16?" Lou asked.

"No, I didn't. I saw him in the hall when I went out for a pop."

"Could you tell if the voices were of a man and a woman?"

"It sounded like it, but I probably just assumed it."

"Are you sure it was a fight or an argument that you heard?"

"It was an argument. My granddaughter even said something like, 'They're not very nice.'"

"Thanks, Mrs. Hogan. You've been very helpful," Lou said sincerely.

"I hope I don't have to go to court. I don't like to do stuff like that."

"I really don't know about that. I'm just trying to find the killer. What happens after that is not in my ballpark, but I appreciate your telling me what you heard. You confirmed that there was a conflict of some kind."

"How was she killed?" Mrs. Hogan asked. "I didn't hear a shot."

"The pathologist says it was suffocation. The killer probably held a pillow over her face."

"Terrible."

"Yes. Thank you, Mrs. Hogan."

"You're welcome."

Lou and Mickey sat across from each other in Chief McFadden's office, discussing what they had learned that day and what needed to be done next. It was decided that Lou would ride his Harley to East Lansing and talk to several people who might have some information regarding the case.

The Billups pulled into the marina in Algoma, Wisconsin. Summertime in Door County, Wisconsin, is crowded and a popular place for Wisconsinites and visitors from all 50 states. LeRoy had called ahead on the ship-to-shore radio to inquire if a slip was available. He learned that a slip was available and immediately reserved it.

With help from Brad and Mary, LeRoy secured the yacht to the mooring and went into the marina office to pay his fee.

"Sure glad you had a spot for us," LeRoy said, extending his hand to the harbormaster.

"We aim to please, Mr. Billups. Normally I wouldn't have a slip open, but there're not many boats your size on the Great Lakes, so chances are better for you to find big slips available," the harbormaster replied.

"By the way, what restaurant do you recommend here?" LeRoy asked.

"Well, to be honest with you, I get in trouble around here when I recommend one place over another. When I get to the Chamber of Commerce meeting, I'm loved by the ones I recommend, and I get the cold shoulder from the others."

"It's tough being between a rock and a hard place, huh?"

"Right. So, I put their information on the bulletin board, and I recommend all of them. You look for what you want. I assure you that you won't get a bad meal in this town. There is a lot of competition for the tourist dollar, and every dining place on that bulletin board will give you service and a meal that will cause you to stop back and thank me. And, now I'll be loved by everyone at the Chamber meeting, the Kiwanis meeting, and at church."

"Your recommendations travel near and far, it seems."

"Well, in a small town, most can actually hear me when I offer an opinion." Both men chuckled. LeRoy thanked the harbormaster for his service and then turned to the bulletin board.

From the restaurant menus posted, he thought he'd choose one with a view of Lake Michigan. LeRoy jotted down the phone number and the web site, thinking he could get a good look at where he would take Mary for their meal.

As he was about to leave the bulletin board, his eyes focused on a missing person poster. There in front of him was the woman he had plucked out of Lake Michigan earlier in the afternoon. He read, "Missing: Peg Lott. Wanted for questioning. Is thought to be dangerous. Anyone with information regarding this woman should call the police."

LeRoy said to the harbormaster, "What's this about?" pointing to the poster.

"That came in this afternoon. I guess there was a murder on the Badger and she's a suspect."

"What's the Badger?"

"It's a car ferry that takes people across the lake from Manitowoc to Ludington – crosses a couple of times a day."

"Murder, huh?"

"Yeah, someone told me a woman was suffocated in her stateroom in the middle of the night."

"Lots of drama in these parts," LeRoy said, becoming quite concerned.

"Hey, nothing surprises me anymore. This world is full of nuts, and I don't mean cashews!"

"Yeah, it's a different time. Thanks for the boat slip. I'll give you a report on the restaurant following our meal."

"Which place did you choose?"

"I think we'll go to the Sand Dune. The menu is appealing, and they have transportation to and from this marina – a big plus."

"You won't be disappointed. But if you don't have a reservation, and I guess you don't since you just got here, you won't get in till after nine."

"I'll call as soon as I get back to my boat and get the wife's thumbs-up on my choice."

"A good evening to you, Mr. Billups."

"Thank you."

When LeRoy got back to his slip, he found his rescued passenger asleep on a berth. Mary and Brad were both reading. LeRoy went to his computer and pulled up the Ludington Daily News to see what he would learn about the murder on the Badger, but the article wasn't anymore informative than the harbormaster.

LeRoy then typed in "Peg Lott" and up came a host of web sites. He chose the one that linked her to Michigan State University. He quickly learned that she was internationally known for her ecology research and had received numerous honors. She had earned a Ph.D. along with a string of degrees. Was this woman a murderer? he thought.

What puzzled him the most was, why was she in the middle of Lake Michigan? He decided not to tell Mary what he had learned at the marina office. He didn't feel threatened by Peg Lott; after all he had saved her life and was her ticket to freedom, if she was telling the truth about being targeted for death.

LeRoy and Mary, fashionably dressed for dinner, went to the Sand Dune in Algoma. They had ordered their entrees when LeRoy felt a tinge of guilt over not sharing what he knew about their passenger. He realized that the news could ruin their evening, but this was a good place to work out the matter, so he began. "When I was in the marina office to pay our fee, I noticed something that startled me."

"The cost of the slip fee?" Mary said, in a teasing way as she picked up her glass of wine.

"No, actually it's pretty serious."

"Ok, let me have it. I can never tell with you, LeRoy, you might really have something serious on your mind or be about to hit me with some insignificant tidbit." Mary took another sip of wine.

"The woman on our boat is a suspect in a murder investigation," LeRoy said. Unfortunately, his timing was not good, as Mary was drinking from her wine goblet. She was able to control her reaction without a scene, but she was taken aback by the comment.

"Is this some kind of joke, LeRoy?" Mary asked, not enjoying the humor, if that indeed was the case.

"It's no joke. A woman was murdered in a stateroom on the Badger, the car ferry service that crosses Lake Michigan. The woman on our yacht is Peg Lott, a distinguished professor at Michigan State University. The stateroom where the body was found was registered to her."

"That's who's on our boat?"

"Yes."

"Well, she'll be off our boat within the hour!" Mary exclaimed. "I'm calling Brad and telling him to get off the dock and into town."

"No, listen. That won't help anything. Brad is not in harm's way."

"How can you say that, LeRoy?" Mary asked. "She's accused of murdering someone on a ship. Brad is on our boat, and she could be a serial killer!"

"Mary, please keep your voice down," LeRoy begged. "People are looking at us."

"Well, maybe they should look at us – we're about the biggest fools in Wisconsin right now, harboring a criminal."

"She is not, in my opinion, a criminal, and as for being a serial killer, she might be, but she is not. I'm convinced she is a victim as she says she is, and I am also convinced that she didn't kill anyone."

"Based on what?" Mary asked, challenging her husband.

"Instinct."

"Oh, right. You and all the shocked people in the world who hear that a pious grandmother has just committed a heinous crime."

"I think we should talk to her when we get back," LeRoy said.

"I think we should get Brad off that yacht, call the police, and have them go out there and put her behind bars or whatever they do when they find someone who's wanted for murder!"

"Mary, trust me on this one. I want to go back to the marina and confront Miss Lott. After we hear her story, if we are convinced that she is a threat to us, we'll call the police. But, if we believe she is a victim and innocent, then we'll take shifts staying awake all night just in case. Tomorrow we'll sail over to Michigan and let her off. Please follow my lead."

"I just hope we find Brad alive when we get back. If that woman is gone, though, I want our ship locked, and we'll leave at daybreak. Understood?"

"Fine."

LeRoy was right when he thought it would ruin their meal. Mary had no appetite once she knew what was going on. LeRoy paid for the uneaten dinner, left a tip following an apology to the waiter, and the two then requested a ride back to the marina.

With a light rain falling, they approached their slip. When they boarded their yacht, they found Brad and Peggy deep in conversation. Mary was very relieved to say the least.

"Have a good dinner?" Brad asked routinely.

"No, we didn't. It was sort of a wasted evening."

"Sorry to hear that. Lousy service? Lousy food?" Brad asked.

"Lousy conversation, son."

"That doesn't sound like you two."

"Normally it isn't, but this evening it was." LeRoy turned to Peggy and said, "We need to talk, and we need to be honest." Peggy could tell by the tone of his voice that she was the reason for the ruined evening and also that she was about to be confronted with some information that would be upsetting.

"Sure. Let's talk," Peg replied.

"When I went to the marina this evening to pay our slip fee, I noticed a flyer with your picture on it. They want to talk to you in connection with the murder of a woman on the Badger last night."

Shaking her head, Peg said in a serious tone, "Please. I am not involved. I don't know anything about a murder. I fear for my life!"

"We want to hear what happened," LeRoy said.

"Did you call the police?" Peg asked.

"No, not yet. We want to hear what you have to say."

Brad interrupted, "Dad, we've got to let the authorities know about her. You can't knowingly harbor a fugitive without paying a price."

"Let's listen to her story, and then we'll decide a course of action," LeRoy said, clearly in control.

Peg pleaded with them. "You folks saved my life, and I owe you a lot. If it weren't for you, I would be dead by now. Who knows if anyone would have happened by? So, I am indebted to you. You have a right to know what happened, and I'll take the risk by telling you things that, if you tell others, could lead to my death."

The Billups didn't promise anything. "You do know that this puts all of us in a bind, don't you?" LeRoy said, looking Peggy in the eye. "Like Brad said, if we keep quiet, we're withholding information from the authorities. But, if we turn you in, you say you could be killed. I guess we'll just have to hear your story."

"What is your story?" Mary asked, wanting to hear the mystery behind Peg Lott.

"I have committed a criminal act, but not murder. I burned down expensive homes that were being built in environmentally sensitive areas of the country."

"Why?" Brad asked.

"I was a member of a group called Ring of Fire. There were four of us. Our leader, we call her the Commander, researches the situations in various parts of the country. She monitors the building of the home, the weather, the chance of being caught."

"Okay, but what were you doing in the lake? Did you fall out of a boat? Were you shoved off?" Mary asked.

"I wanted out of the Ring of Fire. At a conference in Arizona, I met a man who helped me see how wrong I was. I contacted the other members of the Ring to explain my change of heart, and they were very upset. They convinced themselves that I would go to the authorities and turn them all in. I didn't have any intention of doing this.

"Last week, the authorities who were investigating these fires announced that the fires were the work of a group calling themselves the Ring of Fire. We never claimed responsibility, as some environmental or terrorist groups do. It was enough for us to just destroy the homes of those who were destroying the environment. Anyway, as I said, they referred to the arsonists as a Ring of Fire.

"The others in my group, when they heard the phrase 'Ring of Fire,' were sure that I had turned them in. Convinced that I had gone to the police, they had every intention of killing me."

"They knew you would be on the Badger?"

"Yeah, I made sure they knew."

"You did? Why would you work to bring on your own death?" LeRoy asked.

"I was convinced that I could set up the man who was going to kill me."

"You knew who would be the killer?" Brad asked.

"I had a good idea. He was the only one in the group who could kill. The others could damage property but would not kill a person."

"So, you set a trap for the guy?" Mary asked.

"In a way. I planned to mess up my stateroom, smear some blood around, you know. I also had with me a magazine with this man's fingerprints which I left in the room."

"Then you jumped off the Badger?" Brad guessed.

"Yes, but I had had training for doing it, and I made certain that nobody saw me. I had a boat ready to get me out of the water, waiting for my signal, but I lost the strobe light which I had hooked to my pants. So the pick-up boat couldn't see me, and the captain must have thought I never jumped."

"So, there you were, stranded out in the lake," Mary reasoned.

"Yes, until you came along."

"Was the murdered woman in your stateroom?" LeRoy asked.

"I don't have a clue," Peg said, still surprised to hear that someone had been murdered on the Badger. "When I left, the door was ajar, and the key was in my pants pocket. No one in his right mind would murder someone on that ship. I'm horrified that a woman was killed, but I didn't think anything like this would happen. I truly didn't."

"So, let me see if I have this straight," LeRoy said. "You set up a guy on the Badger. You made your stateroom look like a murder had occurred there and then jumped overboard expecting to be picked up and taken to shore. But, the guy who wanted to kill you murdered this other woman?"

"I guess that's what happened. For all I know, I'm wrong, and the other woman was attacked by someone who was after her. I don't know who she was."

"Now, because your car was abandoned in Ludington, because this woman may have died in the stateroom assigned to you, and because you are missing, the police assume that you are the murderer," Mary said.

"I guess so. But I didn't kill anyone. Please believe me! I could never do that!"

"But you could set up a stateroom to lead the police to believe that you were killed, so that a member of this so-called Ring of Fire would be arrested for your murder."

"That's true, but there is a big difference between setting a trap and killing someone."

"I agree, but you hoped he would be tried for murder and put in prison for life. That, to me, is a form of murder," Brad replied.

"Yes, I see that, but I was acting in self-defense, and I couldn't kill him or turn everyone in."

"That was my next question. Why don't you pick up the phone and call the police and tell them everything you just told us?" LeRoy asked.

"Because there are two more members in the Ring, and the odds of my escaping from one, let alone three, are very low. My plan was, and still is, to get to shore, assume another identity and begin a new life."

"But you are an internationally known scientist," LeRoy said.

"I was one, yes. But circumstances now dictate a change in my life, a big change. To live again, without fear of death, I'm willing to drop my old identity and assume a new one."

"You've got the makings of a novel, a full-length motion picture, or at least a made-for-TV movie when you decide to tell your story," LeRoy said, shaking his head in amazement. "Yeah, I guess I do, but that'll never happen. Once I get to shore and assume a new identity, the book is closed, with your rescue being the last chapter. I'll never say another word about the past. If you do, I'll have to run again, and that is why I am hoping you kind folks will not turn me in. If you allow me to get off your boat and get on with my life, I'll thank you eternally for giving me that new life to live."

LeRoy, Mary, and Brad were quite sympathetic to Peggy's story and fully believed that she was telling the truth. Each believed that she deserved a chance to start anew.

"We'll help you. Where do you want to begin this new life? Here in Wisconsin or in Michigan? We planned to stay here in Wisconsin for a few days, where Brad needs to do quite a bit of work. If you want a ride to Michigan, I suggest you stay here on the yacht and out of sight for a few days."

"I think I'll just get off here and make my way to Green Bay and fly to Colorado."

"Peg, you couldn't get out of Algoma without being picked up. Your picture is everywhere," Mary said. "The major transportation services will be on the lookout for you. Going to the Green Bay airport is just like walking into the police station and announcing your arrival."

"I guess you're right. I didn't think of that."

"You've got to be out of sight for a while, and when you do go ashore, you'll need a disguise. You'll almost need to become a different person," Mary explained, as the others nodded.

"I know. Well, because I am more familiar with Michigan, I think I would appreciate a ride over there whenever you decide to go. Thanks for your offer to care for me till then."

"We're taking a risk, but we believe you, and we want to help," Mary said.

"I will never forget your kindness."

Thankful to be alive, Peggy now needed to let Len know that she was okay despite the fact that her plans had been totally rewritten. She didn't know Len's cell phone number, although she knew she could get his Gunnison phone number from Directory Assistance. She also knew that Len wasn't expected back from China until the middle of next week. He would probably call home to get any messages, but then she remembered that he had given Martha and Phil the week off. Still, she was sure he would call home daily to get messages on his answering machine.

Peggy asked LeRoy if she could use his phone to make a call. She tried Len's number in Gunnison, but for some reason the answering machine didn't come on. Martha, she reasoned, had turned it off, as no one would be home to get the message, and she didn't want messages backing up, giving the impression that no one was home.

The original plan had been for Peggy to drive Len's car from the airport to his home. She knew where a key was hidden, so she'd make herself at home until Len returned from China. Frustrated that she couldn't connect with Len, she believed that, as far as he knew, she was safe, except that she was on a yacht in Wisconsin instead of at a mountain retreat in Colorado. At this point Peggy figured there would be nothing she could do but to call Len when he was expected to be home.

On the other side of the world, Len had tried unsuccessfully to reach Peg since she didn't pick up the phone in Gunnison. He recalled that Martha routinely disconnected the message machine. Len couldn't figure out why Peggy wouldn't answer or wouldn't call him. Something was undoubtedly wrong, but he had no way to figure it out. Being a positive person, he simply accepted the premise that no news was good news, and that once he returned to Gunnison, Peg would be there to greet him.

CHAPTER FOURTEEN

Monday, July 15, 2004
East Lansing and Okemos, Michigan

Lou had a lot to do in the East Lansing-Okemos area. A man by the name of Bill Yancy had contacted Chief Grether and said he might have some information about the lady who died on the Badger. Grether talked to him and then called Lou, who made arrangements to interview Mr. Yancy while he was in East Lansing.

Lou and Bill sat in the Sip'n Snack restaurant on Okemos Road. Lou had the soup of the day, split pea, and A Half A Val, a delicious salad that had a reputation among the regulars; it bore the name of the owner and cook, Val Korrey.

"Thanks for meeting with me."

"Sure. Hope I can help."

"Information is always helpful. Tell me what you know and I'll take it from there."

"Okay," Bill said, consuming a mouth-watering slice of lemon meringue pie. "I struck up a conversation with a woman from MSU while the Badger was still in dock in Manitowoc. My wife and I were standing by the rail watching the storm off in the west when this woman came and stood a few feet from us."

"Peg Lott?"

"She said her name, but I don't remember it. She said she taught at MSU. I do remember that. I work in the Attorney General's office in Lansing so the fact that we were neighbors stayed with me."

"Okay, please continue."

"I suppose I got a little carried away with my Badger stories, but she was a good listener, so I just relived a lot of good memories from my time working on car ferries almost forty years ago. Anyway, we went our way, the wife and I and this woman. Then about three-thirty in the morning, I saw her outside on the deck, walking toward the rear of the ship. I recalled another story about my early days on the car ferry. I decided to go over to her and tell her, being the good listener that she was."

"You saw her standing at the rail of the ship?"

"No, I saw her walking toward the back of the Badger. I was inside and couldn't see her after she went past a couple of windows."

"I see."

"I waited a few minutes and then decided I'd stroll out and strike up another conversation, but when I spoke to her, she didn't want to hear a story. Actually, she was rude and almost nasty telling me she just wanted to be alone. So, I left."

"What happened to her? Where did she go?"

"I haven't a clue. As far as I know, she didn't come inside, she didn't walk back down the deck where she came from, and she didn't walk around the deck because she would have to come right by the window where I was sitting playing solitaire. She couldn't go down because that is where the cars are stored, and she couldn't go up without coming inside. So, where could the woman go?"

"Any chance you fell asleep for a moment?" Lou asked.

"No way. I was wide awake like it was the middle of the day."

"Then where did she go?" Lou asked.

"Over."

"Over?"

"She had to," Bill replied. "Unless she was a ghost, or had some magic power that enabled her to transfer her body from one place to another. The only place she could have gone was overboard."

"Did you ever see her again during the rest of the voyage?"

"Nope, disappeared off the face of the earth. I didn't contact anyone because I figured she was the one who was murdered, but when I heard she was not the victim and was missing, all I could conclude was that she went over."

"Thrown over?"

"Well, that I don't know, because I don't know who else was out on the deck where she would have been. I couldn't see because I was inside."

"Was there any chance, Mr. Yancy, that you could have been mistaken, that the woman who walked by the windows may not have been Peg Lott?" Lou asked, searching for an explanation.

"I suppose that's possible, but I'm very sure it was her."

"Anything else seem suspicious?" Lou asked.

"I wouldn't say suspicious," Bill replied. "The three guys playing poker were my main source of entertainment on the crossing. Actually, I guess there were four. Yeah, there were four. One guy was up and down, looked like he had a bad cold, or maybe allergies. He'd play a few hands and then leave, trying to find some relief for his cold, I guess. The scene reminded me of watching old westerns with tough guys playing poker, expecting an ugly confrontation at any moment."

"Thanks for the information, Bill," Lou said, folding up his notebook. "I think I'll have a small dish of ice cream and chocolate sauce. I saw the waitress walk by with someone's dessert, and it sure looked good."

"Everything they serve in this place is delicious," Bill said. "That's real ice cream, too. I'll be on my way. I need to get back to work, but I wanted you to hear my story."

"I appreciate it, Bill. Let us know if you come across any additional information, okay?"

"Will do. Give me a call the next time you're in town; we'll have another lunch here in the Sip'n Snack," Bill said, handing Lou his business card.

"I'd like that. Thanks," Lou replied.

Mickey had arranged for Lou to be present when Chief Grether and the East Lansing Police entered Peg's apartment. A search warrant was issued because Peg was not only a missing person, but also a suspect in the death of a person.

Once inside, the investigators unplugged the computer and removed it from the apartment. Bills and private papers in her desk were confiscated. The apartment was very neat and organized.

Lou was very observant. He opened the refrigerator and noticed that it contained practically nothing. All he saw was a container of catsup and half a jar of sweet pickles. The freezer section was empty, and there weren't even ice cubes in the trays.

Lou noticed that, although there was a litter box, there was no cat anywhere. He also noticed a stack of videotapes. As the others were about to leave, Lou asked, "Mind if I take these tapes?"

"Not if you think they'll be helpful. We looked at the titles and they seem to be newscasts."

"I'll take them then. I'd like to see what she finds worth taping."

"Sure. Take 'em."

Lou had recalled the TV Guides with Fox news programs highlighted, which he'd found in Peg's car. There could be some connection. It was a long shot, but a shot, nonetheless.

Lou couldn't get over how unlived-in the apartment had looked. He knew that the world had all kinds of people. Maybe Peg Lott only used the apartment as a place to sleep and watch TV. Maybe she ate most, if not all, of her meals in restaurants. Her closets were almost bare, but she did have a reputation of being a simple woman and may have only had a few outfits.

Also lacking was anything personal. He hadn't seen any photos of people. The walls held no art work, either. The bathroom was hardly functional as far as having a box of Band-Aids or other common health items.

As Lou walked out, he wasn't sure whether he had just been in a basic, no-frills apartment used only for sleeping and existing away from the university, or if this Peg Lott left the apartment as if she never intended to return.

Lou called Dr. Hutchinson. He wanted to talk further with her, and if Dr. Lott had a graduate assistant, he asked if that person would come along. Lou was early at the Harrison Roadhouse at the corner of Michigan Avenue and Harrison Road in East Lansing. He sat in a quiet booth sipping coffee and reviewed all of his notes on this case to date. He had written down some things he wanted to check out when suddenly Dr. Loraine Hutchinson appeared with a young man.

"Mr. Searing, good afternoon."

Lou stood up, "Hello. You must be Dr. Hutchinson?"

"Yes. I'd like you to meet Gregory Tan. Mr. Tan is Dr. Lott's graduate assistant."

"Hello, Mr. Tan. I'm pleased to meet you," Lou said, with a handshake and a slight bow.

"My pleasure," Mr. Tan replied, returning the bow with a head nod and a smile.

"Please join me. Can I order you something to drink or eat?"

"No thanks," Lorraine said. "I can only stay a few minutes."

"Nothing for me either. Thank you. I have to go soon as well."

"OK, we'll get right to my questions then."

"Thank you," both replied in unison.

"I wanted to talk with you in the hope that I could learn as much as possible about Dr. Lott: her habits, friends, personality, that sort of thing."

Dr. Hutchinson began. "Dr. Lott is a very private person. She is a loner and I get the impression that she would be very happy living as a hermit. She rarely comments in staff meetings, and I never see her at any type of social function."

"You agree, Mr. Tan?" Lou asked.

"Yes. She is very private."

"Does she talk with students?" Lou asked.

"Oh, yes. She lectures. She has office hours," Mr. Tan replied. "She meets with students and is good with them, but she is to-the-point, all business."

"Wouldn't it be safe to say, that you, Mr. Tan, are about the only person she talks to informally?"

"I think so. I mean, she has to since I run the lab, prepare some of her talks for conferences, and things like that."

"I see. Mr. Tan, does she ever talk about anything other than subject material or university responsibilities? Was she afraid of anyone? Did she have hostile feelings about anyone?"

"You are asking a lot of questions, sir."

"Sorry, I just want to learn about this woman."

"She is a private woman, as I said. She never talked about anyone in an angry manner. I know of no one who doesn't like her. I mean, most students think she is different, but they would all tell you she is to be respected for what she has accomplished and for her knowledge of the subject matter."

Dr. Hutchinson added, "I agree with Mr. Tan, but you asked about emotions. Peg Lott is an environmentalist, and while that ties into her subject matter, she is emotional about the environment. She has little if any patience for developers buying up land and putting houses up. She is passionate about animals and plants. In fact, I think that she bonds with animals and plants better than with humans."

"I see. So, we have a quiet, reserved, intellectual, private woman who does her job, but outside of her job she is not social, at least as far as you two are concerned. Am I painting an accurate picture here?"

"Yes," both replied.

"Mr. Tan, have you ever been in her apartment?"

"Yes. Once. She asked me to come over one evening to pick up lecture material for the next day."

"Describe her apartment, if you will."

"Messy, but controlled messy, an extension of her office. She can immediately put her hand on anything she needs. If you mention some research study, her hand will move like a magnet as she goes into the right pile and quickly pulls out the correct manuscript. Let's see, she has a cat. Let me make something clear: when I said 'messy' I didn't mean dirty, I meant that books, papers, manuscripts, drafts of reports were everywhere."

"Did she cook or eat out?"

"I can help with that," Dr. Hutchinson replied. "She prepares all of her own food. She is fanatic about eating organic foods, and she doesn't trust anyone to prepare the food that she eats. I've never been in her apartment, but she commented to me that she would need to get home to prepare her meal, which always seemed to be an extensive undertaking. And, as you can see, she is not skinny as a rail, so she's eating more than enough food."

"Yes. Are you sure I can't get you something to drink or eat?" Lou asked.

"No, in fact, I really must be going," Dr. Hutchinson said, sliding from the booth and standing up. "You can always reach me on my cell phone, Mr. Searing."

"Okay, yes. Thank you for meeting with me. I'll let you know if and when I learn anything."

"Thank you."

"I suppose you need to be going also?" Lou asked Mr. Tan, who had remained seated.

"Yes. I have a section of Dr. Lott's lab and the students are probably wondering if I am coming to class."

"One last question then. Why was Dr. Lott going to Minneapolis?"

"She was to present a paper with Dr. Willard Lowe of the University of Washington. The two of them have been studying a common hypothesis and have been e-mailing their thoughts and data for the past six months. They decided to submit a joint paper, and it was accepted."

"I see," Lou replied. "Thank you, Mr. Tan."

"You are welcome. I'm sorry I have to go, but please understand."

"I do. If you think of anything else let me know. Here is my card." Mr. Tan took the card, glanced at it and put it in his shirt pocket.

"Oh, one more thing, if Dr. Lott contacts you, please try to find out where she is and then let me know, okay?"

"Yes, sure. I will."

"Thanks."

Lou set a few dollars on the table to pay for his coffee and a tip, stood up and walked to his motorcycle. The information was helpful but hardly what he had hoped to get. Since he was close to the Valvoline Oil Change place in Okemos, he decided to stop in and talk with the manager. Lou got on his Harley and headed to the shop.

The place was busy, but Lou was able to locate the manager Priscilla Leach.

"My name is Lou Searing. I'm a private investigator looking into a missing person case over on the west side of the state. The person we're looking for came in here a few weeks ago to get her oil changed."

"Yeah. How do you think we can help?" Priscilla asked, anxious to get to the customer whose car was in the first bay.

"I would like the mileage and date of service of her vehicle."

"Can't help you," Priscilla replied. "That's personal information about one of our customers. Nobody's business. Excuse me, I've got customers."

"Sure," Lou replied. "But I do want to talk about this some more. I'll wait."

Priscilla served some customers and could see that Lou was not going to leave until he talked with her again. She approached. "I don't think we can help you."

"If it is confidentiality you are concerned about, that isn't a problem. I know the person and the car. I'm not asking you to identify anyone or tell me anything about that person."

"You want the mileage on the car, that's personal," Priscilla said.

"Not in the sense of a phone number, address, age, name or anything like that. They are facts, the odometer reading and the date the service was provided."

"I don't think so. I'd have to call the owner and I don't have time. People are lined up."

"Listen, a woman is missing, and you've got information that could help us locate her," Lou said, getting upset with the manager's stubbornness.

"The number of miles on an odometer can help you find someone?" Priscilla asked. "No way."

"Indirectly it can. The police have her car, and we know the mileage when it was abandoned, but we don't know how many miles she drove it after getting service here. The information is quite important, actually."

"I'll be right with you, sir!" the manager shouted to a gentleman who was about out of patience in the far left bay. "Listen, give me your card and I'll call you."

"Thanks. Here is a little gift to show my appreciation," Lou said, handing her a twenty dollar bill. "All I need is the mileage and the date of service. My cell phone number is on my card. Also I wrote down the letter and number code that was on your sticker inside her windshield." Priscilla nodded and immediately went to the less-than-patient customer.

"I'm coming! Sorry."

Lou knew that she'd call. He probably could have saved the twenty dollar bill, but he knew that giving it to her would ensure that he got the information. Lou pulled out of the oil change place and went back to Peggy's apartment building. He sat on his Harley, reading a paperback, patiently waiting for one of Peg's neighbors to come home. Lou had some questions to ask.

About ten minutes later, a car pulled up beside the apartment complex. Out stepped a middle-aged gentleman with a briefcase. Lou got off his bike and approached.

"Excuse me. May I have a word with you?"

"Me?"

"Yes. Do you live here in this complex?"

"Yes."

"My name is Lou Searing. I've been asked to assist in locating a missing woman who lives in this building, and I was wondering if I could ask you a few questions."

"Who are you talking about?"

"Dr. Peg Lott."

"Perfect neighbor. Never here, and when she is, she's quiet as a mouse."

"Never here?" Lou asked.

"Well, I mean, I think she teaches nights at the university, goes back there early in the morning. That's what I mean."

"I see. Did anyone ever come to see her?" Lou asked. "You know, someone who may be upset with her, like a student to whom she gave a poor grade, or someone she may have upset in some way?"

"A couple of environmental nuts drop by once in awhile."

"Environmental nuts?" Lou asked, not sure he heard right.

"Yeah, you know, hippie types. I saw them demonstrating at some 'Save the Turtles' rally about a month ago. They're not my kids, so what do I care? I think they are misguided, but then, I'm a deer hunter. I'll tell you this: if I hung my buck each fall in the garage over there, she'd pass out," he said laughing.

"That can be upsetting to non-hunters," Lou said.

"Yeah, I know. All them radicals are hard to read. But, hey, I'm no psychologist, but I tell you, it's the quiet people who end up killing little old ladies. Know what I mean? It's always the ones who would never hurt a fly that do the killing, and that professor you're trying to find – she'd never hurt a fly."

"Thanks," Lou said.

"Sure. That your Harley?"

"Yeah. Good bike."

"I love those things. I had one when I was 30 years younger. I loved the speed, the noise, the glances from the girls."

Lou smiled. "I know about the speed and the noise, but the only glances I get are from Harley wannabees. Some of them come over and drool all over the chrome."

Lou had gotten all he was going to get from the resident, so he brought the dialogue to a close. "Thanks for the information."

"Sure, hope you find the lady. She's different, but hey, some people think I'm different. Takes all kinds."

"Thanks," Lou said as he walked toward his bike. He almost had his helmet fastened when his cell phone rang.

"Lou Searing."

"This is Priscilla at Valvoline Oil Change."

"Oh, yes. Thanks for calling."

"The mileage was 45,606 and the date of service was June 29."

"Thanks."

"Hope I don't get in trouble for giving out that information."

"You won't," Lou said.

Lou turned off his phone, fastened his helmet, and headed for I-96 and the two-hour trip to Grand Haven. The day had been a good one. He'd learned quite a bit about Peg Lott, seen her apartment, talked to people who knew her, and even gotten her mileage when she changed her oil.

Carol was glad to see Lou and was always thankful for his safe arrival. She lovingly worried about him every time he rode his motorcycle and, especially when he was going over 75 mph on the interstates. She was confident in Lou's riding ability and his promise to her to always use good judgment, but it was the nuts on the road that concerned Carol. All it took was someone not seeing him at an inopportune moment, and their lives would be changed forever. But, she thought, the ride brings Lou joy, and he has every right to make choices, so she'd do her best to accept his passion, even though to her it made no sense whatsoever.

When she thought of how she'd like to control Lou, she was reminded of a joke a priest told one Sunday. A bride was exceptionally nervous before her wedding. The priest told her that her feelings were normal and he had some advice that might help her. "While you walk down the aisle, concentrate on the aisle, nothing else, and say, 'Aisle, aisle, aisle.' When you look up to the front you should concentrate on the altar and say in your mind, 'Altar, altar, altar.' If you still need help, you are to concentrate on the hymn and think silently, 'Hymn, hymn, hymn.'" The advice worked well, and she was able to get through the ceremony without fainting. At the reception she was stopped by one of the guests who said she was beautiful coming down the aisle, but it looked like she was repeating some phrase. When he asked her what she was saying, she replied, "I'll alter him, I'll alter him, I'll alter him."

Carol didn't want to alter Lou and hide his bike for the rest of his earthly days, but on the other hand, she didn't want his days to be fewer than the Maker intended because of his need for speed.

The evening was ideal for having a small fire on the beach by the water's edge. Lou and Carol invited their neighbors for S'mores and conversation around the glow of the fire. Before setting the fire, Lou and Carol took their evening walk up and down the shore of Lake Michigan, walking hand-in-hand as always. They shared what had happened during the day. Lou told Carol what he had learned in East Lansing, and Carol talked about her day volunteering at the Ronald McDonald House close by the hospital. Samm was content to chase sticks.

The sun appeared to paint the summer sky before calling it a day and sinking into Wisconsin. Nature did a good job of earning some "Ooohs" and "Aaahs" with the changing colors along the horizon. As soon as the flames leapt into the sky, neighbors started appearing with blankets and food. The next couple of hours were spent talking and relaxing around the fire.

CHAPTER FIFTEEN

Sunday, July 16, 2004
Grand Haven, Michigan

Lou was up early, as usual. He put one of Peg's videos in his VCR. All he saw was a series of Fox News Programs. There was nothing that caught his attention or explained why Peg would want to save a series of news broadcasts. As soon as the sun lit the beach, he and Samm went out to the water's edge for a walk.

Around eight o'clock, Lou called Mickey to report what he had learned in East Lansing.

"The odometer was at 45,606 when she changed the oil the day before her trip to Ludington. It's about one hundred and eighty miles from East Lansing to Ludington, assuming she took a direct route."

"I'd agree with that," Mickey replied. "That means she had ninety miles to drive before getting back to Manitowoc."

"She'd have to go out and back, so half that in an arc from Manitowoc would be a maximum of forty-five miles," Lou reasoned.

"Of course, she could have driven around Manitowoc all day for all we know."

"Right, but we know she didn't drive to Minneapolis," Lou said.

"Let me tell you what I learned while you were in East Lansing," Mickey said. "I called the alumni office at Harvard University to see if I could locate her parents. The director of the alumni office was sympathetic and wanted to help me, but said that confidentiality rules and policies forbade her from giving me the information."

"Yeah, I can see that," Lou replied.

"I told her that I was the Chief of Police and that Peg Lott was missing and next-of-kin needed to be informed. I explained that I could get our prosecutor to talk to a judge and get the skids greased for obtaining the information. I could do all that, and she'd end up giving me the information anyway, but valuable time would be lost, and every minute I didn't have the information, Peg Lott's parents would not know of the crisis in their daughter's life."

"She gave you the information, right?" Lou guessed.

"Yup. Peg's parents live in New Jersey. I called and talked to her father who by the way was thankful I reached him because Mrs. Lott is not well and getting news that Peg was missing and perhaps dead would have probably killed her."

"So, they obviously don't know where she is or if she is safe?"

"No. I got the impression that the relationship has been strained, and that there is guilt around it. There is no question that the father is concerned and upset with the news."

"Did he give you any information that would help us understand this strange woman better?"

"Not really. He said she is a very private person, different, plain, passionate about the environment, brilliant, you know, what we've heard before."

"Anybody ever threaten her? Any violent tendencies?" Lou asked.

"I didn't ask. I didn't want to press my luck. My goal was to locate her parents and I accomplished that. The father was willing to cooperate and will help in any way we ask. So, we can follow up with questions when they've had some time to adjust to the news."

"Sounds like we had a successful day."

"I think so."

"Anything else?" Lou asked.

"Oh yeah, the crime lab got fingerprints off the magazine, and the hair strands are going to be helpful if we can ever find a head to match them. The hair strands do not belong to the victim. Some of the prints on the magazine match Dr. Lott's, but that's no surprise, since she was assigned to the stateroom. We can't find a match of the victim's prints, except on the door knob to the stateroom. The blood isn't the same type as the victim either. So, we've got hair and blood that don't match the victim, and prints that don't match the victim or Peg Lott."

"You've got a lot of nothing, Mickey," Lou said, shaking his head.

"Right, for now. But once we get a suspect or two, that evidence will come in handy."

Chief Grether had faxed the phone log from Peg's number to Lou in Grand Haven. There were several pieces of the puzzle that didn't fit, but the one that did was two calls to a Betty Taylor in Green Bay. The police had learned that Betty was a veterinarian.

Lou called the number and asked to speak to Dr. Taylor.

"Hello. Is this Betty Taylor?" Lou asked.

"Yes. Who is calling?"

"I'm Lou Searing, a private investigator in Grand Haven, Michigan."

"What can I do for you, Mr. Searing?"

"Dr. Peg Lott of East Lansing is missing. We've learned that she called you recently, and I'm curious about the nature of those calls."

"She is a client of mine. She was calling to get advice about a health problem for her cat, if you must know." Betty didn't sound cooperative which was odd. When contacted by police or investigators, every person in the medical area is usually extremely cooperative. This doctor seemed to be inconvenienced by Lou's call.

"I see. You're her vet in Green Bay?"

"I used to work at the Small Animal Clinic at MSU and knew her there. I moved to Green Bay and like people who feel comfortable staying connected with their doctors, Dr. Lott wanted my advice."

"Uh-huh. What was wrong with the cat?" Lou asked.

"Now, is this really any of your business, Mr. Searing?"

"No, I guess not, just curious."

"Well, doctors don't share the condition of your family's health with strangers and I don't feel it is my place to share the information with you."

"Did Peg Lott visit with you in the past couple of weeks?"

"No. I talked to her on the phone a few times about her cat. That's all."

"I see. Thanks for talking with me. If Dr. Lott contacts you again, would you please call me?" Lou gave her his cell phone number.

"I have patients to see. Goodbye."

"Yes, certainly. Goodbye." Lou heard the phone go onto the cradle.

Lou was more interested in the doctor's reaction than in what she said. When someone hears that another is missing, there is almost always some concern, some compassion, some reaction of sympathy. In this case there was none. Lou interpreted this to be that the vet knew of Peg Lott's status and was unconcerned. In fact, he had a hunch that the vet was playing a role, doing what she could to throw him off. He wouldn't have been surprised if Peggy had been in the office listening to the conversation.

Lou received permission from Mickey to call Peggy's parents in New Jersey. After he and Carol arrived home from church, he called and asked to speak to Mr. Lott.

"Hello, this is Samuel Lott."

"Mr. Lott, this is Lou Searing in Michigan. I'm working with the police to try and locate your daughter."

"Yes. Thank you."

"I'm calling to see if you can help me know your daughter a little better."

"I'll try. What would you like to know?"

"Who is her best friend, for starters?"

"She doesn't have one, unless you could call her cat a best friend."

"No good friend? Nobody to go to to share a huge problem or a cup of coffee?"

"Not that we are aware of. Since middle school she has been exceptionally shy and quiet, and seems to have no desire to communicate. We thought she might be autistic as she simply didn't relate to others. Our doctor assured us that she was not autistic, but an extremely brilliant girl who has a personality that chooses to be aloof and private."

"I see. Do you have any other children?"

"Yes, we have a son who is two years younger than Peg."

"Does she relate to him?"

"Yes. In fact, she is closer to him than she is to either her mother or me."

"Can you give me some way to contact him?" Lou asked.

"His name is Charles. He lives in Muskegon, Michigan."

"That's about twenty miles north from where I live," Lou said, noting the information in his notebook.

"You are welcome to contact him, but you will have trouble communicating with him. He is deaf, doesn't talk. Unless you know sign language, or take an interpreter with you, you will not be able to talk with him."

"I see. How does Peg communicate with her brother?"

"She signs to him. She was quite protective of Charles when he was young. Peg's world in her younger years was consumed by her thirst for knowledge, her cat, and her deep love for Charles."

"That's helpful. Please give me an address or phone number for Charles. I can find an interpreter who would go with me. Is Charles married?"

"No. If you are thinking of driving up to see him, forget it, Mr. Searing. Charles is in the men's correctional facility in Muskegon."

"I see. Can you tell me what he is serving time for?"

"Murder."

"Murder?"

"It's a terrible story and one I don't want to share because I am sure it has nothing to do with Peg's being missing. In short, Charles was abused by someone when he was at a state school for the deaf. The experience was traumatic, to say the least. Several years later he thought he saw the man at a deaf club. He lost control of his emotions and attacked the man, choking him to death in front of several people. The victim was not who he thought it was."

"How did Peg react?"

"Protective, unconditional love, always at his side. She saw that he got legal help and all the accommodations he needed for his trial and his incarceration."

"When did this happen?"

"About five years ago, I'd say."

"She keeps all of this to herself, I would imagine," Lou said.

"Oh my, yes, she is a very quiet and private person as I said, but all of this business with Charles was kept quiet. I wouldn't be surprised if she used an alias during all of her work. She worked closely with someone at the Division of the Deaf and Hard of Hearing in your state capital. I don't recall her last name but it is something like Wilson."

"Trina Williams?" Lou asked, familiar with the staff.

"That's it."

"I know Trina. She is a marvelous advocate for people with hearing loss."

"Anyway, she took a liking to Peg and did a lot of work to see that Charles got the legal services he needed."

"She would," Lou replied. "That's consistent with her personality and professionalism."

"The case got a lot of media coverage. The trial was on Court TV actually. But, Trina protected Peg, so there was never any sign of her involvement."

"Didn't she have to testify at the trial?"

"Yes, but it was all done behind the scenes, tape recorded."

"Why Peg's desire for privacy on this?"

"You know, I really don't know. I suspect she didn't want to have her career tarnished in any way. She was becoming world famous for her research at that time, still is by the way, and I have always thought that she didn't want to wear that part of her family on her sleeve."

"But I've learned that she protests environmental issues," Lou said.

"Oh yes, she is a flag burning radical when it comes to the environment. That topic gets more of her attention than any of us in the family. I'd rank it this way: her cat, the environment, her career, Charles. Then we'd be much further down the list, with several more activities ranking between us and the most important parts of her life."

"Flag burning radical?" Lou asked.

"Oh, not literally. You know what I mean. She's just passionate, quite a bit more passionate than what I would call normal, but she is entitled to her passions, I suppose."

"Her cat is really at the top of her list?"

"Yes, that is a long story as well. She has called all of her cats Flame from the time she was a little girl. The first Flame was a tabby, and she called her Flame because she would sit and stare at a candle flickering. She wouldn't try to play with it or attack it or anything. She'd just sit staring at the flame. Finally, Peg started to call the cat Flame since that's all she seemed interested in when she wasn't eating or sleeping."

"Interesting. Since then, every cat has been named Flame?" Lou asked.

"Yup. Don't ask me why. I quit trying to understand Peg years and years ago. I love her, but I'm afraid the feeling is not mutual. We haven't talked in years, and frankly, I don't know what we did to deserve this. My wife and I sort of gave up trying to figure it out. She is just different, and we've come to accept that and maybe some day we can reconcile. We hope so."

"I do too. Thanks for talking with me," Lou said. "I don't need any information on how to contact your son. I can find him."

"I hope you can find Peg. She's a beautiful person, once you get past her idiosyncrasies."

"We'll find her," Lou said, with confidence. "Thanks, we'll be in touch."

CHAPTER SIXTEEN

Wednesday, July 19, 2004
Pentwater, Michigan

LeRoy guided his yacht into the marina in Pentwater, a perfect example of a port city on Lake Michigan with much charm and personality without hordes of people to disturb the tranquility of the community.

Peggy decided to wear a disguise and walk off the yacht and begin a new day. "If I am recognized and turned in, I'll simply have to play those cards when they're dealt."

"You sure you'll be okay? Do you have money?" Mary asked.

"I'll be fine," Peg replied. "No, I don't have any money, but I'll be just fine. I'll manage somehow. I have a brother in Muskegon. I'll probably take a bus down there and stay with him for a few days."

"We'll give you a couple of hundred just to get you started, and you can keep the outfit you are wearing now," Mary said, trying to be as helpful as possible.

"Thank you. I'll pay you back as soon as I can."

"Keep it, Peggy," Mary said. "It's our gift to wish you well."

"Thank you for everything. You folks saved my life in so many ways. I'll never forget you."

"I have one favor to ask," LeRoy said.

"I should have known there would be some contingency," Peg said, offering a rare smile.

"When your story is picked up by Hollywood, I'd like to play myself in the movie."

Peggy smiled, shook her head and said, "I'm afraid I can't control that. But, if I can have a say in who stars in the flick, you'll get the call. If you win the Academy Award for playing your part, I'd like my picture taken with you in a tux. Deal?"

"Deal!" LeRoy said chuckling.

Peg hugged LeRoy, Mary, and Brad as she set off on her new life. It was almost two o'clock in the afternoon on a hot summer day when she stepped from the yacht onto land. She didn't look the same. Most of her hair was cut off, and a wide-brimmed hat hid some of her face. She had a coin purse, a gift from Mary, which contained two hundred dollars.

"Good luck to you, Peg," Mary said.

"Thanks. Again, please don't say anything."

"You have our promise. We only wish you happiness and peace of mind," LeRoy said, touching her shoulder.

"Goodbye now."

"How was that for a strange experience?" Mary said to LeRoy and Brad as Peg walked down the dock.

"Very strange. I suppose we could sail for years and years and never know an incident quite like that," LeRoy said.

"Do you suppose we'll hear the end of the story?" Brad asked.

"Oh, yeah," LeRoy replied. "Not much can happen any more without people getting access to people's lives. We'll follow the story in Michigan newspapers. Plus, this story is bound to get on one of those major network news shows."

"Think we'll be on it?" Mary asked.

"No. I think that as much as Peggy hopes we keep quiet, she will do the same for us. She knows we took a huge risk in protecting her and saving her life. She won't say a word to anyone about our involvement."

As Peg was walking through town, the thought struck her that her new identity should be that of a person who was profoundly deaf. She would take the name Charlene, as it approximated her brother's name. Her last name would be the name of her cat, which she would miss for the rest of her life. Having established her name and her new personality, she walked to the Pentwater Library where she would plan her next move.

She took a copy of the Ludington Daily News from the newspaper rack. She was curious to see what the media had been reporting about the murder and her being a suspect, or at least missing. It was eerie to read about herself on the front page. She noted that she was being sought by the team of Lou Searing of Grand Haven and Maggie McMillan of Battle Creek in addition to law enforcement agencies. She was very certain that Todd Baxter had mistaken this woman for her and, in the darkness, killed the wrong person. Peg believed that Todd and the others realized by now that she was alive. What would happen next? she wondered. Would they still try to kill her?

After reading the paper, Peg went to the row of Michigan phone books. She picked out the Lansing book and looked up the number for the Family Independence Agency – Division of Deaf and Hard of Hearing as well as the means to access the relay system. When Trina Williams of the Division helped her and her brother Charles, Peg never met with her face to face. She planned to arrange a meeting with Trina, as a deaf person, to see what assistance she could receive. She decided she would be Charlene Flame, an abused wife who had walked away from her husband with only a couple of hundred dollars and who needed to start over.

She called Trina using the relay system in which a person who is deaf can "talk" to another via a keyboard and an intermediary at the phone company, who serves as the means by which someone without the technology can reply.

Peg dialed the number for the relay service and, when the operator answered via a digital printout, she asked to be linked to Trina. Trina answered and the two conversed through the intermediary even though Peg heard everything said. Peg asked for help with finding housing and a job in the Ludington area, and she was told to go to the County Office for Families and Children. She was to tell them she needed an interpreter and, if she encountered any problems, to call back.

Next, using the library's computer, Peg typed in "Maggie McMillan" and up came a variety of items. She learned that Maggie's husband was Tom, a prominent oral surgeon in Battle Creek. Next she went to the white pages and easily found the home phone of Thomas McMillan, D.D.S. Then Peg called Maggie McMillan and left a voice message. The message was, "If you attend to the captioning on Fox News at five o'clock, you will be led to the terrorist group setting fires around the country."

Unbeknownst to Peggy, just as she walked from the Pentwater Library, an Oceana County Sheriff's cruiser pulled up to the Pentwater marina. The sheriff turned off the engine and entered the marina office.

"Morning, Billy" said Connie Van Strat, the harbormaster.

"Hi, Connie," Billy replied. "I need some help."

"That's what we've got a lot of, especially for our friends in the sheriff's office."

"I understand you have a pretty good size yacht in here. Came in early this afternoon."

"Yes. It's a beauty, isn't it?" Connie said, pointing out the window toward the end of the long dock.

"I'd like to know who owns it." Billy said with authority.

"Why? Is there a problem?" Connie replied.

"Don't know. I want to talk to the owner, but I wanted to stop in here first and see what I could learn."

"I talked to the man who filled out a registration form. Just a minute, I'll get it out." A few seconds later she had it in hand. "Here it is. His name is LeRoy Billups. His yacht is based out of Los Angeles. He paid for one night. He lists the people who are with him as his wife Mary and son Brad. That's all I have. He seemed like a nice guy. Asked for a restaurant recommendation telling me he and his wife always enjoy a wonderful on-shore meal while his son studies for some doctoral program he is in at Southern Cal, I think."

"Okay, thanks." Billy turned and started toward the door.

"Hey, wait a minute. If I've got some criminal in my marina, I'd sure like to be warned."

"As you can imagine, we've a citizen or two with nothing better to do than watch people. One gentleman in particular is very observant. He'll call often, telling us he's seen someone wanted for something or other. He thought he'd seen a couple of people on that TV show, Unsolved Mysteries. Anyway, he thinks he saw the woman involved in the Badger murder. Says she stepped off that huge yacht docked here. I wanted to check it out."

"Okay, please stop in before you leave. I'm always curious what you guys are learning."

Leaving the harbormaster's office, Billy walked up to the Billups' boat and called, "Anybody home here?"

LeRoy walked topside and greeted the sheriff. "Yeah, we're home. Didn't expect a greeting from an officer of the law, but happy to see you, I guess. Was I speeding out there on Lake Michigan?"

"No, not speeding. That's not our department anyway – you'd have to deal with the Coast Guard on that front."

"Want to come aboard?"

"No, but thanks. We got a call from a citizen shortly after you settled in here. Seems a woman got off your boat and walked into town. The caller said she might be the woman who is missing in these parts, so I decided to check it out. Who was the woman on your yacht when you arrived?"

LeRoy's heart began to beat rapidly, his palms began to sweat. He knew he had to think fast and say something that would be convincing without implicating Peggy. He tried to stall a bit while thinking of something to explain Peg's presence on his boat.

"A woman is missing? I haven't heard about that."

"Yeah, there was a death on the Badger a few days ago. The woman who was assigned to the stateroom where the body was found is missing, and her car was abandoned. She's obviously someone the investigators want to talk to."

"I see. We came here from Wisconsin, spent last night in Algoma."

"First time sailing the Great Lakes?" Billy asked.

"Yeah, our son is doing a dissertation on how these lakes were formed."

"I see. So, tell me, who was the lady that came over with you?"

"Oh, yeah, sorry. This is going to sound strange, but you know, I don't know her name. The harbormaster approached me this morning and asked if I would take her to Michigan since we were coming over here. I thought it a strange request but said I'd check with my wife. It was a bit awkward, but we thought we could put up with a stranger for a few hours."

"Why did the harbormaster ask you to take her?" Billy asked.

"I think there was a death in the woman's family. We didn't talk much. The harbormaster said she couldn't afford to fly or drive around the lake, and she needed to get over here as soon as possible, so she couldn't take that car ferry you mentioned."

"She going to visit someone in Pentwater?"

"No, actually, I forgot where she's going."

"How would she get wherever she is going?" Billy asked.

"Got me. I was just asked to bring her over here. Maybe she'll call a relative from town or something. Hey, I was just doing the lady a favor. If I'd known I'd be interrogated by the law, I never would have offered."

"Oh, everything's okay," the sheriff replied. "I'm just doing my job, checking out a citizen's call, is all. I'll report that you didn't know the lady's name but were giving her a complimentary ride to Michigan."

"Thanks. I didn't mean to get upset, but I wasn't real excited about giving her a ride, stranger and all, sort of like picking up a hitchhiker, and I don't do that. You can tell that citizen caller that I'm glad he is observant, but my passenger lives in Wisconsin and didn't commit any murder."

"Thanks, Mr. Billups. Enjoy your stay in Pentwater. Sorry I wasn't much of a welcoming committee."

The deputy walked away knowing that something was not right with that story. He thought, In the first place, I didn't mention any car ferry and if the guy is from L.A., I doubt he knows that the Badger is a car ferry. Secondly, a harbormaster would never suggest that a client give a free ride to a stranger. He'd direct the woman to social services. Asking favors of paying customers is a terrible business practice. Last, I never said the woman on the Badger was murdered.

The sheriff walked into the marina office and asked to use the phone and a directory to find the name and number of the harbormaster in Algoma, Wisconsin. When he got through, the assistant on duty said he knew nothing about a woman needing a ride across the lake. He promised the harbormaster would call back when he returned from a meeting at City Hall.

When he hung up, Connie asked, "Well, have I got a problem at my marina?"

"I'm not sure, but I have good reason to doubt what Mr. Billups said. There is no threat to you or any of your guests at the marina, but I'm going to ask you to pay attention to everyone who comes into this marina, especially from town. Take a good look at the woman on that poster on your bulletin board and if you see her or anyone who resembles her, call our office."

"You mean that Badger murderer was in my marina?" Connie asked.

"I don't know that, and I wouldn't start that rumor, because that is all it would be, a rumor. In fact, please don't say anything, okay?"

"Sure."

"From some of the things Mr. Billups said, I have reason to question that what he told me is true. We just need to be observant. I'm going to put out a Be On the Lookout bulletin in the county and up and down the coast here for a single woman without transportation. It might be a waste of time, but it could be helpful. If I am going to err, I want to be extra cautious. I don't need to be a source of embarrassment for the mayor. His challenger in this fall's election doesn't need any ammunition."

"Got it. Thanks, Billy."

"Sure." Billy tipped his hat, turned and left, feeling quite curious about the lady who had gotten off the Billups' yacht.

Lou called Maggie. After he asked her how her aunt was doing, he briefed her on what he had learned on the case. "I have a question for you, Maggie."

"What's that?"

"Peg collected a lot of videotapes of news shows," Lou began. "I can't seem to figure out why."

"I guess she wants to save the material," Maggie said rather sarcastically. "I mean, that's why people record shows."

"I know that, Maggie. Get serious with me here. I'm trying to go deeper. Why does she want to save the material?"

"Well, one reason could be that she wants to keep up with current events and has a class at MSU at that time and misses the broadcast."

"OK, that's logical."

"Or, she's following some news story and wants a collection of comments about it."

"Yup, that makes sense, too," Lou said.

"Or, she is saving the material, not for herself, but for somebody else, somebody who doesn't have a VCR or a television."

"Uh-huh."

"Or, within all that video is some clue as to why she is missing."

"That's what I think," Lou said. "Assuming none of your suggestions are reasons for her taping the news shows, what could be a clue as to why she is missing?"

"Are the shows captioned?" Maggie asked.

"Yes."

"Well, there you have it."

"There I have what?" Lou asked.

"Lots of potential is what you've got."

"What is that supposed to mean? Come on Maggie, don't treat me like a fool. What's on your mind? As far as I can tell, all I've got is a transcription of what the commentator said."

"Maybe, maybe not," Maggie replied. "Someone is typing what you read on that screen, Lou. It isn't done by machine, at least not yet."

"You know, Maggie, you are so bright, so out front when it comes to seeing the patterns, but I still don't get it. Come down to my level is what I'm saying."

"What I'm trying to tell you, Lou, is that she could be getting information from the captions in those news shows."

"You mean the person who is doing the captioning is sending Peg Lott a message?" Lou deducted.

"Yup. Now, I'm saying could be. Conjecture on my part," Maggie replied. "It would seem to me that, if you took the time or paid someone to take the time to match what the commentator says with what appears as captioned, if it is the same, my theory is useless. But if the two don't match, all I'm saying is that there could be a message there, that's all."

"I watch captioning on my TV at home, and there are mistakes all of the time," Lou replied.

"So do I, and I see them too, but what we want to know is if the mistakes are logical."

"Logical?"

"Yeah when the commentator says 'Baghdad' and you see 'Bag Dad,' it's logical, but if he says 'Bush' and you see 'Harris,' it's not logical."

"I got it," Lou replied. "Well, I suppose it might be worth the effort to find someone to analyze them."

"Don't blame me if all of your efforts take you down a blind alley," Maggie said. "All I'm doing is trying to think of something that would cause her to want to copy a show, every night, for future study or review, and so far that's my best shot."

"Thanks, we might be heading right for the bull's eye."

Peg looked up the Catholic church in the phone book. She called and asked to speak to someone who handles St. Vincent DePaul emergencies. The secretary/receptionist said she would be that person.

"How can I help you?"

"I'm calling for a woman who is profoundly deaf. She doesn't talk and from the notes she writes it seems that she is homeless. I think she left her husband, has little if any money and really doesn't know where to turn to or where to go for help."

"About all we can do is pay for one night in a local motel. We don't have resources to help beyond that. We can see that she gets some clothes and maybe a gift certificate for food in the amount of twenty dollars."

"I see."

"We are a get-through-a crisis service and not a long-term caregiver. I'm sure you understand."

"Yes, I do. I think any help you can give her would be greatly appreciated."

"I can send a couple of our members to meet with her. Where is she now?"

"We're near the city park. She's scared. I think she's afraid her husband will find her and hurt her."

"Can you bring her here to the church?"

"Yes. I could do that."

"Let's do that then. When she gets here, we'll need her name, address, basic information like that."

"Does she need to be Catholic?"

"No, no, there is no requirement like that. If someone needs help, we try to give it."

"That's good. I'm not sure if she even goes to church. If she does, it would have to have a deaf ministry. Do you have that, a deaf ministry?"

"No, we don't. I'm sorry."

"I'll drop her off. She has written her name on a piece of paper. It's Charlene Flame."

"Flame? Like a candle flame?"

"Yes."

"Okay, have her come to the church office, and we'll see that she gets help overnight. Then we'll probably point her toward some county service or something."

"Thank you. Wait, she's writing something down. I think it's meant for you. She has written, 'Thank you.' She'll be there soon."

Peg was extremely frustrated in not being able to talk to Len. She knew he would be in Beijing for several days, and they had made no allowance for contingencies in case things didn't work out. They had no mutual friend for her to call, nor could Peg remember the cell phone number for Captain Warren. She knew she couldn't explain to the authorities who she was, because to do so would mean she would be arrested, and that would end her chance to begin a new life in obscurity. For the time being, she would play a deaf and indigent woman and try to figure out how to connect with Len.

She walked to the church, entered, and followed the signs to the office. It was time to play the part of a deaf woman and a shy one at that; the role would match her personality so that wouldn't be difficult. But to pretend not to hear anything or to say anything lest her cover be revealed – that would be a challenge.

CHAPTER SEVENTEEN

Wednesday, July 19, 2004
Denver, Colorado and Pentwater, Michigan

Maggie had gotten a call from her husband Tom back in Battle Creek telling her about a tip from an anonymous caller. Tom relayed the message word for word.

Maggie had some time on her hands. She was a god-send to her aunt, but her mind needed a challenge, and while she couldn't be with Lou in Grand Haven or in Ludington or wherever the action seemed to be, she still could be of some help.

Maggie was intrigued by Lou's question about Peg Lott's collection of videotaped newscasts. This along with the phone tip caused Maggie to go to the Internet to find out as much as she could about Peg Lott. From having watched hundreds of evening news shows over the years, Maggie knew that the world events depicted were not of any scientific interest and rarely presented anything to interest a scientist unless it was earthshaking news, and that was rare.

Maggie's idea that the captions might hold a clue stayed in her mind. She contacted a television station in Denver and asked to speak with the person on staff who would know about television captioning.

"Hello. This is Rhonda Gomez. You have a question about our captioning?"

"Yes. My name is Maggie McMillan. I'm curious about how the captioning works and thought I'd satisfy my curiosity by asking a few questions. Do you mind? Have you got the time?"

"Sure. I like to talk about it, and I don't go on the air for an hour so ask your questions."

"I guess my first question is, do you have a person right there in the studio who captions your programming?"

"Well, not right in the studio," Rhonda replied. "We contract with a captioner who works out of her home."

"I see. Does this person do the network shows?" Maggie asked.

"Oh, no. That's a network service, and the networks handle all of that."

"So, let's say for the CBS News, CBS hires the captioner for that, and the same captions go all across the nation. Correct?"

"Yes, but once again, the network will probably contract with a company to provide the captioning service," Rhonda explained. "A company employs several full and part-time captioners around the country who work out of their homes, or perhaps a studio."

"I see. So, the captioner might sit in a home in Ohio somewhere and caption the live news. The captioner types in what is said, and it gets fed into the transcription of the program. Right?" Maggie asked.

"I don't want to get too technical, but there is a second or two delay in the signal, but yes, for all practical purposes, the captioner feeds the signal to the network, and the network sends it out with the newscast."

"That person must type fast, given how quickly those news people talk."

"They don't type," Rhonda explained.

"Really?"

"No, it is a court reporting transcription format. The same skills and machine are used. As a court reporter needs to keep up with testimony, a captioner needs to keep up with the news reporters. These people are skilled and very good at what they do."

"Well, now some mistakes make sense," Maggie said, trying to understand how the system worked.

"Mistakes?" Rhonda asked, confused.

"Yes. Sometimes I see words on the screen that are not said but sound similar."

"Yes, that's because the captioner is really typing keys that represent phonemes or groups of phonemes."

"You're getting too technical now, but I think I have a basic understanding of how the process works."

"Glad I could help," Rhonda said. "Any other questions?"

"Yes. Is the captioning supervised?" Maggie asked.

"How do you mean?"

"I mean, does someone observe the work and evaluate the accuracy of the captions?"

"I think so, that would be logical and an important assurance that the captioning company puts out a quality service. However, I don't know the ins and outs of how that is done."

"That's okay. I've got far more information than I need. Thank you for your time."

"You're welcome. Call me again if you think of any other questions."

"I will. You've been most helpful."

Maggie recalled that when she was in therapy following her attack, she was a member of a disability support group. During that time she met several interesting and courageous people, one of them being Andy Bloom. Andy, an electrical engineer by trade, had experienced a sudden loss of hearing in both ears.

Maggie and Andy hit it off, since both were professionals who had experienced a sudden disability. Maggie lost her ability to move her legs, and Andy lost his ability to hear. When the support group ended, the two stayed in touch, meeting for lunch on occasion.

Maggie knew that Andy was an analytical thinker and would be willing to help her out. In fact, Andy was always very interested in the cases that Maggie and Lou solved together. He secretly yearned to be involved in some way with a murder investigation.

Maggie called Andy using the telephone relay system. "Andy, this is Maggie. I'm in Denver helping my aunt who is quite ill. How are you?" asked the relay operator.

"Fine. It's good to hear from you, but I'm sorry to hear of your aunt's illness."

"Thanks. I'm trying to be supportive emotionally, as I'm not really much help physically."

"I'm sure you are a great help."

"I hope so. I'm wondering if you would be willing to help Lou and me with a case we're working on."

"Sure. I've wanted to do this for a long time. What do I do?"

"Well, it isn't very glamorous, but, if I'm right, your work could reveal information that might help solve this crime."

"Tell me what to do, Maggie, I'm ready to go," Andy said. "Am I going to the scene of the crime?"

"Andy, I said it isn't glamorous, and I mean it. But, I do need your help."

"Not a problem. I'll help no matter what you need."

"Thanks. We need you to watch the Fox Evening News every night at five o'clock EST. Can you do this? Are you free then?"

"Yeah, but that's it? Watching TV?" Andy asked.

"Lou found some old TV Guides in a suspect's car, and during a search of her apartment, he found and confiscated several videotapes. He then learned that all that was on the videotapes was one Fox Evening News show after another. The shows were captioned too. We can't understand why anyone would record this show day after day."

"Yeah, sounds strange. I agree."

"I thought that if you could watch these shows, maybe even record them yourself for further study, you might figure out our mystery."

"Well, the watching is easy – probably she likes that network or announcer. The saving – that's difficult."

"I told Lou I think that maybe there is a clue in the captioning."

"Could be. But, you know, just talking to you, I think this is a wild goose chase. I think the suspect can't be home at that time and doesn't want to miss the news, so she records it and then just doesn't erase it. It's easier to just have it record day after day from five to five thirty and let them accumulate, than to record, watch, and erase, over and over. I'll do what I can, but it seems a huge waste of time for me. Besides, I'm a Peter Jennings fan, myself."

"I know Lou would appreciate your looking for a pattern, and if you're right, and I tend to agree with you, we can cross that off as something not needing further investigation."

"Okay, but I was really hoping for chasing a suspect at a high rate of speed," Andy said. "You know, some action."

"Our work isn't like that, Andy."

"Lou got shot on one investigation. You got shot on another. Wasn't that action?" Andy asked.

"Oh well, if it is being shot you want, we can arrange that."

"Very funny. You know what I mean – something with a little excitement."

"The excitement will come if you find something helpful, and I promise you that we'll involve you if something exciting results from your work."

"I'll start this evening and let you know what I find. Can I include a friend who has a hearing loss as well, or is this some secret work?"

"You can include a friend. All I want to know is whether there is something in the captions that might be a reason for this suspect to want to save them. If it is a wild goose chase and maybe it is, I'll apologize for asking you to do such mundane work, but you could also be the key to solving this murder. You never know."

Mickey called Lou in Grand Haven. "I have a report of the dust and stuff on the floor of 16. Ready?"

"Yeah. What do you have?"

"Dust and hair."

"That's no surprise."

"We picked up nothing else. We have seven strands of hair. Worthless at this point."

"Right, at this point. But as soon as we get a suspect or two, the information will come in handy."

"We'll keep the hair and toss the dust."

"Fine."

Peg Lott, in her new identity as Charlene Flame, walked into the Catholic church office. With her newly cut hair and change in makeup, plus her demeanor as an abused woman, she didn't think anyone could possibly recognize her.

"Hi. You must be Charlene?"

Peg simply stood there wearing a weak and nervous smile. She wrote on her pad, "I am Charlene. Friend called you about help."

The receptionist wrote back, "Yes. I'm Mrs. Logan. I talked to your friend. Can you read my lips?"

Peg wrote, "A little. Notes, please."

The receptionist took a pencil and wrote, "We can put you up at a local motel for one night, and give you a gift certificate for some food at a local supermarket. Do you need some clothes?"

"No clothes. Thanks. What do tomorrow?"

"I can ask a social worker to see you. She will have advice on where to go or what you need next."

"Ok, thanks."

"Do you have a car?"

"No."

"I'll drive you to the motel. I've called, and they will give you a room."

"Thank you. God bless you."

"Glad to help."

The two women got in Mrs. Logan's car, and Peg was driven to the Four Seasons Motel on the outskirts of town. Mrs. Logan went into the office, talked to the lady at the registration desk, and then came back to the car to give Peg a key to Room 12 and a twenty dollar gift certificate for food.

Mrs. Logan wrote on Peg's pad of paper, "The lady in the motel office will drive you to the supermarket if you want to go. Just go into the office and let her know you want to go."

"Thank you," Peg wrote back. "Will the social worker come tomorrow?"

"Oh, I forgot to tell you. Yes, she will be here about nine in the morning."

"Thanks."

Peg got out of the car and walked toward Room 12. She opened the door to the simple but clean room. She had decided not to go to the supermarket since she could be recognized there. She could get some pop and a couple of packages of cheese and crackers or candy bars from the vending machine. Peg also decided not to go into the motel office. She knew that often these folks are on the lookout for people wanted by the police.

While Peg lay on the bed pondering her future, the motel clerk was calling the Oceana Sheriff's Department.

"Sheriff's office."

"This is the Four Seasons Motel in Pentwater. Is that woman you are looking for deaf?"

"No. Why?"

"I've got a guest here who is a single woman without transportation. She meets your description except she is deaf."

"Are you certain of the deafness? She could be faking that."

"She came here with Mrs. Logan from the Catholic church in town. She was representing St. Vincent DePaul and assisting the lady."

"Is she credible?"

"Oh, yes. Very. She says the woman has left her home and fears her husband. They communicated by writing notes."

"Doesn't sound like the woman we're looking for."

"Okay, just wanted you to know."

"Thanks. I would suggest you try to monitor her, keep an eye on her, and try to find out where she goes if she decides to leave the motel this evening."

"Mrs. Logan asked me if I would take the lady to the grocery store, and I offered to drive her there if she wants to go."

"Let us know if you suspect anything after driving her and observing her more closely."

"Will do."

"Thanks for calling."

"Sure."

Lou tried unsuccessfully to reach Dr. Willard Lowe at the University of Washington. He left a message requesting that Dr. Lowe call as soon as possible. About an hour later, Lou's cell phone rang.

"Hello. This is Lou Searing."

"Mr. Searing, this is Willard Lowe from the University of Washington. I'm returning your call."

"Thank you, Professor. I'm a private investigator working with the police to try and find Dr. Peg Lott of Michigan State University. She has been missing since she took a car ferry from Wisconsin to Michigan and has not been heard from."

"I'm very sorry to hear that. Peg's a marvelous scholar."

"I'm sure she is. Could you please tell me about seeing her in Phoenix at your conference?"

"Sure, what do you want to know?"

"What was she doing, whom did she see, did she say she was being threatened, was she nervous? Those kinds of observations."

"I see. Peg is a very quiet person, stays to herself, doesn't socialize at all. She didn't say anything about being threatened or anything like that."

"That's helpful."

"There was something strange though. I've seen Peg at many conferences over the years and she is always reserved, never smiles that I can recall, very much a recluse. But at the conference in Phoenix I did see her a couple of times with a man whom I would say might be five to ten years older than she is."

"Do you know his name?"

"Oh, no, and she didn't say anything about him to me. But, I do remember it because it was so unlike her even to talk to anyone."

"Do you know where this man was from?"

"No, like I said, she didn't say a word to me about him."

"Can you describe him?"

"Oh, my. I only saw him a couple of times. Let me see. He was tall, wore cowboy boots, I do remember that about him. He was well dressed. Gave the impression of having a lot of money. I don't know why, but that's how he struck me."

"Might he have been a threat to Peg?" Lou asked.

"Again, I don't know, but I will say this: I saw Peg smile a couple of times when she was with this man, and as I said a moment ago, I don't think I've ever seen her smile."

"Do you know anyone else at this conference who may know who this man was?"

"No. I doubt anyone could help you with that."

"Was he registered for the conference?" Lou asked.

"I don't think so, and I say that because he didn't have a name tag, which you need to get in to just about anything associated with the conference. He might have been a family member who lived in the area, maybe an uncle or someone. I have no idea."

"Did you see him in the audience when you and Peg gave your presentation?"

"No. I'm quite certain he was not in our session. We spoke to approximately fifty people, and we knew most of them from our research and professional meetings. No, he was not at our session."

"Thanks, Professor. Oh, one more question. I understand you were to present a paper with Dr. Lott in Minneapolis. What happened with that?"

"Peg called and asked me to present our paper. She said she would not be able to attend."

"Did she offer a reason?" Lou asked.

"No, and I didn't ask. I hope you find Peg. She is a marvelous person, quiet and reserved, but she has a pure soul."

"I'm sure we'll find her. You have my phone number; if you recall anything else that you think might help us find Peg, would you contact me?"

"Definitely."

"Thank you."

Lou pondered the conversation with Dr. Lowe. The strange man in Phoenix could be a factor in this mystery. Lou wasn't sure how to get more information about the mystery man, but he was grateful for what he had learned from the professor.

Mickey McFadden called Lou. "Chief Grether called me a few moments ago with something I thought you would want to know about."

"What's that?"

"The forensic folks have finished their analysis of Peg Lott's computer."

"The purest form of having your rights to privacy violated," Lou said, to Mickey's astonishment.

"You really feel that way?"

"Oh, definitely. This Dr. Lott has not been charged with any crime. All we know for sure is that she is missing. We only have some circumstantial evidence that she might be involved, and I emphasize might. All character references we have indicate that the woman is peaceful and would have no part in the murder of a woman. So, because of a little circumstantial evidence, we have the right to thoroughly invade her computer, and most computers hold a tremendous amount of private information."

"I see your point," Mickey replied. "But anything we discover is helpful in finding Peg and getting to the bottom of the case."

"I understand; it just hit me how we are violating this woman's rights. Sorry for the soap box. Now watch me change my tune once you give me some fantastic information that turns this case around. What did Harry have to say?"

"Most of her files seemed to be lectures on professional papers. There were a couple of listserves and these were with students in her classes and a group of professors who share her academic subject – Ecology."

"So, nothing out of the ordinary."

"Well, not really. I'm not finished yet. They found a list of her favorite web sites, and most of them relate to academia, including some that might be suspect."

"For example?" Lou asked.

"The ELF."

"The ELF? What does that mean?"

"ELF is an acronym for Earth Liberation Front, an environmentalist extremist group. They often resort to burning and destroying operations that they see as detrimental to the environment."

"You're suggesting she's a member?"

"No, just something that you don't see often would be my guess."

"But for a professor of ecology, and one who demonstrates at environmental rallies, this doesn't strike me as odd," Lou said.

"Just pointing it out, Lou. Hey, pal, lighten up," Mickey said. "What's got you by the tail this evening?"

"Didn't take my Zoloft this morning, I guess," Lou replied. "Sorry, maybe I'm just too busy with this case and missing my evening walk with Carol along the shore of Lake Michigan. Let me count to ten and take a deep breath, and we can start over."

Mickey chuckled. "They also have in their report that she had a favorite site related to deafness."

"That makes sense since her brother is deaf, and she is quite close to him. Anything else catch your attention?"

"I guess that's it, except for a visit she made to a web site in Gunnison, Colorado."

"The web site for the community of Gunnison?" Lou asked.

"It appears so. She looked at a map of the area, but other than that, she probably read a number of the sections in the web site."

"Ok, nothing I'm hearing is helping any. Any personal e-mails that stand out?"

"Like I said, most are students. She has one group called Warriors, whatever that means. There are three names in there: Todd Baxter, Eve Summers, and Carrie Willoughby."

"Give me those again, and give me the e-mail address too."

Mickey complied with Lou's request, repeated his advice to loosen up a little, and then finished their conversation.

Lou called Bob Carter and asked to speak to the person who could give him a passenger list for the trip across the lake on July 14th. He was put through to the reservations office.

"Reservations," said a polite and nice-speaking woman.

"Hello. Mr. Carter has authorized me to get some information from you."

"Yes, he told me to cooperate with you."

"Fine. Thanks. I need to know if some people had a reservation and if any of them had a stateroom and, if so, the number of the stateroom."

"OK. Their names?"

"Todd Baxter, Eve Summers, and Carrie Willoughby."

"One moment, please."

"Thank you." Within fifteen seconds Lou heard, "I don't see any of the names you've mentioned. However, there is a Todd Adams on that crossing, and he did have a stateroom, it was number 20."

"What is the mailing address for this Adams?"

"Pittsburgh, Pennsylvania."

"Hmmm, that could be Baxter using a phony name. Any other passengers named Todd on the crossing?"

"No, he's the only one."

"Ok, thanks. I assume 20 is four down from 16 where the body was found?"

"No, two doors, the staterooms are even on one side and odd on the other."

"Ok. You have the registration information for Mr. Adams?"

"Yes, I do."

"I'd like his address and phone number, please. Also his car registration."

"Sure. He gives his address as the University of Pittsburgh. The phone number is area code 498 and the number is 555-9999. His car is a 1999 Ford Escort, license plate HIT, the number 2, and the word KILL. Repeat, HIT2KILL."

"Kind of odd isn't it?" Lou asked.

"My guess is he's on the boxing team, the hockey team, or a football linebacker."

"Good guess. Thanks a lot."

"You're welcome."

Peg was watching television at eight o'clock in the evening when there was a rap on the door. Her heart jumped. How should she react? She was supposed to be deaf and shouldn't be able to hear the knock. There was no peephole in the door. When the knock came again, she decided to part the curtain a bit. Peg saw the motel clerk who smiled and motioned for Peg to open the door.

The clerk greeted Peg and showed her a note which read, "Do you want to go to the store?"

Peg felt she needed to accept the kind offer. She wrote on her pad of paper, "Yes. Thank you." She took her purse and walked out to the car. Once at the supermarket, Peg went her own way and was looking at some fresh produce when Brad Billups approached her.

"Listen to me and do what I say. After you walked from our yacht, the sheriff came to our slip and asked Dad a lot of questions about you. Dad lied around it, but maybe something of what he said may have tipped them off."

"Why did the sheriff come to him?"

"Somebody called in thinking you might be the missing woman in the Badger murder."

"I'm doing okay, Brad. You go back, thank your dad for his kindness and tell him I'll be all right. People think I am deaf, and no one will recognize me."

"I'm not going to do that. I have to do as he said. Dad made that very clear."

"What does he want me to do?" Peg asked.

"We've got to leave here on my scooter. We are to go up to Ludington, where Mom and Dad will pick us up at the marina there."

"That's right next to the Badger. The police will be sure to identify me there."

"Let's go. We will do as Dad says. We'll go out the delivery door."

Peggy owed the Billups her life, and it was not her place to refuse to go along with what LeRoy felt was in her best interests.

While the motel clerk was waiting for Peg to finish shopping, she picked up a copy of the paper; on the front page was a photo of Peg Lott. The deaf woman staying in Room 12 looked a lot like her. When Peg didn't appear in a reasonable time, the motel clerk walked through the store looking down each aisle. The clerk went to the manager of the store and asked to use the phone. She called the sheriff. "I'm pretty sure Peg Lott is or was in the grocery store. You had better get here in a hurry! The clerk said she looked outside and saw a woman riding on the back of a scooter. She looked too old to be a girlfriend of the kid driving."

"Thanks for the tip," Billy said. "We won't have a problem picking them up. He can only go north, south, or east from Pentwater and we'll cover every road."

Brad drove his scooter into Pentwater and, following the map of Pentwater his father had printed out, he knew exactly where he could go. Once, a little ways out of town, he headed north, but, instead of taking the road where, up ahead and unbeknownst to him, was a roadblock, he turned toward the state park, and was able to get the bike down to the water's edge. The sand there is not loose, but wet and packed. The lake was calm, so he didn't have the lasting effect of waves to contend with.

"Hang on, Peg. We're going up to Ludington."

When Peg could take her mind off the crisis, which wasn't for long, the ride was exciting. The stars and moon provided a nice ambiance over the lake which sped by as Brad moved the bike as fast as he could, given the weight of two passengers.

When Peg was a teenager, her brother Charles owned an old Indian motorcycle that he had fixed up. She was often a passenger on his bike. This trip to Ludington brought back memories of those enjoyable rides.

LeRoy did not inform the harbormaster in Pentwater he was leaving, as there was no requirement to do so. Yachtsmen often take their boats out into the lake at all hours of the day and night. When a ship is as big as the Billups', it can be quite stable, even on a rough Lake Michigan. LeRoy and Mary slowly pulled out of the slip, turned their yacht toward the harbor, and soon were out in Lake Michigan.

Brad called his parents on his cell phone and reported he had found Peg and the two of them were traveling up the coast. The plan was for LeRoy to stop at the marina to get gas in Ludington. At that point, Brad and Peg would board the ship, and if all went as planned, Peg would be safely out of sight in a matter of hours.

At this point, the only potential problem would occur if Brad was stopped before meeting his father. But all went without a hitch. The only lead the authorities had to go on was that the woman spotted in Pentwater could be the missing Peg Lott. The authorities had no proof that the mysterious woman was Peg Lott, but they believed it was an important tip.

The theory was confirmed the next morning when the Sheriff showed Mrs. Logan a photo of Peg Lott. "That's the lady. For sure. She's not deaf?"

"No, ma'am."

"Couldn't have proved it by me. Well, I'm embarrassed, and I'm sorry," Mrs. Logan replied. "We do get some questionable characters from time to time, but our policy is to serve all of God's people and to try not to judge."

"You did just fine, Mrs. Logan. At least we know that the woman we are looking for is alive and, as of last evening, was in Pentwater. We're getting close to finding her."

LeRoy and Mary Billups got to Ludington before Brad and Peg. The attendant at the marina was filling the tanks with gas when the scooter pulled up. Peg quickly boarded the yacht, where Mary sent her directly below. Brad and LeRoy put the scooter on board.

LeRoy said to the attendant, "Our kids, never happy to stay in one place. They wanted to shake their sea legs and ride up the coast a bit. I told them to meet us here."

"Yeah. Anything else you're going to need?"

"I don't think so. I usually pay by credit card, but I'm coming close to my limit so I guess I'll pay with cash. What do I owe you?"

"That'll be fifty-two dollars."

"Ok, here's a hundred," LeRoy said, putting the bill into the hand of the attendant. "Listen, I wasn't here if anyone asks about this boat pulling in for gas. Understand?"

"You in some kinda trouble, mister?"

"I've been breaking some no wake requirements in harbors south of here, and I've probably been a bit reckless on occasion. I figure the Coast Guard may be looking for me. I'd appreciate your keeping this quiet – so keep the change."

"You weren't here, mister. I never seen this boat or you and your family."

"Thank you."

LeRoy left the gas area of the marina and slowly made his way out into Lake Michigan. Peg looked out of the porthole and thought, This could be the last time I ever see the state of Michigan. So long; you've been a good place to live and work.

"I was doing fine, but Brad demanded that I come with him," Peg said, once the four were together.

"You may have thought things were okay, but I'm convinced you were on the verge of being picked up."

"Because?"

"Well, the sheriff came to our ship shortly after you left and began to ask a lot of questions. Apparently someone saw you and thought you were the missing lady. I told him no way, but I may have let on that I was lying by something I said. I told Brad to take his scooter to town and see if he could find you and, if he could, to keep an eye on you."

"I never saw you, Brad," Peg said.

"I know. I saw you come out of the library and call someone in the downtown area. I followed you to the Catholic church, and then I followed you and that lady to the motel. I came back and told Dad what was going on, and that's when he said you needed to be brought back on board, and we'd get out onto the lake for a couple of days. Once you were alone in the store, it was easy to get out and get to Ludington."

"You're taking a risk being seen with me," Peg said. "But, I'm grateful, and thankful for your concerns."

"We believe you, Peg. We're afraid that if they find you before the truth comes out, you'll be branded for more than you probably are now and all the publicity will be horrendous. We agree with you, if you are going to lead a new life you need to get far away and soon."

"I don't know how to make that happen," Peg said.

"My plan is to sail under the Mackinac Bridge, go through the locks, and over to Duluth, Minnesota. Brad will take you to the airport, and we'll fly you one-way to Anchorage or Juneau or wherever you want to go. That way, you'll be in a better position to make it."

"I'll pay you back," Peg said.

"That's not on my mind. What is on my mind is getting to Duluth without the Coast Guard stopping us and finding you. After all, the authorities know this ship from the Pentwater Marina, and it will be quite easy to find me out here. We'll find a way to protect you if that happens."

"But this is disrupting your plans and Brad's research," Peg replied.

"Right now, you are our priority. You concentrate on working with us to keep you out of sight. We'll get back to Brad and his research once you're on your way to freedom."

"But you could be arrested for helping me," Peg said, sympathetic to her friends' commitment to help her.

"Sure we could. Remember, we believe you, and we believe that you didn't kill anyone, and that that eventually will be found to be true. We're not concerned. I've got friends who are lawyers, and they are itching to get some of my money. We may need to give them the chance. Don't be concerned about us, Peg. We'll be just fine."

LeRoy pointed his yacht north, and the four began their trip to Duluth.

The Pentwater police and the Oceana sheriff were befuddled at what had happened to the scooter with two passengers. Peg hadn't had time to escape and each road out of town was blocked. They realized that a scooter would have more possible escape routes than a car, but then again, a scooter is not an all-terrain vehicle capable of going over sand or rough ground. The beach was out of the question. A scooter would certainly be unable to get through sand with two passengers on it; it would surely spin down like it was in quicksand.

The alert went beyond Oceana County. Mickey McFadden received the alert as soon as it was issued. He contacted Randy Herbert and asked him about it. "The guy probably drove it on the shoreline," Randy offered.

"The police probably didn't think that was an option, I suppose."

"Probably not. You can lift that scooter over the main parts of the beach, you know, the soft sand, but the wet and packed shoreline would support a small bike."

"And two adults?"

"Sure. If it's moving, he'd have a safe ribbon of driving anywhere from a couple of feet to six feet wide or so."

"I see your point."

"Oh yeah, and if he can stay out of the water and out of the sand, it's like driving down a highway."

"Let's see, are there any inlets or harbors outside of Pentwater?"

"Not till you get to Ludington going north, or not till you get to Stony Creek going south. That is quite a ride, but to get around a roadblock, yeah, that's what he must have done." "Thanks, Randy. I'll call the sheriff and explain your theory."

Mickey called and the sheriff sent an officer to check the shoreline north and south for tire tracks. Sure enough, the bike went north along the shoreline. The Oceana sheriff contacted the Mason County sheriff and explained that they had a scooter with two passengers who had escaped a roadblock and were either coming into Ludington or were already in town.

The Mason County Sheriff issued an alert, and all law enforcement eyes were watching for a scooter with two passengers. One squad car pulled into the Ludington Marina and talked to the kid who seemed to be tending the store.

"You see a scooter with two people on it around here?" an officer asked.

"Yeah."

"Where are they now?" the officer asked.

"They buzzed the dock area and left. Two adults, man and woman on a scooter, 125 cc type bike, right?"

"Yeah, I think so."

"Yup, about fifteen minutes ago. I seen 'em come through here on a joyride, and they took off. I don't know who they are. Tourists with too much to drink, I figured."

"Okay, thanks."

As the cruiser left the marina, the kid didn't feel good about lying to the cops. His uncle was a cop and he respected him, but forty bucks in his pocket was worth a little lie. After all we're not talking murder here or anything, he thought.

CHAPTER EIGHTEEN

Thursday, July 20, 2004

The evidence was mounting against Peg Lott. Most, if not all of it, was circumstantial, but the tide of opinion was not in her favor. A meeting was held between Joan Nelson of the Federal Bureau of Investigation, Mickey McFadden, Harry Grether, and Lou Searing to discuss the status of the case.

"Peg Lott is suspect number one, and I'm quite certain she murdered Stephanie Brooks," Joan offered.

Lou was not sure. "If the woman spotted in Pentwater is Peg Lott, that means she is alive. We haven't found anything on the Badger to indicate that she killed Stephanie."

"I think the opposite is the case," Chief Grether said. "If she were not guilty, she would immediately contact us and announce her innocence. She has to know that a murder was committed on the ship. Guilty people run and stay hidden from the law. If she is the Pentwater woman, she is running and not cooperating."

"Absolutely," Joan added. "The stateroom was hers and the body was found in her room.

Peggy killed the woman in her stateroom, and when the Badger got to Ludington, she took off on foot. I don't buy the jumping off the boat theory," Joan hypothesized.

"It seems that we've forgotten the possibility that Moe, the drug runner, killed Stephanie," Mickey added.

"That's right," Lou agreed.

"We've got no evidence to suggest he did," Joan said. "We have no witnesses, no physical evidence, only the belief that he could be a suspect, but we could apply the same thoughts to anyone on that crossing."

"Mrs. Hogan said she heard an argument," Lou added. "Thinks she heard a male voice. Says she saw a big guy in black leather."

"I keep coming back to Peg as the murderer," Chief Grether said, dismissing Lou's comment. "If she is alive and is running from us, as it appears she is, then she is digging herself a grave that goes deeper with each minute that she fails to contact us and tell us what happened."

"Precisely," Joan said.

The meeting was adjourned with little left to discuss except that Peg hadn't come out of the meeting looking innocent.

Mickey and Lou got into Mickey's cruiser, and after several seconds of silence, Lou said, "Peg Lott didn't kill Stephanie, Mickey."

"I don't think so either."

"I keep going back to Bill Yancy," Lou said. "He said Peg walked past the window of her own volition. She was not with anyone, and then she disappeared. He said there was no screaming. If someone were forcing a human over a ship out at sea, the person would be kicking and screaming."

"I agree," Mickey replied.

"So, let's assume she jumped. Either she drowned, or she was picked up and spotted in Michigan."

"Agreed, and of those two, I say she's back in Michigan, because I believe she was in Pentwater. I talked to the sheriff, and he has several good points about inconsistencies in the information Mr. Billups gave him. Besides, we've checked with the harbormaster in Algoma, and neither he nor anyone on his staff asked Billups to take a woman across the lake."

"Okay, so let's agree that she is alive and in Michigan," Mickey said. "Now the question is, why did she jump? As far as we know, she did not know Stephanie Brooks and therefore had no reason to kill her. If she did kill her, why would she try to escape by jumping? Wouldn't she wait till she got to Ludington and then go into hiding somewhere? That makes a lot more sense than jumping."

"Absolutely, Lou. I agree. The mystery seems to be locked on the answer to the question, why did she jump?"

"I think so," Lou replied.

"Jumping is a form of escape," Mickey said. "If she didn't kill Stephanie, then she jumped to escape something or someone."

"Agreed, but why so drastic an escape?" Lou asked. "It is almost suicidal to try an escape by jumping off a car ferry, in the middle of the night, in the middle of Lake Michigan."

"It seems to me that we need to talk to Billups," Mickey said. "He has to be somewhere on the Great Lakes or in port somewhere. My guess is, he has the answer to this whole thing."

The fact that Todd Baxter could have been on the same crossing as Peg was a bit higher than chance. Lou called Mickey and asked if he could do a floor sweep in Stateroom 20 like he did in 16 the next time the Badger was in port.

"If two hairs match, one in 16 and one in 20, and the hairs belong to Todd Baxter, we've got ourselves a man with some explaining to do," Lou said. "I'm going to contact this man, or at least try to."

"Okay, let me know what you find out, Lou," Mickey directed.

Lou dialed the number for Todd given to him by the reservations office at the LMC, Inc. in Ludington.

"Athletic Office. To whom may I direct your call?"

"I'm trying to reach a man by the name of Todd Baxter."

"One moment, please." The operator pushed the extension for the football office.

"Football program, Alice Reinhart speaking."

"Hello. I'm trying to reach Mr. Todd Baxter."

"I'm sorry, coach will not allow players to talk with people who call this office."

"But, I…," Lou began.

"Sorry to interrupt, but it's policy. If you are the media, you can attend our weekly press conference or contact our sports information office. Would you like to be transferred?"

"Yes, please."

"One moment."

"Sports Information Office. May I help you?"

"I hope so. This is Lou Searing. I'm calling from Michigan. I'd like to talk to Mr. Todd Baxter."

"I'm sorry. Mr. Baxter is participating in our conditioning clinic for high school coaches right now. Is there something I can help you with?"

"Advice, I guess. How can I reach Mr. Baxter to talk with him? Will he respond to phone messages? Does he have voice mail? Can you give me his home phone number?"

"No, I can't give you his private phone number. Are you an agent?"

"No, I'm not."

"A reporter?"

"No."

"May I ask the nature of your call?"

"I want to talk to the man. How about e-mail, does he have e-mail?"

"I'm sure he does, but we are not authorized to provide that either. I can leave him a message that you called and ask him to call you, but I can't assure you that he will. He is very busy, gets lots of these messages everyday. I'm sure you understand."

"Popular guy, I take it."

"Very. Since you're not some woman looking to get a date, you've got a better chance than most to get a call back."

"Ok, let's try that. My name is Lou Searing and my phone number is area code 616 and the number is 555-7778."

"May I tell him what this is regarding?"

"No. It's a private matter."

"I'll give him your message, Mr. Searing."

"Thank you." Lou hung up, certain that curiosity alone would press Todd to call back. He was right. The receptionist in the Sports Information Office must have gone to the clinic and told him of Lou's call, because the cell phone rang within the hour.

"Hello."

"Mr. Searing, this is Todd Baxter. I understand you wanted to talk with me. I'm curious, what is this about?"

"I'm a private investigator looking into the disappearance of Peg Lott, and I'm curious whether you know anything about this."

"Why would I know something about the disappearance of a woman?"

"Because you know her, and you were on the ship the night of the murder," Lou said.

Todd was surprised, to say the least, that this stranger knew about his connection to Peg. His hands began to perspire and his heart rate increased. He felt like he did before kickoff in a game against rival Syracuse in the Currier Dome.

"I'm afraid you're talking to the wrong person," Todd said.

"Are you telling me you don't know Peg Lott, and didn't sail on the Badger the night of July 14th?" Lou asked, getting right to the point.

"No to both questions, and even if I did, it wouldn't be any concern of yours."

"Well, I beg to differ with you. It is a big concern of mine. Your deciding to lie about your trip across the lake and knowing Dr. Lott tells me quite a bit about your involvement. Sometimes I learn more from people by how they answer questions, Mr. Baxter, than from the information they provide."

"Okay, yes, I know Peg Lott and I was on the Badger that night. When I found out that she was missing, I didn't want to get involved, so I've been trying to keep it all to myself."

"Why would you do that?" Lou asked. "Are you involved?"

"No, of course not. I just got scared."

"What is this Warrior connection you have with Peg, Carrie and Eve?"

Todd was shocked. How did this man know about his connection to Peg and crossing Lake Michigan? Now, how does he know of the Warriors? Todd thought, while trying to come up with a response. The moment of silence was telling.

"We are interested in the environment. We share a concern for clean water, less pollution and things like that."

"I see. That's admirable. What is meant by being Warriors?" Lou asked.

"I don't know. Does Peg call us Warriors?" Todd was surprised at his comment. He was not good at answering a question with a question, but he had just done it at a most opportune time. It caught Lou by surprise as well.

"The three of you are identified as Warriors and I was wondering what this could refer to, a Warrior of what?"

"I guess you'd have to ask Peg. She created the word for the three of us." Once again, Todd was amazed at his answer. He successfully averted the opportunity to release something very important. Also, he implied that Peg was alive to be asked. He was on a roll in dealing with this man.

"Mr. Baxter, do you know where Dr. Lott is right now?" Lou asked.

"No."

"Did you have anything to do with the death of the woman in Stateroom 16 of the Badger the morning of July 14th?" Lou asked bluntly.

"No." Without being able to watch a stylus wriggle on a piece of graph paper, Lou could not tell whether Todd was telling the truth.

Within fifteen seconds after speaking with Lou, Todd was on the phone with Carrie.

"The jig is up big time."

"Calm down and explain yourself," Carrie replied.

"I just got off the phone with a private investigator who is looking for Peg. He knows a lot, Carrie."

"What do you mean?"

"He knows the three of us are Warriors."

"You mean by name?"

"Yup. He asked me why Peg called us Warriors, and he asked if I killed her. He knew I was on the Badger that night and that Peg was a friend of ours."

"Too much information for this guy to have and live," Carrie said in anger. "Who was he, Todd?"

"Lou Searing. He gave me his number to call him if I changed my mind. It is 616-555-7778."

"Let me see, 616, that's western Michigan. Listen, I want this Searing guy dead. Understand?" Carrie said forcefully

"Yeah, but I don't know anything about him."

"You will. Stay tuned. I'll research him and get back to you," Carrie replied. "You could get to western Michigan in twelve hours couldn't you?"

"Oh yeah, I'd say about nine to ten hours max."

"Listen, I want you to head there and I'll call on your cell phone with the exact location and what I want you to do."

"But, I've got...."

"Do as I say! If you aren't successful on this trip, Todd, whatever you have to do can only be done from prison. Am I clear?"

"Yes. I'll leave in a few minutes. How do you want him killed?"

"Be prepared for anything."

"OK."

Carrie went to the Internet to see what she could learn about Lou Searing. Getting information was easy, for his web site had a photo and a bio. It contained his address and a statement of how to reach him. She read, "Call (616) 555-7778, and if you can't reach me, I am either investigating the next soon-to-be-solved murder, or walking on the Lake Michigan shoreline behind my home."

Todd was about to leave the outskirts of Pittsburgh when his phone rang. "Yeah."

"He lives in Grand Haven on Lake Michigan. He lives in a fashionable home, four homes south of the Dunes With A View condos on Lake Michigan Drive. This is about six miles south of Grand Haven on the only two-lane road that links Grand Haven with Holland. It follows the Lake Michigan shoreline for the most part. He takes walks on the beach in the evening. He rides a Harley."

"I've got it," Todd replied.

"I want him and his information dead, understand? I want you to kill him as you killed Peg. I want anyone working with him to get a message, too."

"He'll be dead by midnight," Todd promised.

It didn't make sense for Andy to see one show a day to see if any pattern existed in the captioning of Fox News. What made sense was for him to get the set of tapes that Lou Searing had and study them.

Using the telephone relay system, he called Lou.

"Mr. Searing. My name is Andy. Your colleague and a mutual friend, Maggie McMillan, has asked me to study the captioning of Fox News." Lou listened to the relay operator and then gave her his response.

"Good. Maggie knows how to get a case solved. I hope you can find a pattern."

"Yes. She wanted me to watch each evening, but I have a better idea. Could I bring the videos to my home for study?"

"I've a better idea. Why don't you come to our home and do your work in front of our TV?"

"That would be fine, except that I was going to do this with a friend who understands captioning."

"That's fine, we have room. Bring a toothbrush and stay here, both of you, while you work."

"Are you sure you don't mind?" Andy asked.

"Not at all. Information is power, and the closer I am to information the better. Besides, I'd like to meet you and watch you work."

"Great. We'll be there in a few hours."

Andy was a member of the Jackson area Self-Help for Hard of Hearing People club. He had been instrumental in inviting Pat Archambault to explain the captioning process. Andy called Pat using the relay and asked him if he was available to go to Grand Haven and spend a few hours analyzing some video clips that were captioned. Pat was available; he would drive his own car and meet Andy at Lou's home.

LeRoy Billups called the Soo Locks on his navigational radio and received permission to enter the lock. Usually yachts enter behind a freighter, but because of the length of the Billups' yacht, it would have to wait and enter with a couple of smaller boats.

Once he was inside the lock with the gates closed, LeRoy was told that the Coast Guard would board for a search of his yacht. When he asked the reason, he was told, "Suspicion of harboring a criminal."

The harbormaster in Pentwater had given the authorities the Billups' boat name and registration number. The police had come to the conclusion that Peg Lott had indeed gotten off the yacht that morning. And, with the early departure of the yacht, they thought it wise to board and look around.

The Billups' yacht had been under surveillance since it left Ludington, where it had been spotted leaving the harbor. The police and Coast Guard tracked its course and waited for a good time to do the inspection. Once they heard the request to go into the lock, they knew they could trap the yacht and prevent any opportunity for an escape.

As the water level in the lock began to rise, the Coast Guard confronted LeRoy and announced they were coming aboard. They then arrested the Billups for harboring a fugitive. They also arrested

Peg on suspicion of murder. An officer took control of the yacht and guided it to a dock west of Sault Ste. Marie where LeRoy and Peg would be transferred to a police vehicle and taken to the county jail for processing before an appearance before the judge. Jurisdiction was federal because the alleged crime was committed on waters of the Great Lakes. It would be up to the judge whether to hand Peg over to the Ludington police or to keep her within federal jurisdiction.

That evening was busy at the Searing home. Lou was working on a chapter of his next book while checking in with Andy and Pat who were watching the videos and comparing observations. Carol was at her quilting group.

"Have you two come up with anything yet?" Lou asked, hoping their effort would not be in vain.

"We've found a few errors here and there, but we don't see any abnormality at this point," Pat said.

"You might not find any. It is a long shot at best. But, as investigators, we try to follow every angle in hopes that something will break the case."

"Got to take the dog out for a walk," Lou said to Pat, knowing that Andy would not hear him. "Make yourselves at home. Help yourselves to drinks and snacks in the kitchen."

"Okay, thanks," Pat replied.

"I'll be back in about a half hour. You two will be okay till I get back?" Lou asked.

"Yeah, we'll be fine," Pat replied. "Enjoy your walk."

Lou opened the door, and Samm shot out and headed for the shoreline. This late evening ritual was predictable. The only difference was that Lou and Samm were usually accompanied by Carol. The two enjoyed being away from the telephone, the television, and all the cares of their separate and active lives.

Todd Baxter had settled himself in the dunes south of the Searing home. He was concealed by a lot of trees and beach grass and out of sight since there were no homes in that area. He lay in the sand, his high-powered rifle resting on a stand, with the crosshairs of his telescope trained on the shore.

Todd soon saw a man with a dog coming down the beach. He trained his binoculars on them. From Carrie's description, the man was Lou Searing.

When they got to the water's edge, Lou headed in Todd's direction. Todd set the binoculars down on his backpack. He lay prone, positioning himself so that the crosshairs were fixed mid-chest on Lou. He checked to be sure that the shell was ready and that the rifle was steady. He looked all around him, not wanting to be surprised by anything. All seemed to be in place.

Lou tossed the stick and Samm retrieved. This toss-retrieve activity was predictable; day after day, week after week, it was always the same.

Todd watched the routine and decided that the best shot would be as Lou stood by the water waiting for his dog to return. Just before he bent down to get the stick, Todd would fire.

Todd watched the routine twice more: walk several paces, toss, stand and wait, bend over and pick up the stick. He would fire the next time Lou stopped, waiting for the dog to return with the stick and put it at his feet.

Lou threw the stick, walked a few paces, and stood waiting for Samm to return. Samm ran back toward Lou, and then, as the shot rang out, Samm jumped up and planted both front paws firmly on Lou's chest. Lou heard the shot as he felt the impact, but he didn't realize he'd been shot.

Lou grabbed Samm's legs to keep them both from falling backward. He thought the punch to his left side had been caused by Samm's paws hitting him. Samm fell to the beach, obviously wounded. When Lou looked down and saw a circle of blood on his shirt, he realized both he and Samm had been shot. He knelt in the wet sand at the shore of the lake, and reaching to comfort Samm, he passed out, his body falling onto the sand.

"What was that?" Pat said to Andy.

Andy shrugged his shoulders, as he didn't know what Pat was talking about.

"I heard a shot," Pat said, looking at Andy so he could read his lips. "I'll be back."

Pat ran out the back door and saw Lou and Samm down by the shore motionless on the beach. When Pat arrived, blood was mixing with the water coming in to shore.

"Oh my God," Pat screamed. He ran to Lou afraid he was dead. There was no movement. He checked for a pulse and finally found one. He quickly covered the wound and tried to talk to Lou, who did not respond.

Andy realized something was wrong and followed Pat down to the shore. He checked Samm and could tell that she had sustained a deep wound to her shoulder. Samm was trying to get up, but her front leg wouldn't hold her up. She whimpered, and Andy knew she was in pain.

Pat got Andy's attention. "You stay here. I'm calling 911." Andy nodded, and Pat ran to the Searing home to get a phone.

Todd was certain he was successful. He hadn't expected the dog to jump, but the shell was so powerful that it would have gone through the dog and Lou. He gathered up his equipment and calmly walked to his vehicle. He tossed the gear into his car and headed for Holland, away from the emergency vehicles he figured would be en route to the scene.

While driving toward Holland, Todd called Carrie to report that what she had ordered had been carried out without a hitch.

Carol was on her way home when she saw flashing red lights in her rearview mirror, so she pulled off the road, giving the two fast-moving vehicles the right of way. She crossed herself and said a brief prayer for the victim. She had no idea that the vehicles were on their way to her husband.

When Carol saw the ambulance in their driveway, her heart fell into her stomach. Her heartbeat quickened considerably. "Oh, God, please. No. No. No," she said as she got out of her car and ran toward the house. There was no one inside, not even Samm, so she immediately went to the back door and saw people down at the shore. By now, several neighbors had gone down the beach to discover what had happened.

As Carol ran toward the shore her first thought was that Lou had had a heart attack but then she saw that Samm was down too and she couldn't figure out what might have happened to both of them.

"Lou, Lou, Lou!" Carol screamed as she ran to his side. An officer stopped her.

"Stay back ma'am, they're working on him."

"He's my husband. Let me see him!" Carol pleaded.

"Not now, please. You can help by letting them do their work."

"What happened? Is he OK?" Carol asked.

"We're not sure. He's alive, I can tell you that. But I don't know anything else."

A neighbor came to Carol and held her in her arms, relieving the officer. He was busy with crowd control as the word of the crisis spread up and down the shore.

"It's going to be all right, Carol," the neighbor said, trying her best to be comforting.

"What happened? What happened to him?" Carol asked.

"I think he and Samm were shot. Several of us heard what we thought was a firecracker, but then we heard the sirens and saw Lou and Samm down at the shoreline. My husband got to him a little before the paramedics and thinks he's alive. He's lost a lot of blood, but they found a heartbeat."

"Oh, thank God." She looked over at Samm, who was whimpering and obviously in pain, unable to stand. A teenaged neighbor held Samm wrapped in a blanket. While the authorities wouldn't let her near Lou, she was allowed to go to Samm and hold her head in her arms. "Oh, Samm, my dear Samm. You're going to be okay, girl, you're going to be okay." She stroked Samm's head and wanted more than anything to comfort Lou, but the paramedics were busy tending to him.

An IV was hooked up, and Lou was soon strapped onto a stretcher and taken to the ambulance. "You can come with us, Mrs. Searing." Carol nodded and was thankful that she would finally get to hold Lou's hand and offer a little comfort; even if he couldn't hear or see her, at least she would be beside him and could hold him.

Samm was also strapped onto a stretcher to be taken to a small animal hospital in Grand Rapids. She was badly hurt, but she would undoubtedly live.

Lou was unconscious. He was breathing, but he had a weak heartbeat, irregular and slower than normal. The missile had missed his heart, according to the paramedics, but it had gone through a lung. He was alive, but Carol was given no assurance that he'd survive this ordeal.

CHAPTER NINETEEN

Friday, July 21, 2004
Beijing, China and Grand Haven, Michigan

Len Miles was disturbed. He didn't think Peg had jumped from the Badger as planned. Since she had not been heard from since before she left on the Badger, he knew something must have gone dreadfully wrong. He would have flown home from Beijing but the weather was bad and the fog was not expected to lift for several hours.

Len got onto the Internet to see what he could find in Michigan newspapers. He typed in "Peg Lott" in the search section, and up came an array of references to her. Ninety-nine percent were related to her professorship and her efforts to conserve the environment, but one referred to an article in the Detroit Free Press. He clicked on the icon and was surprised to read that a woman had been murdered on the Badger. The article noted that the stateroom where the murdered woman was found had been assigned to Peg Lott, and that Peg's car was found abandoned at the dock of the Badger. He read further that Peg was missing and was a suspect in the suffocation of the woman in her stateroom.

Len was shocked. He couldn't believe what he was reading. There was no way that Peg could be involved in all of this. Since he hadn't been contacted, he was beginning to fear that she might be dead. Surely she would have called him to explain why the plan had failed and to let him know that she was alive and okay.

He continued to read the article, which ended with, "The case is being investigated by the FBI and the Ludington city police. Noted private investigator Lou Searing is also looking into the mystery of the missing Dr. Lott."

Len then put the words "Lou Searing" into the search box and up came numerous references to him, including newspaper articles about solved murders – all in Michigan. There were also references to the many books he had written. Len found what appeared to be a personal web site, opened it, and took down information for contacting Lou.

Finally, Len was able to board a plane from Beijing to the United States. The long flight seemed interminable. When Len finally arrived home, he immediately dialed the number for Lou, and after four rings, he heard the common message, "Sorry, there is no one here to take your call. Please leave your name and number and a short message, and we will return your call as soon as possible."

Len said, "Mr. Searing, this is Len Miles of Gunnison, Colorado. Please call me at your earliest convenience, Area code (723) 555-9876. Thank you."

From the moment Lou was wheeled into surgery, he had been listed in critical condition. Following surgery, Carol talked at length with their family doctor as well as with the chief of surgery who gave her guarded hope that Lou would survive. The next 24 hours would be critical, but Lou was in good shape for a man his age, and the surgery had been successful. The doctors recommended that Carol go home and get some sleep. There was nothing she could do at the hospital, and Lou would be under sedation for several hours.

Carol had called their son Scott Searing in Grand Rapids and their daughter Amanda in St. Louis as soon as she could. She called again after the surgery so her follow-up call was somewhat hopeful that Lou would live. Scott immediately drove to the hospital and Amanda would be on a flight in the morning.

Carol called a few other close friends, as well as Maggie in Denver and Mickey in Manistee. A neighbor came over to stay with her and to handle phone calls and reporters.

Carol was not thinking about Lou's investigation, but only about her hope that he would live. When she listened to Len's message, she didn't give it much thought. The words "Gunnison" and "Len Miles" meant nothing. She jotted down his number; she would tell Lou when he could handle the message.

Len waited all day for Lou to call. He called again and got the same recorded message. He couldn't stand not knowing anything and not being able to reach Mr. Searing. He didn't want to call the FBI or the Ludington police because he didn't want to foil any change of plans that Peg may have successfully managed. By contacting a private investigator, Len expected to be able to keep what he knew out of the public sector and the media.

In the background CNN was giving the news of the day. Len heard the name "Searing" and turned up the sound. He learned that Mr. Searing was gunned down near his home on the beach south of Grand Haven, Michigan. "The police believe a sniper shot him from the dunes. The man's dog was also shot." The reporter went on to say that Mr. Searing was in surgery late last night. "He's still alive, and his vital signs are stable, according to the hospital spokesperson."

Len turned off the television and prepared to fly to Michigan. He packed a few things, drove to the Gunnison airport, completed and filed his flight plan, inspected the plane, made sure the fuel tanks were full, checked the weather reports, and all was ready for an uneventful flight to Michigan. His Lear Jet roared down the runway and ascended on a course that would take him over the eastern edge of the Rocky Mountains and across the Plains to the Great Lakes.

Once Mickey heard that Lou had been shot, he quickly moved to take over the investigation. He was fairly certain he could handle the case as well as the murder of FBI agent Stephanie Brooks. Mickey's inclination was to go to Grand Haven to see Lou and provide any comfort he could to Carol. One of his officers had been shot several years before, and he knew how devastating the situation is for the spouse who normally lives in a chronic state of worry anyway. Once the event occurs, and for Lou this was the second time, the spouse needs a lot of gentle and supportive care.

However, instead of heading for Grand Haven, Mickey called Maggie in Denver. He had worked with her on the Marina Murders case and knew that she was vital to Lou's success in solving crimes. He needed to console her as well, and to get any advice she might have.

Mickey was lucky in that he was able to reach Maggie. She was staying close to the phone, thinking each call might be Carol, or her husband Tom in Battle Creek, with an update of Lou's condition.

"Maggie, this is Mickey McFadden."

"Hi, Mickey. Have you heard that Lou's been shot? It doesn't look good."

"I know. Carol called me too. Lou'll be OK. He's been down this road before, and he's in good shape, so I expect the medical team to win this one."

"I sure hope you're right."

"By the way, this is Lou's last investigation," Maggie said.

"How's that?" Mickey asked.

"Carol will never let him work another case. The last time he was shot was traumatic enough, and now that it's happened again, Carol will insist. And Lou loves her so much that he'll end his private investigations."

"You're probably right."

"She went along with the Harley, and she went along with the previous investigations, but I know she worries every minute Lou is away on these assignments. She wants him to follow his dreams, but she wants him alive. I'm sure this will be Lou's final case."

"He's probably finished now. I'm going to try and solve this thing, and I hope I can do so before Lou is well enough to get home and recuperate."

"Wish I could be there."

"Well, you can be indirectly by helping me."

"Tell me what you need," Maggie said, eager to help.

"Advice. Do you know anything about this shooting?" Mickey asked. "Did he mention a threat from anyone?"

"No, but I hadn't talked with him in several hours. We talked about the strange collection of captioned videotapes, but that was all. He wasn't onto any suspect that I know of."

"Any general advice then?" Mickey asked.

"Find his small notepad," Maggie advised. "He writes down everything that is important on that notepad. It's sort of his shorthand journal of the case. He uses it to remind him of what he's learned about his investigation. And, it also serves as reminders for him when he writes the book after he's solved the murder."

"Good advice. I'll call Carol and see if she knows where it is. Anything else?" Mickey asked.

"You know that if Samm was hit first, the shooter was south of the Searing home. I'm sure the police have gone over that area with a fine-tooth comb," Maggie responded. "You might suggest you use a metal detector in case the weapon ejected the casing and buried it in the sand."

"I'll talk to the chief of police in Grand Haven to see what his staff is doing about that. Anything else, Maggie?"

"Nope. Good luck. My guess is that there is something in his notebook to tie the shooting to someone."

"I'll let you know what I find out, and I'll call if I think you can help in any other way," Mickey said.

"Don't assume I know about Lou's condition. It only takes a phone call so if you hear anything you think I should know, please call."

Mickey called the Ottawa County sheriff who had jurisdiction in the Grand Haven shooting.

"I'm calling because I need your help."

"What can I do for you?"

"I need a notebook belonging to Lou Searing, the man who was shot south of Grand Haven. He was working with me on a case out of Ludington. I think there may be information in that notebook that will help me solve the case."

"Not a problem. Let me put you on hold and I'll check his belongings." A few moments later the sheriff came back on the line. "Chief?"

"Yes."

"I have Mr. Searing's notebook. It was in his shirt pocket when he was shot."

"Good. Can you tell me what's in it?" Mickey asked.

"You want me to read his most recent notation and work to the front?"

"I guess that makes sense. Start reading from the end, and I'll stop you if I need more information."

Mickey already knew much of what he heard until the sheriff read, "Todd Baxter on e-mail listserve as a Warrior, also Carrie Willoughby and Eve Summers. Baxter was on Badger when woman was killed. Info on Baxter: U of Pitt football player; Pennsylvania license plate HIT2KILL. Talked to him via phone. Definitely a suspect to keep track of."

"That's all I need," Mickey replied. "Looks like this is your case too with the shooting in the dunes. But what Lou means is that this Baxter guy is someone Peg Lott knew well enough to have him on her e-mail list, someone who was on the ship when the murder took place, and someone who Lou thinks might have further information about Peg's whereabouts."

"We'll put out a Be On the Lookout Bulletin on this Baxter," the sheriff said. "If he did the shooting and is traveling in his car, we have a good chance of pulling him over."

"Good. Thanks."

Mickey wrote down the names, Carrie Willoughby and Eve Summers. If this Todd Baxter fellow is involved, then the chances were good that Carrie and Eve were also involved.

It didn't occur to Todd Baxter that a registration form for crossing on the Badger would mount a bull's-eye on his back when it came to finding him. But Todd was certain that Lou was dead and obviously unable to tell the cops that Todd might have been his attacker. Therefore, in Todd's mind, he was "Out of Dodge," so to speak, and he only needed to get back to Pittsburgh to await the next assignment from Carrie.

Andy took the videotapes and went home because staying at the Searing home was not an option once the shooting occurred. He felt a bit guilty for wanting to be around some action, and he certainly didn't mean to be on-site when Lou was shot. Back in his home in Battle Creek, he and Pat began watching the videos again. Suddenly the two hit on something.

"Look at that," Andy exclaimed. "That's no error." He stopped the video, backed it up 30 seconds, and said to Pat, "Read the caption immediately after the photo of the President shaking hands with Putin."

Pat watched intently. "You're right. That's not a mistake. That looks like some type of code. Keep the tape going, and we'll see what happens."

About three minutes later Andy said, "There it is again! It has to be some message or something. It has nothing to do with what the newscaster is saying, and it's not a phoneme error in transcription." Pat nodded in agreement.

"This is nothing a supervisor or a viewer would pick up on. It's nothing to us, but to someone who knows what they're looking for, it is probably very meaningful." Again, Pat nodded his head in agreement.

Andy called Maggie and used the relay operator to tell her that he and Pat had discovered something that resembled a code being sent by the captioner. Maggie confirmed that the material being captioned was the 5 o'clock News on the Fox Network. She called Mickey immediately and told him what they had discovered.

Mickey took the call in his cruiser in the parking lot of the Ottawa County Hospital where he had just arrived to see Lou. He entered the hospital, asked for Lou's room number, and made his way to the second floor. He entered, gave Carol a hug, met son Scott and daughter Amanda. He shook Lou's hand and with his head shaking said, "I'm very sorry, partner. Very, very, sorry."

"Comes with the territory, Mickey. You know that."

"Yeah, but I promised your bride that I'd deliver you safely home," Mickey said, with his arm around Carol's shoulders.

"Well, so you didn't follow through," Lou said. "Looks like you'll owe her one."

"Let me tell you and your family this, Lou. I'm going to nail this guy. I owe it to you, Lou."

"Well, now that I've done all the work, it shouldn't be hard for you to wrap it up, Chief," Lou said with a smile. Mickey wasn't laughing.

"In this job, we do our best not to let emotions get in the way of our work," Chief McFadden said. "I'll tell you this, Lou. I'm going to be going on emotion, and I'll not let up till the guy who did this to you and Samm is in a place where there's not a lot of fresh air and sunshine. It's my promise to all of you."

"Aw, don't be so hard on yourself, Mickey. I'll be okay. We'll take care of Samm, and the guy who did it will pay a price. We always get our man, so it's just a matter of time. But thanks for the promise, Mickey. You're a good man. Your old man would be mighty proud."

As soon as Mickey left the hospital, he called the Fox Network station that served northern Michigan.

"This is Manistee Chief of Police Mickey McFadden. May I please speak with Tom, the station manager?"

"Yes. May I tell him what this is regarding?"

"I have a request to make that is very important."

"One moment, please."

"Hello, Chief. I owe you so many favors for information you have given us. You tell me what you need, and the world will stop while I get it."

"Whoa, I'm not cashing in all my chips, Tom, only a few, but this could be important in solving a case."

"What do you need? I'm at your command."

"I need the name of the captioner who captioned the five o'clock Fox Network News on July 21. I need the name and where this person works."

"If you can give me a minute, I'll have it for you. I only need to call Network Headquarters in New York."

"I'll stay on the line."

It took a bit longer than a minute, but Tom came back on. "The captioner's name is Carrie Willoughby who is employed by Captioners International out of Louisville, Kentucky. She works out of her home and her home phone number is area code (756)-555-5252."

"Excellent. Thanks, Tom."

"Sure, glad to help. Now, are we all even in the favors department?"

"We can be. You know I'll always be here for you guys. I'm not counting."

"Neither are we. Glad to help," Tom replied. "Call if you need more information."

"Thanks. Oh, I might have a hot tip for you soon. As you folks say in your business, 'Stay tuned.'"

CHAPTER TWENTY

Saturday, July 22, 2004
Gunnison, Colorado; Louisville, Kentucky and Ohio

Eve had told Carrie of Peg's new friend Leonard Miles the owner of a huge estate in the mountains northwest of Gunnison, Colorado. As an act of revenge, Carrie assigned Eve to destroy his home. The assignment was difficult for Eve because of her affection for Peg, but the Ring of Fire needed to survive for the cause and Eve realized that Peg needed to be punished for being a traitor.

The Gunnison County Sheriff's Department decided to stake out the Miles estate because a tip had come in about a possible arson attempt. The sheriff had put the stakeout in place with no fanfare, no sirens, no obvious police presence at all. He was able to round up a number of volunteers with rifles and camouflaged outfits, who quietly and effectively took up stations surrounding the complex where the arsonist might strike.

The sheriff, with support from the Federal Department of Alcohol, Firearms, and Tobacco, had determined that catching the arsonist in the act was the most efficient way to gather enough evidence to prosecute the suspect. They didn't want any slip-ups so that the arsonist could get away to "torch" again.

It was the middle of the night, and Eve didn't have a campfire to give her light or warmth. She had learned the obvious at Outward Bound that light and smoke would quickly alert others to her presence. Eve sat on a rock and thought about Peggy. She missed her friendship and felt lonely. She wondered if Peggy ever regretted her decision to leave the Ring of Fire. Even if she didn't, did she miss her or their talks of their passion for the environment?

The night was perfectly quiet as she sat on a rock under the moonlit sky. Out of the blue, she heard an unmistakable snap of a twig. She scanned the area to see what made the noise. Initially seeing nothing, she revisited the feeling she'd had since dusk that she was being watched. Eve quickly grabbed her headlamp, knowing that a beam of light would increase her chances of seeing who or what was out there. She looked up into the eyes of an animal. Fear grabbed hold of her and she instinctively activated the headlamp. The light reflected from a cat's green eyes. A cougar! A mountain lion! A catamount! Eve thought, as her heart raced inside her chest. As the cat stared fearlessly into her eyes, she knew without a doubt that she'd been considered potential prey for several hours already.

The huge cat, hissing low in its throat, moved forward and down the rocks toward her. Each leg made slow and deliberate movements, bringing it always closer. Its rhythmic gait drew her attention to the cat's front leg, disfigured from some old injury. The shadows cast by the headlamp onto the ribs of the beast showed Eve that the cat was starving. Obviously hunger was the reason the cat stalked her.

Eve knew she had to act, and almost instinctively she remembered listening to the Outward Bound instructor lecturing about what action to take when confronted by a predator in the wilderness. Her instructor would have been proud of Eve because she acted exactly as she had been trained. She became a wild woman. She stood up, waved her parka like a bullfighter. She jumped up and down, made loud noises, threw rocks and sticks – whatever she could find around her campground. Had anyone seen her, they would have thought she had simply gone crazy.

The big and injured cat must have figured that this prey wasn't worth it. The cougar stopped, surveyed the craziness, hissed, turned, and limped away, leaving Eve alone in her campsite.

Eve took a breath of fresh air and listened to her pounding heart, imagining the adrenaline pumping into her circulatory system, causing every organ to be on full alert.

At 2 A.M. on Sunday, July 23, without a clue that she was being watched, Eve Summers silently walked up to the home of Len Miles and began to spread gasoline around the base of the house. The police pounced on her. She was caught red-handed and the police had all the evidence needed to convict Eve of intent to burn the building.

Eve really didn't know what hit her. Immediately, she was handcuffed and read her rights, and a waiting squad car took her to the county jail for booking.

When Carrie did not get a message that the mission had been accomplished, she knew a problem had occurred. Maybe Eve had made the decision to cancel the arson for some reason, or it may have meant that she had been arrested.

It hadn't taken long for the FBI to break the code of the Ring of Fine. The Ohio Highway Patrol found Todd's car in the parking area of an eastbound service center. Turnpike and Ohio State Police officials spotted him in line at Taco Bell, followed him back to his car and arrested him. He was surprised at the arrest, thinking that he had gotten out of Michigan undetected.

Early the next morning a police car pulled up in front of Carrie Willoughby's home outside of Louisville, Kentucky. Neighbors noticed the police cruiser in the driveway of the Willoughby home.

The police knocked on the door and when Carrie opened it, she was apprised of her rights and arrested for masterminding a ring of arson, and charged with the destruction of eighteen homes in environmentally sensitive areas around the country. She was handcuffed and led to the squad car with neighbors gawking.

The neighbors couldn't believe their eyes. Carrie Willoughby was the consummate mother, neighbor, community volunteer, and housewife. If ever the police had made a mistake in arresting a woman, it was now!

While some of the mothers gathered outside on this warm morning to talk about what had happened, a newspaper reporter and camera crew appeared and interviewed the neighbors. Readers and viewers would once again be shocked when they heard that a least-suspected person had been arrested in a quiet and perfect community.

The Billups' attorney flew in from Los Angles, arriving about the time that the case was falling together like a line of dominoes. He presented his brief to the judge, explaining that while his clients did harbor a murder suspect, they acted out of compassion and saved Dr. Lott's life. The judge gave a short lecture about the importance of always involving the law when confronted with a possible crime rather than taking on the solution alone, and then dismissed the case. He authorized the Coast Guard to release the Billups' yacht and to return anything that had been confiscated.

In a matter of hours, the Billups were on their way back to the northern part of Lake Michigan, and Brad was back working on his thesis while LeRoy and Mary planned their next stop. Once in port, LeRoy called a producer friend in Hollywood and told him of a fascinating story that would make a good movie. The producer told LeRoy to keep it in his back pocket, and they'd talk about it over lunch when he returned to Los Angeles.

Strangely and luckily, it all came together quite well. When Peg arrived in Ludington, the news was out that members of the Ring had been arrested. Trials would follow.

EPILOGUE

Lou Searing recovered from his wound and vowed to Carol that his crime investigating days were over. He would now write his novels from his imagination and not seek plots from his actual experiences. He would remain a consultant to any law enforcement office that believed he could help; but for Carol's sake, he decided that life was too short to put himself in harm's way. His oncologist gave him good odds of surviving his cancer. If he were a cat, he'd have seven more lives, but he wasn't a cat. He was a vulnerable human being who loved life, Carol, and the opportunity to write.

Samm lost her right front leg. She was fitted with an innovative prosthesis from an experimental program at the veterinary clinic at Michigan State University. She could walk with a limp, but her days of chasing sticks along the beach behind the Searing home were over. She took some short beach walks with Lou and Carol, but for the most part, she lay at Lou's feet while he wrote his novels.

Mickey McFadden and Joan Nelson together successfully conducted a multi-state drug bust.

Randy Herbert shaved and traded in his motorcycle for a stint at traffic enforcement.

Moe, Jeff, and Lucky were convicted of trafficking drugs and were all sentenced to terms in the state penitentiary. Moe took pride in letting fellow prisoners know that he killed an FBI agent. He was so dominant a presence that no one would rat on him. When asked to explain, he said that "Big Guy" Renaldo knew from an informant that Stephanie would be on the Badger. She was watched by the informer who signaled Moe. When the coast was clear and Stephanie was vulnerable, Moe overpowered her. There was a brief scuffle, and then powerful arms held a pillow tight over her face until oxygen deprivation led to death. Moe walked out of the room, closed the door, and returned to deal the next hand of poker. The other players figured he went to the bathroom and never suspected that Moe had just snuffed out the life of a woman in Stateroom 16. Moe was allergic to feathers and being close to the feather pillow gave him a sinus attack. Moe figured out that the note was wrong. The room assigned to Stephanie was Stateroom 19, which looked like 16 upside down, and the guy wrote "16" on the note before passing it to Moe.

Todd Baxter was not charged with the murder of Stephanie Brooks. DNA and fingerprints put Todd in Stateroom 16 where the dead body was found. During his interrogation, Todd told all under a plea-bargaining agreement. He exposed the Ring; he told of Peg's decision to leave, and his order to kill Peg and Lou because Peggy was believed to have informed the police about their burnings. He maintained his innocence of the murder of Stephanie Brooks, even though there was hardly a soul who believed him. The prosecuting attorney didn't believe he could convince a jury beyond a reasonable doubt that Todd had suffocated Stephanie Brooks. Todd was charged with the attempted murder of Lou Searing. A jury found him guilty, and he is currently serving a life term in Jackson's Southern Michigan Correctional Facility. He was also convicted of setting fires and destroying many homes in the East.

Eve Summers was tried for her role in setting a number of fires. She is currently serving time in a prison in Colorado.

Carrie Willoughby was tried and found guilty of masterminding the Ring of Fire and using interstate communication technology to commit a crime. As a final act of revenge, Carrie admitted assigning Eve to burn the home of Len Miles. Her family and friends are supportive of her, but everyone in the family has suffered greatly as a result of her crime and imprisonment.

Peg Lott was found guilty of setting six fires in the Midwest. She was sentenced to 20 years in a women's correctional facility in southeastern Michigan. She was a model prisoner, and she expects to be released within two to five years.

Len Miles remains deeply in love with Peg and was committed to being supportive of her during her trial and incarceration. After her release, they plan to be married and live in his mountain home for the rest of their lives.

The S.S. Badger continues its reputation of excellent service to passengers as it enters its 51st year of service.

Finally, Betty Taylor was able to contact Len who made arrangements for Flame to be transported to his home. Len committed to having Flame present when Peg was released from prison and walked in the door of her new home.

THE END

GRAND RAPIDS, MICHIGAN

"Hi, Nana. Nick would like you and Grandpa to visit his preschool during grandparents' week. Can you come? Any morning next week would be fine," Patti Searing said.

"We'd love to come," Nana replied, thrilled to accept any invitation to be with her grandchildren. "You tell Nick that Grandpa Baldwin and I will be there and we'll be the proudest grandparents to visit his school. OK?"

With camera in hand and a thank-you gift for the teacher, Lou and Carol walked into Nick's preschool. When Nick saw Nana, he lit up and smiled. He then stood up and came over to give Nana a hug. It was a special and innocent moment, one that Lou and Carol would not forget.

The morning evolved with Nick doing a wonderful job cooperating with his classmates, attending to his teacher, and appropriately participating in the activities of the morning. Carol was invited to work alongside some of the children while Lou took some photos for the family album.

When the visit was over, the plan was to go to Bob Evans Restaurant on 28th Street for lunch. The occasion was a special one for all present which included Nick's mother Patti, and his 2-year-old brother Jack. An older brother Ben was in first grade all day.

Nick sat between Carol and Lou. After lunch, Lou suggested a small hot fudge sundae, which in actuality was a selfish gesture on his part, but Nick accepted the suggestion. Soon the delicacies were delivered and Lou and Nick savored every mouthful.

Since Lou got to the bottom of his sundae first he was the one to discover a small Reese's Peanut Butter Cup nestled in the bottom of the glass container. Rather than allowing Nick to discover the treat on his own Lou announced, "Hey, Nick. Wait till you get to the bottom. You'll find a peanut butter cup and boy is it good with some ice cream and chocolate sauce."

Nick continued to inch away at his dessert and like a Texan discovering oil, Nick eventually hit his peanut butter cup. With a grin, he got his spoon under it and lifted the treat bathed in melted ice cream and chocolate sauce to his mouth. He closed his lips around it and then went directly into heaven with the overflow oozing from his little mouth.

"You were right, Grandpa. It was there. It's good."

"I knew you'd like it, Nick. It's very good, huh?"

"Uh-huh. It's very good," Nick said as his puffed cheeks returned to normal while the tasty treat slid toward his stomach.

As Lou and Carol pulled away from the restaurant, with Nick riding in the backseat, Nick could be heard saying, "That Bob Evans sure has good ice cream, Grandpa."

"You got that right, pal," Lou said. "It was delicious!"

Lou found a lot of satisfaction in solving a crime and in bringing some justice to what often seems to be an unjust world, but nothing could match the joy of sharing a hot fudge sundae with a hidden Reese's Peanut Butter Cup under a mound of ice cream and chocolate sauce with his grandson Nick, of whom he was very proud.

As the Searing car headed for Nick's home, Lou smiled and felt at peace. All was right with the world and he was blessed, and thankful, and most fortunate to share life with Carol, his children Scott and Amanda, their spouses Patti and Joe, and his five delightful grandchildren.